THE WOMAN IN COMPARTMENT 13

ANTHONY PATHFINDER

Published by EastSouth Publishing LLC
www.eastsouthpublishing.com

The cataloging-in-publication data is on file with the Library of Congress.

ISBN:979-8-9885126-2-2 (paperback)

This book was printed in the United States of America.

For more information, or to contact the author:
anthonypathfinderr@gmail.com
www.anthonypathfinder.com

Every story begins with a single moment, small yet full of meaning.

The world is made richer by the tales we choose to remember.

Even the simplest experiences can shape the deepest truths.

Life is a collection of moments, each one worth noticing.

PROLOGUE

The town of Kramden slept under a heavy, restless moon, unaware of the shadow stirring beyond its borders. In the quiet of the church, the priest's hands trembled as he clutched the parchment. He had seen it all before, omens, whispers, strangers with vengeance in their eyes. Some whispered that the town itself was tied to ancient bloodlines, legacies that shaped more than just its streets, stretching beyond oceans and centuries, linking the living and the dead. A voice, old and trembling, spoke from the shadows: "A girl and her family will come. They seek retribution." The priest's mind raced, his heart beating. He had dismissed warnings before, but this time, it felt different. Something ancient was waking, and when it did, no walls, no barricades, and no mortal fear could hold it back. Outside, the wind whistled low and faint but continuous, like the mournful cry of a train passing through realms unseen. Forces unseen, bloodlines long forgotten, and battles yet to come would soon converge. Kramden was about to be tested, and the town would not know what hit it until it was too late.

FIRST BLOOD

In the Old World, ancient bloodlines lived and fought among themselves for thousands of years. The Barrs, a name claimed by one of the first three families to settle in a remote European village, were vicious and cruel. Their ethereal and living ancestors battled constantly with other bloodlines. The Abyss, dark pits of shadow dwelling in the hidden places of death, was their domain. A bloodline of power and secrets, it held knowledge of forces beyond mortal comprehension.

It was in this world that Abby Barrs, the youngest of four sisters, who would later be called Lady, was born. She came into being beneath a sky alight with storms, stars, and shadowed forms that rose from the earth to claim her. Among the bloodlines of the underworld, this was seen as a deed of favor. Even as a child, she carried the past in her bones. From the moment she drew her first breath, whispers traveled through the dark world of power. Elders of the hidden bloodlines spoke her name in guarded reverence, recognizing the power she had been given, a force that would shift the balance of both the living and the spirit world. Her parents, keepers of the Barrs' legacy, watched over her carefully, knowing that the world outside would test her in ways no child should face.

When whispers of the new lands across the seas reached them, Abby's parents chose to bring some of their bloodline to America. It was there, in the untamed reaches of the New World, that Abby arrived as a young girl, small, yet already marked by her heritage. Every lesson, every watchful glance from her elders, was meant to guide her toward the role she was born to play: a guardian of her family's power, a force that would one day shape destinies beyond her own.

Even in her youth, Abby understood that her life would not be ordinary. Her bloodline demanded vigilance, cunning, and courage. Kramden, quiet and unsuspecting, would soon witness the stirring of a legacy centuries in the making, a girl whose small frame carried the weight of the Barrs' history and the promise of what she would one day become: Lady, the heir to a power that could not be ignored.

SECOND BLOOD

Long before the streets of Kramden whispered with tales of missing townsfolk and midnight travels, Alias Siobhan moved through the old forests of Eastern Europe, a young man with eyes too old for his age. His family had long been tied to secrets that most considered superstition, and he had been raised to recognize the invisible threads that connected blood to power, spirit to flesh, life to death. As a boy, he learned from his father the subtle art of listening, not just to words, but to the force behind every move, every heartbeat, and what it meant to their bloodline.

Doris Siobhan, by contrast, had grown up in a quiet village where the river met the rolling hills, her childhood steeped in the soft hum of ancestral chants. Her mother, a woman of calm but iron resolve, taught her that the world was not just what it seemed: every stone, every shadow, every gust of wind carried whispers of those who had come before. Doris had inherited a gift that ran in her blood, a connection to the spirits of the departed, the ability to sense them before they arrived. Yet she had always felt incomplete, as though some part of her soul was waiting for its counterpart.

Though both carried the Siobhan name from birth, their union was more than coincidence: it was the joining of kindred lines, a continuation of a family legacy that spanned both blood and spirit. Together, they became a living bridge between the mortal and the ethereal, their bond destined to shape the course of the generations that would follow.

Their paths crossed on a night thick with frost and fog. Alias was traveling between villages, carrying messages for his father's network, an intricate web of families united under one of the ancient bloodlines.

Doris had been tending to a sick child in her village when a gust of wind brought the stranger to her doorway. Their meeting was silent at first, an exchange of glances; however, the bloodline stirred, and it recognized the other. There was no need for words; their bloodlines spoke to one another before either dared to speak.

They lived simply, aware that they were part of something greater than themselves. Then the wars came, bloodline against bloodline, each fighting for control. In those moments, they were more than young lovers; they were guardians, warriors of a lineage older than any village record. Some of the most powerful bloodlines fled, fearing extinction. But when word came from across the seas that parts of their line had settled in a new world, several members of the Siobhans followed, leaving behind a lineage they could always return to.

And when the time came, they knew they would pass this legacy in the flesh of their children. The first was Demetria, born under a crescent moon, her cries cutting through the night as though announcing the arrival of a force that had waited long to step into the world. Eva and Mattie soon followed. Alias and Doris understood that their children were not simply daughters; they were heirs to a bloodline that would one day connect them to one of the most powerful bloodlines, the Barrs.

The Siobhan

The Siobhan family had been a mysterious presence in Kramden for as long as anyone could remember. Their true identity was a well-guarded secret, carefully concealed from the prying eyes of the townspeople. Living a reclusive life, they chose to marry among themselves, keeping their lineage within their bloodline. However, one family member couldn't escape the townsfolk's attention: Demetria, the eldest daughter. With her ethereal beauty, Demetria stood out from the crowd. Her slender frame, fair complexion, long dark locks, and penetrating brown eyes made her an enigmatic figure in the town. Towering at almost six feet tall, she was a striking sight in an era when women were typically shorter. The townspeople couldn't ignore her presence.

Demetria was often seen alongside her sisters, Eva, and Mattie, as they made their way through town, walking to the Aldan Circle train station under the cover of darkness. The sisters' nightly excursions had long intrigued and unsettled the townspeople, especially considering the eerie rumors surrounding the sealed-off Compartment 13 train stop. Whispers and lingering gazes from a few locals followed the sisters wherever they went. Despite the speculations and concerns of the townsfolk, the Siobhan family had always dismissed the gossip as baseless rumors. They urged Demetria and her sisters to ignore the prying eyes and continue with their nightly walks.

On one moonlit evening, as the sisters made their way toward the train station, several curious townsfolk seized the opportunity to approach them. An elderly woman with a loose tongue, and no stranger to the sisters, gathered her courage and called out to Demetria. "Well, well, if it isn't Demetria Siobhan! What brings you and your sisters out at this hour? Are you off to the forbidden train stop, perhaps?"

Demetria, maintaining her calm demeanor, turned and faced her with a polite smile. "Good evening. We're simply taking a stroll, enjoying the calmness of the night. There's no truth to the stories surrounding the old train stop, I assure you."

"Is that so? Then why are people dying? It has been said that the train station is the cause of the missing people and deaths," the woman responded.

"Where did you hear that?" Demetria asked.

With a shrug, the elderly woman stated, "We know that's all."

A middle-aged man with a penchant for ghost stories chimed in, his voice tinged with skepticism. "But what about the barricade? The tales say it's sealed for a reason. Are you telling us it's all a hoax?"

Eva, the middle sister, stepped forward, her voice calm and composed. "The barricade is there for safety reasons; it has nothing to do with the death of our neighbors."

"Now, see, that's where you're wrong," he responded, turning to the crowd.

Eva sighed, "It's best not to venture near it if you feel this way. The stories attached to it are nothing more than figments of your imagination." The middle-aged man's wary eyes bore into Eva's.

Mattie, the youngest of the sisters, added with a mischievous twinkle in her eyes, "If there were anything truly sinister lurking behind that barricade, I assure you, we wouldn't dare go near it!"

The townspeople exchanged vague glances, torn between their fascination and apprehension. Demetria, sensing their hesitation, spoke softly, her voice carrying a touch of melancholy. "We mean no harm. Our family has chosen to live a private life, away from prying eyes. I beg you to respect our desire for privacy and let the mysteries surrounding our family remain as such. But as far as the deaths in our town, someone or something is responsible for it, and that's the sheriff's job."

The crowd fell into a thoughtful silence, contemplating Demetria's words. Finally, the elderly woman spoke up, her voice softened. "Very well, Demetria. We shall respect your family's privacy. But promise us one thing."

"What's that?" Demetria asked.

"That you'll never judge us like some of the other people in town. We are afraid, and we only want answers."

A smile played on Demetria's lips, tinged with a hint of suspicion, as she replied, "Oh, no, certainly not! And we want answers as well."

As the sisters walked away from the townsfolk, their footsteps muffled by the darkness, they huddled together, their voices low but filled with relief and concern. Demetria cast a glance behind, making sure they were out of earshot before saying, "That could have gone worse, I suppose. Those two seemed genuinely curious."

Eva nodded. "Yes, they were, but they're all the same to me. I hope they heed our words and respect our family's privacy."

Mattie chimed in with a playful tone. "Oh, I do enjoy a bit of mystery. The more they speculate, the better our nightly walks are."

Demetria chuckled softly. "You always find the silver lining, Mattie. But we must remember to be cautious ourselves. We don't want to draw unnecessary attention."

Eva added. "True. Our family's secrecy is crucial. We've managed to keep our true identity hidden for so long, and we must continue to do so."

Demetria placed a comforting hand on Eva's shoulder. "Don't worry, dear sister. We have always been discreet, and we'll remain so. The townspeople have grown accustomed to us, and they won't suspect anything."

Mattie's eyes glinted mischievously. "Besides, the mystery adds a certain charm, doesn't it? We're like characters from a forgotten tale."

Eva sighed. "Just remember, our safety comes first. No matter how tempting it may be, we must be mindful of the chilling tale surrounding the concrete barricade that sealed off the old Compartment 13 train stop and its secrets."

Demetria agreed with her sister. "It's forbidden for a reason. But like many in town, we're in the dark about why so many people are dying." Eva and Mattie nodded. "Let us continue our walk and enjoy the stillness of the night."

The sisters vanished into the night, their graceful figures blending with the shadows, leaving the curious townsfolk with lingering questions.

2

Strange Happenings

Demetria, like many townspeople who commuted to Evansville and its surroundings, worked as a librarian in the city, a forty-five-minute commute from Kramden. One day, during her walk to the train station, a dense mist suddenly emerged. Unfazed, she continued to the station, bought her ticket, and talked briefly with the clerk, paying no attention to the strange weather.

As she walked toward the platform, the sound of the approaching train grew louder. The dense mist obscured her vision, creating an eerie ambiance, and a wave of unease washed over her as the train came into sight. The door opened, and she entered. She smiled uneasily. The conductor welcomed her. "Your seat is in Compartment 13." The passengers, cheerful on the surface, smiled and greeted her warmly, but beneath their friendliness lingered something strange, something she couldn't quite put her finger on.

Stuttering she said, "A compartment?"

"Yes. There's no need to be nervous."

"Oh, no. I'm not nervous. I'm just surprised by the welcome and the look of this train."

"I understand. Most first-time passengers react this way. Don't worry, there's nothing to be worried about. And our next stop is the Evansville stop. Please, here," he pointed her to the compartment.

"Wait a minute? You said, first-time passengers?"

"I did."

"I'm not a first-time passenger. I travel this route all the time."

The conductor smiled. "I understand, but I assure you that it's your first time on this train."

She couldn't make sense of what he was saying. "There were people on the platform, where did they go? What happened to them?" she asked curiously.

"They are in the other cars. You're the only one who entered this car. Is there a problem?"

Unsure of what to say, she answered, "I guess you're right."

A heavy stillness filled the compartment as she stepped inside. She sat down, her eyes darting around. Something felt wrong. Someone was watching. She could feel it. A soft shuffling came from the path leading to the door. It wasn't the train rocking; it was something else. She couldn't see anyone, but the sound was there. It grew louder. A whisper. Then another. She rose, drawn to the door. Her hand trembled as she gripped the handle. The whispers turned into a frantic hiss. Her chest tightened. Any sane person would run. But she couldn't.

Collecting herself, Demetria glanced at her watch, relieved to discover she was still on time. Walking back to her seat, she settled in once again. Shortly thereafter, there was a knock on the door. It was the conductor, she opened it.

"Your stop is coming up."

She found it strange that he would say that, but she only smiled and replied, "Oh, thank you," before walking beside him and leaning against the side of one of the leather sofa seats nearby.

"How did you find the ride, even though it was a short one?" the conductor asked, looking into her eyes.

"I enjoyed it. Nothing to be frightened about," she said, hiding how she felt.

Giving her a good look over, and with a straight face, he said, "Glad you enjoyed your ride. Will we be seeing you again?" he asked, knowing the answer, as the train pulled into the stop.

She smiled but didn't answer. As she exited the train, the remaining passengers smiled and waved at her as she walked into a thick fog. She watched as the train rumbled on, wondering why fewer people got off. Normally, a lively crowd would get on and off the train. However, as she approached the ticket windows and clerks, there was no sign of the passengers who had just left.

As she strolled the short distance to her workplace, a look of confusion was on her face, leaving her unsure of how to explain everything that had happened. Arriving at her workplace, she took a deep breath, ready to confront whatever lay ahead, though she didn't have all the answers. Throughout the day, she kept playing the whole thing over and over in her head, wondering if she was losing her mind or had already lost it. She was more than ready to go home when her shift ended. She walked the short walk to the train station. But one thing was clear to her: who would believe her, other than her sisters? As far as anyone else, she wouldn't dare chance it by telling them, fearing they would think she'd lost her mind.

Surprisingly, there was no mist to obscure her view as she waited for the train on her return trip. She heard the familiar rumbling sound, but as the train approached, she realized it wasn't the same one she took to work. She boarded and settled into her regular seat. But something felt amiss. She felt like the other passengers were staring at her. She thought she had lost her mind. To escape the uncomfortable situation, she closed her eyes, pretending to be asleep.

Demetria's make-believe slumber was abruptly interrupted as the train jolted to a halt. Startled, she realized it was her station. Hastily, she rose from her seat, anxiously awaiting the opening of the doors. As soon as they slid open, she hurriedly made her way through the small group of passengers, eager to escape the intrusive stares and prying eyes that had left her feeling uneasy.

Once home, she made a beeline for the shower, offering only a brief hello to her parents and sisters. The sound of running water offered her temporary refuge. After her shower, her mother asked if everything was alright. She told her yes. Her sisters saw the telltale signs and sensed something was wrong.

"What's wrong with you?" Eva asked her, out of earshot of their mother.

"Is it these nosey ass people?" Mattie added.

"If it's them, you shouldn't let it get to you," Eva said before Demetria could answer.

"No. It's not them. It's more than that," she said to them with an uncertain look on her face.

"You have to tell us what it is," Mattie said.

"She's right," Eva stated. "Come, let's go outside." The three walked to their usual spot, a place they had been going to since they were children. They were floored by what Demetria told them. They suggested that she tell their parents, but Demetria would have none of it. Vowing them to secrecy, they agreed that if word got out, they would be looked at differently.

3

Renegade Jones

As the sun began to set over Kramden, casting an orange glow across the town, the sisters walked hand in hand along the narrow path that led to the train station. They had grown accustomed to the suspicious gazes and hushed whispers that followed them wherever they went, but tonight felt different. The tension in the air was unmistakable, and they knew Renegade Jones and his followers were behind it.

Demetria tightened her grip on Mattie's hand and glanced over her shoulder. "Do you see them, Eva? Renegade and his clan seem to be lurking around again."

"Yeah. I see them. I don't like it."

"Me neither," Mattie added.

Demetria's eyes scanned the surroundings, catching sight of Renegade's dark figure standing at a distance, his piercing eyes fixed on them. "They're always watching, Mattie," she replied in a concerned voice. "But we won't let them intimidate us. We have to stand up against their false accusations."

They quickened their pace. As they neared the train station, a group of townspeople gathered, their faces etched with suspicion and anger. Renegade stepped forward, his voice booming through the crowd. "People of Kramden!" he declared, his voice dripping with malice. "We have suffered enough at the hands of these sisters and their family members. The deaths and disappearances cannot be ignored any longer. It's time to take matters into our own hands!"

"What the fuck is he talking about?" Eva asked with an incredulous look on her face.

"I don't know," Demetria responded. Her heart sank as she heard the familiar accusations being hurled their way. She knew they had to address the crowd, no matter how dangerous it was. She climbed onto a nearby crate, her voice projecting over the murmurs of the crowd. "Listen to me, Kramden! We are not the monsters they claim us to be. We have been here for generations, protecting and caring for this town just like you."

A skeptical voice shouted from the crowd, "Then why are people dying? Why do we find bodies and never any answers? Don't you find it strange?"

Eva stood next to Demetria and said firmly, "We didn't cause these deaths and disappearances. We want to find those responsible as much as you do."

Renegade scoffed from his position, a sinister grin creeping across his face. "You can't fool us. We know your true nature. Your family's history speaks for itself."

Demetria's voice trembled with frustration. "You speak of history, Renegade, but what about your own? Your family has a long line of killers, and you continue their evil legacy. You blame others to deflect attention from your dark deeds."

The crowd fell silent, their eyes shifting between Renegade and the sisters. Doubt started to creep in, and whispers of skepticism began to rise. A brave voice emerged from the crowd. It was a member of one of the families that Renegade despised. "Enough, Renegade! We have suffered long enough from your lies and hatred. It's time to face the truth. Leave the sisters and the Siobhan's bloodline alone."

Others in the crowd nodded in agreement, encouraged by the man's words. Renegade's face twisted with rage; His eyes were red, burning like fire, and just as suddenly, it stopped as he continued. "You will all regret this!" he bellowed; his voice filled with bitterness.

Renegade's eyes locked with the man as he gazed at the sisters. For years, he had managed to manipulate the townspeople, playing on their fears and suspicions, and he didn't like what he was hearing.

"Enough of your lies," Demetria continued, picking up where the man left off, "We know the truth about your family's dark history, Renegade. Your ancestors have terrorized this town, spreading fear and violence for a long time."

One of Renegade's followers stepped forward, his voice trembling, "Is it true, Renegade? Have we been deceived all this time?"

Renegade stared at the man. He knew the sister and her family knew the truth, and he was not going to let them or anyone else disrespect his bloodline. "You fools!" he spat angrily. "How could I have deceived you when you are of my blood? You think these sisters, these outsiders, can save you? They're just trying to divert attention from their wickedness!"

"Outsiders, we're not," Eva said.

Renegade's eyes darted around as his right-hand man, Burt Long, and several of his loyalists quietly pleaded with him to leave the sisters alone and walk away.

The sisters stood tall, their resolve unshaken. "We will not be silenced, Renegade," Demetria proclaimed. "And you, the people of Kramden, don't be fooled by his false narrative." The crowd slowly scattered while talking under their breath.

****

The girls returned home after their encounter with Renegade Jones, their hearts still pounding with the events that unfolded. Their parents, Alias and Doris, who were sitting at the dinner table talking, looked up from their conversation, concern etched on their faces.

Doris rushed forward, her eyes widening with worry. "Girls, what happened? You look distressed. Is everything alright?"

Demetria took a deep breath, trying to steady her nerves. "Mother, Father, we need to tell you about what occurred during our walk to the train station."

Alias motioned for them to sit, his voice filled with curiosity and concern. "Take your time, my darlings. We're here to listen. What happened?"

Demetria began, "Renegade Jones and his followers confronted us, accusing us once again of being responsible for the deaths and disappearances in town."

Doris's eyes widened as she glanced at Alias. "Oh no, not again. How did you handle the situation?"

"We stood up to him and his false accusations. We addressed the townspeople, telling them the truth about his family's dark history and their role in spreading fear and violence."

Alias looked at his daughters. "And how did the townspeople react?"

Demetria smiled faintly. "At first, they were hesitant, still swayed by Renegade's manipulation. But slowly, some started to question his claims, including Andy Asher, who spoke out against him."

"Andy Asher? He's of his bloodline. Renegade must have done something to him that only the two of them know about. Andy Asher wouldn't have any doubts or question him in front of the townspeople. You girls are aware that this is only the beginning?" Alias stated. The sisters nodded as they explained everything.

Once the girls left the room, Alias turned to Doris in a low voice. "Do you think it's time for them to know the truth?"

Doris paused, folding her hands. "Maybe we should . . . but then again, why not give it some more time? What do you think?"

Alias shook his head slowly. "Hmm. Give it some more time."

"Are you sure?" Doris asked, searching his face.

"I am," he replied in a quiet voice.

4

The Family's Origins

Their journey began on a small ship, their cloaks hiding their faces. No one knew who had paid for their passage, and they kept to themselves. After several hours at sea, they and the other passengers transferred to a smaller boat. The trip was grueling, with mist and cold leaving everyone shivering. Through the cold evening mists, the lowland swamps came into view. Once they reached the shore, the passengers disembarked and were led to a makeshift checkpoint by villagers whose faces revealed no emotion.

The town seemed a relic of the past, yet beneath the old façades, it had been modernized for the times. The villagers determined who could stay and who must go; the newcomers were lined up and examined for disease, the women, men, and boys checked thoroughly, while the girls were spared. Two figures slowly made their way through the crowd, the town's priest and his assistant, keeping a watchful eye on the newcomers.

Afterward, they were handed two brown bags, one with toiletries, the other with food, before being led to the town's church, a building that had seen better days. As they stepped inside, the voices of the locals rejoicing echoed through the worn hall. The local priest's eyes widened at the sight of the newcomers. The singing broke off as his voice cracked into a shout: "What do you want here?" He and his flock had once been warned that a girl and her family would come seeking vengeance. They had called the messenger a madman, mocked him, and even run him out of town several times. But now, with the newcomers before him, the memory of those warnings was on his mind.

"I came for you," Abby Barrs said, removing the cloak as her parents and sisters stared at him with a scowl.

"Me?" he asked nervously. "Why?" Suddenly, the old, worn doors and windows of the church slammed shut on their own, the iron locks snapping into place as if commanded by an unseen hand.

The Priest called on the name of the Lord. She only smiled and said, "You're useless. Is that all you can do?" With no mercy, she and her family unleashed their wrath, brandishing blades of fire hidden in their garments as they cut through the church members and the outsiders who had entered with them. Their true target was the Priest. Abby extended her hand toward her father, who drew a sword from his waist and handed it to her. With one swift motion, she severed the Priest's head, flames bursting as it fell. Her father lifted the corpse and hung it upside down on the pulpit. Opening the church door, they revealed their gruesome handiwork to the men and women waiting outside, who fled in terror. After making sure no one was left alive, the family walked to the outskirts of town, their footsteps slow and deliberate.

****

In the wake of the horrific church massacre, the Barrs sought refuge in the quiet confines of Kramden, Maine, a quaint town nestled amidst the picturesque countryside. Home to a close-knit community of approximately a thousand people, Kramden was once a beacon of hope, renowned for its laid-back atmosphere, amicable populace, and nostalgic old train that rambled through the heart of the town. The train was old and rickety, but it was the only way to get from one end of the mountain range to the other. The train had been running for generations, and it was a beloved symbol of the town's history. But there was a dark side to the town.

The Barrs wandered into town, a family of five. Their eyes didn't tell much as the townspeople of Kramden stared at them. Their peering eyes watched from half-draped curtain windows and their open front doors. No one made eye contact with them. There was something in their eyes that terrified them. No one knew who they were or where they came from.

The residents were fearful of strangers. Visitors to the town said the residents behaved strangely, and discernible signs and unseen forces haunted some of the older residents. Others describe it as a cursed town. The town was devastated by a string of murders over eight days many years ago, and some of the residents who lived through it said it was repayment for the evil that is rooted in the town.

Some of the townspeople refused to accept that it was their evildoings that gave the town a bad reputation, while others say the town had a reputation before the Barrs and other families' arrival, such as the Wicks.

Seeking refuge, a handful of the residents fled into the swamp area, where they built their community. Yet like many in the town, they brought their evil with them, including the Priests, who some felt weren't doing the work of the Lord. There were whispers that he was a womanizer and a practitioner of black magic, and was known for his close relationship with many of the ethereal and dark forces in town. And this, the Barrs were aware of.

Gerome Wick, head of an old bloodline that stretched back through the Americas and into the Old World, was said by some of the locals to be an evil man, as were his supporters. He came to town many years ago, establishing himself and his followers. When one of the seven Priests in town died, the church refused to let any of the remaining six conduct their services; instead, they used a church member with a questionable past. When Gerome told the townspeople that the man wasn't a good person, no one believed him. And why would they, when he himself couldn't be trusted? Taking matters into his own hands, Gerome and his followers lured the unsuspecting man and the Priests to a gruesome death.

After hearing the circumstances behind the man's death and the death and disappearance of others in town, Gerome warned the people that the town was a killing garden, cursed, and only he could fix it. Gullible and afraid, the townspeople believed him, unaware that he was going on a murderous rampage. Gerome and his supporters murdered as they pleased, passing their bloodstained ways from one generation to the next. They practiced black magic and sorcery, using it against both the living and the spirits of their enemies. It was said that some were buried alive near the old Compartment 13 train yard. So, when the Barrs arrived on their killing spree, Gerome and his followers vowed revenge, not so much for the people they killed at the church, and would kill later on, but for fear of being replaced.

5

The Barrs And Siobhans' Ties

The Barrs and the Siobhans shared a bond that went back to the Old Country. Tied by blood and tested during the early wars, their bloodline fought as one. The Siobhans had settled in Kramden before the Barrs arrived, welcoming them into the community. What grew between them was loyalty, rooted in generations of shared history. The Siobhans despised Gerome just as much as the Barrs did, even though all the families were equally involved in the town's murderous sprees. The Siobhans and Barrs would one day make plans to get rid of Gerome.

Several families led by the Barrs and the Siobhans met along the sleepy, hilly terrain where the Aldan Circle now stands. In those days, it was the old Compartment 13 train stop. The town's hilly location was ideal for any suspecting eyes as they marched a small group of men, women, and children to their deaths. The men and women weren't backing down, enraging the Barrs, the Siobhans, and their followers.

"Hogtie them," Mr. Barr said to the men.

Lying them side by side, the group used swords, daggers, and knives to surgically mutilate the bodies, the blood-gurgling cries and pleas for mercy echoing through the night, until the earth came alive beneath them, branches unfolding like ghostly arms, dragging the mutilated remains into the depths. The rural dread of the sleepy hillside terrain had once again lived up to its reputation as a place of evil and death.

****

Gerome was aroused from his sleep as his wife told him some of his followers were waiting in the parlor for him. Still groggy, he greeted the men. "What is it that brings you here?" he asked them with an uneasy look on his face.

"Sorry to bother you," the man taking the lead said.

"Okay, hurry up, it better be good waking me up this time of the night." The man told him that a neighbor of theirs was snooping around when he saw and heard the Barrs, the Siobhans, and their followers slaughtering a group of townspeople, some of the very same people that Gerome was planning on getting rid of.

Gathering a band of armed men and women and summoning the spiritual force of their bloodline, Gerome and his blood went from house to house, rounding up all who were involved. When word reached the Siobhans, many of their bloodline fled, abandoning their homes and possessions. The Barrs, too, saw many of their kin and followers scatter, though not before killing several of Gerome's bloodline. Yet the patriarch of the Barrs stood his ground, fighting tooth and nail, until he and his family were overwhelmed by the spirits Gerome and his blood had called forth. The Barrs were taken alive.

With their hands bound by an ethereal force, shadows, and whispers from the underworld, the group was led back to the place where they had committed their acts only hours earlier, and where they would meet their fate. But of all the people in the group, Gerome focused most of his attention on Abby. He told his men to bring her to him.

"It was said that when you were born, the shadows rose from the ground to claim you, and your name was whispered by the spirits of your bloodline and the ancient ones. But where are they now?"

"The souls of our lineage will soon find you and your bloodline," Abby's father shouted in rage. Her mother's incantations struggled to pierce the veil of the spirits Gerome and his blood had summoned.

"I do not fear you, wicked one," Abby snarled, struggling against the ethereal bonds that held her.

"Then we will see if the legends speak true," he said, with bloodshot eyes. The shadows and ghostly whispers swept over her as Gerome dragged her to the Compartment 13 platform. He assaulted her with a mixture of dark force and ritual, tearing at her defenses, the ethereal energy of their bloodlines entwined with the shadows. Her gargled screams drove her father to call upon his bloodline in a forceful voice, trying to shatter the ethereal hold that bound them. Suddenly, bullets of fire tore through the air, striking her father and hurling him backward. Round after round ripped into the others. Gerome and his men seized Abby, still alive, her mouth gagged, and buried her alive in the old train yard behind the Compartment 13 stop. One by one, the bodies of the others were dropped into the earth beside her. Over the graves, Gerome and his blood chanted their incantations in unison, sealing both the living and the dead beneath the soil.

When word of what happened got back to the local sheriff, he did nothing until he was pressured by some of the townspeople. But what some of the townspeople didn't know was that the sheriff and his department knew what was happening. It wasn't long after the investigation ended in Gerome's favor that things took a turn for the worse.

Gerome and his blood should have known better than to celebrate so openly. The victory that had filled them with pride became their undoing. As Gerome, his family, and their loyal followers returned home from one of their gatherings, they were ambushed. There was a stillness that clung to the skin like a cold sweat, and they felt it.

Gerome's right-hand man leaned in close and whispered, "Something doesn't feel right."

"I feel it. Something is following us. Whoever it is, its eyes are on us. Come, gather," Gerome ordered as they formed a circle and began their incantations.

The silence broke into a smoking fog of black magic and dark sorcery that swallowed their terrified screams. *Tonight, you will feel our wrath and see that we speak truth,* a voice of many thundered through the fog. Knives, daggers, and machetes of fire flashed in the fog, tearing through flesh with sickening ease. The ground trembled under their feet as the shadows themselves battled against Gerome's bloodline incantations. Blood soaked the earth as they were cut down where they stood, bodies crumpling like broken dolls. Even their dogs, once fierce protectors, fell silent, their lives snuffed out by the sorcery.

The massacre left behind a nightmarish vision of violence and death. By morning, the mutilated remains of Gerome, his family, and his followers were found scattered in the river and along its bank. The townspeople were shaken, terrified, especially those not bound to the bloodlines of the evil lineages.

****

It wasn't long after the horrific murders of the Barrs that strange things began to happen. The townspeople started to see ghostly figures in the train yard, and on the local train, and what stood out more than anything was the woman with long black hair and a pale white dress. At first, they thought it was just their imagination, but soon the sightings became more frequent. There were whispers that the woman was Abby Barr, who had returned as a vengeful spirit. She was angry and wanted revenge on Gerome's bloodline and his followers.

The townspeople were terrified as Abby and her blood began to wreak havoc on the town. At times, the townspeople couldn't tell the difference between the local train and what would later be known as the Compartment 13 train. It appeared mostly at night, and those tied to Gerome's bloodline, and others, would vanish, their remains scattered along the tracks or in other places.

The train was no longer a symbol of the town's history or pride, but of fear. The townspeople tried everything to rid themselves of Abby and the other vengeful spirits, but nothing worked. Even when they blocked parts of the track, it still chugged through the town, with Abby's ghostly figure leading, and haunting every step of the way.

A group of townspeople and a Priest steeped into the occult decided to take matters into their own hands. They gathered in ritual, chanting incantations as a circle of black surge spread over the old train yard. The sound of an oncoming train pierced the night. It slowed. A door creaked open, and the group stepped inside, facing the unknown.

Several ghostly figures waited for them. "You requested to meet, Lady, for what?" a malevolent voice asked.

"Lady? We're here to see Abby."

Stepping from the shadows, she emerged. "It is I, Lady. You'll address me as such. Now, what is it you want?"

"The spirits have warned us that there are too many killings."

"The spirits? Your bloodline? And you dare bring along a priest?"

she sneered as an eerie sound filled the train. Suddenly, the priest began clawing at his throat, strangling himself, his eyes bulging before he crumpled to the floor.

Seeing what happened to the priest, the others panicked. Men and women shoved past one another, calling on their spiritual bloodlines. A chain of fire encircled them as they rushed for the door. They tried prying it open, but it would not yield. A woman fell to her knees, her hands grasping for air as the flames burned her to a crisp. The train hummed, drinking in their cries. One by one, the townspeople doubled over, their eyes wide and mute, fingers clawing at collars and their throats as though invisible hands were choking the life from them. Their breathing thinned, shallow, then gone. Bodies slid to the floor and lay still.

The leader who had come to prove his bravery staggered, clutching his chest. His face went limp, the color draining as if the life had been sucked through the seat beneath him, then a sword of fire split him in two. Abby watched with a smile, her figure levitating. She moved among the fallen with the calm of someone who wasn't in a rush. She paused, speaking to no one in particular. "You called me. You have your answer. From this night until forever, they will refer to me as Lady."

She smiled coldly. The doors open, and a wind swept the ashy remains from the car, before moaning shut, as if pleased. The Compartment 13 train resumed its slow, inevitable course into the night. Nothing much happened after that night, and the townspeople thought things had returned to normal. However, that was not the case. Every thirty years, Lady and her bloodline would reappear, resume their killing spree, and then vanish.

Years later, some townspeople reported hearing the rumbling of a train and seeing figures sitting and talking on the Compartment 13 platform. The town decided to seal off the station. These stories were passed down through generations. Renegade Jones, a descendant of Gerome, would take up the mantle of the evil that plagued Kramden, targeting anyone claiming to be a relative of the Barrs while keeping a close watch on the Siobhans and their bloodline, and others.

6

The Present

As Demetria walked to the train station, her steps echoing against the empty streets, she couldn't shake off the eerie feeling that something was amiss. The same dense mist that had encircled her before obscured her vision, but the familiarity of the ticket takers and passengers waiting alongside her sent shivers down her spine.

Muttering to herself, *this is strange . . . I could have sworn I've seen these people before. Are they following me? Or is it just a coincidence?*

As the train approached, she hesitated for a moment before stepping aboard. Inside, the atmosphere felt disturbingly familiar, just like before. *The train conductor, those passengers . . . they're behaving exactly the same. Is this some kind of prank? Or is there something more sinister at play?* she asked herself.

Demetria's heart raced as she searched for answers, her mind spinning with possibilities. The stares of the passengers' expressions and the conductor's friendly demeanor only fueled her growing fear. *I don't understand . . . This can't be real. It scares me, but I need to stay calm. Maybe I'm just imagining things,* she said, her voice trembling.

Despite her attempts at self-assurance, Demetria couldn't shake the feeling that she was trapped in a nightmarish loop. The rhythmic clickety-clack of the train wheels and the persistent mist outside only intensified her unease.

She whispered, her voice shaky, *is this some sort of twisted illusion? Am I losing my mind? No, I have to keep my wits about me. There must be an explanation.* As the train rumbled on, she tried talking to the other passengers, hoping for reassurance or a sense of reality.

However, their responses were vague and emotionless, as if they were merely programmed robots. Now desperate, she wondered why they wouldn't respond. The conductor was his normal self, and as he ushered her back inside the compartment, she was convinced that she had to find a way off the train before it was too late.

Settling into her seat as she did before, the same forces she experienced and the faint shuffling, noise, and intelligible whispers were more intimidating. *I won't let this consume me. There's something wrong here, and I need to find out what it is,* she muttered. Determined to unravel the mystery, Demetria braced herself, ready to confront whatever awaited her at her destination. With each passing moment, her confidence grew, even as the reasons behind it remained unclear. Soon, she and her sisters would uncover the truth about their family.

Racing through the fog-drenched scenery, the train rattled along its tracks when a sudden knock echoed upon the compartment door. Startled, Demetria turned to find the conductor standing there, reminding her that Evansville was fast approaching. As expected, everyone in the car reacted the same way. Stepping off the train, a deep sense of déjà vu hit her. The conductor, the passengers, and those who exited with her all repeated their actions exactly as before. The conductor's words sounded the same, and everyone mirrored their previous gestures. It was as if time had looped back, trapping her in a strange cycle.

The workplace buzzed with its usual energy, and everything seemed in order. The daily routine flowed smoothly, and the walk to the train station after work felt like any other day. But despite everything feeling normal, an unusual excitement urged her to hurry home and tell her sisters about the strange experiences.

Demetria's sisters couldn't help but notice the worried expression etched across her face as she walked through the door, prompting them to ask questions.

"Is everything alright?" Eva asked. "You seem quite worked up about something."

Nervously, Demetria responded, "Today has been quite unsettling. I can't shake off this feeling of unease."

"What's going on?" Mattie asked.

"Something really strange has been happening to me lately, and it's starting to scare me. It's like I'm stuck in a never-ending loop. Every morning when I leave for work, the same events keep happening over and over again. It's unnerving."

Eva, with a confused look on her face, asked, "What do you mean by a loop?"

"Every morning when I go to the train station, I see the same people. There's always this strange mist lingering around, and I can't shake off the feeling that something's not right."

"The same people? Are you sure it's not just a coincidence?" Mattie said.

"No, it's more than that. The conductor always greets me the same way and escorts me to the same compartment."

"Did you say a compartment?" Eva asked.

"Yes. Compartment 13."

"There are no compartments on the train that runs through town. We've been going to the Aldan Circle since we were children, and the only Compartment 13 I've heard of is the one that the townspeople talk about."

"I know. But I thought it was something new."

"Why didn't you say something much sooner?" Mattie spoke.

"Okay, okay, go ahead, finish up," Eva said, eager to know more.

"And when I step inside, all the passengers smile at me. It's the same smile, Eva, every single time."

"That sounds unusual."

"It sure is, and inside the compartment, I hear these eerie sounds, like the train is carrying secrets. But it's when I exit that things get even stranger. The same people who get off with me, I never see them again as I walk away from the station. It's like they vanish into thin air, and then I see them on the train the next morning."

Concerned, Mattie asked, "This is starting to sound really disturbing. Are you okay?"

Demetria, shaking, responded, "No, Mattie, I'm terrified. It feels like some sort of loop or a never-ending cycle. I can't explain it, but the shit sends shivers down my spine every time."

"Well, I won't let you face this alone. I'll take a day off from work and come with you tomorrow. We'll figure out what's going on together."

Relieved, Demetria said, "Thanks, sis. Your support means the world to me. This is bizarre, and I need to find out what's going on."

Mattie, offering support, added, "Count me in, too. We're sisters, and we'll face this together. We won't let you go through this alone."

"No, Mattie," Eva responded. "It's best if you go to work. Demetria and I will fill you in later, okay?"

"Okay," she said, not liking the idea at all.

Eva's Train Ride

With each step toward the train station, Demetria and Eva walked into a thick mist that gave off a strange energy. Curious, Eva turned to Demetria and asked, "What do you think this all means? What could be happening?"

"Give me your hand," Demetria whispered, reaching out to Eva. As their palms met, they walked together through the mist. Eva was surprised by the experience. The mist clung to them like a thin veil. Demetria, always alert, pointed out the ticket taker and passengers boarding the train up ahead. "Look, Eva! There's the ticket taker. We're almost there."

Eva's eyes swept over the scene. The mist was heavy around the open train door, and she felt an unsettling force pulling her back. She tugged on Demetria's arm. "Demetria, something doesn't feel right. It's like . . . something is trying to keep me away from that train," she said, a worried look on her face.

"Hold on and step forward with me," Demetria said, as she locked her arms tightly around Eva, refusing to let her go as they inched closer to the door. "Don't worry. We're going to get in."

"Sis, this is crazy!" Eva responded.

Finally, despite the strange pull, they pushed forward and entered the train. The mist faded as they crossed the threshold, and the conductor greeted them. He smiled at Demetria with a sly look and acted as if he hadn't noticed Eva beside her.

"How rude it was of me not to introduce myself when we first met," he said to Demetria, smiling. "You can call me Elias," he replied, a slight smile tugging at his lips.

With raised eyebrows, Demetria nodded and mumbled, "Okay."

Elias pointed in the direction of the compartment. "Your seat is in Compartment 13." The passengers, seemingly cheerful, smiled at her and greeted her warmly, just as they had before.

"What you just heard and what you're seeing happens to me every morning for weeks," Demetria said.

"There's something creepy about everyone onboard," Eva said. Eva's curiosity got the better of her as she stepped forward. "Excuse me, sir."

"It's Elias."

"You greeted my sister, but not me. Was there a reason for that?" Eva asked, a hint of suspicion in her voice. Demetria watched closely, curious to see how things would unfold.

"Good evening, miss. Welcome aboard. What brings you to our train today?" Elias asked, his voice warm and welcoming as he addressed her. His eyes widened momentarily, then he chuckled softly. "My apologies, miss. You see, this train is a peculiar one. It's only here for those who have a reason to board. The young lady here had a reason, and that's why she was acknowledged," he explained, gesturing toward Demetria. "Now, tell me, what is your reason for boarding?"

"I'm here because of my sister," Eva explained in a firm voice. "Wherever she goes, I follow. I couldn't let her face this alone."

Elias' eyes wandered, as if nothing were inside. He silently guided them down the corridor, stopping at a compartment door. Eva looked at Demetria. With a nod, he opened it, and they both stepped inside.

"Demetria, we have to get off this train," Eva said nervously. "I don't like it. It's spooking me. This is not a normal train."

Just then, the same sensation that had gripped Demetria during her earlier rides returned. The faint shuffling sounds and unintelligible whispers sent a chill through Eva, leaving her frightened.

As the train whistle blew and the wheels creaked into motion, an eerie uneasiness settled over the compartment, stifling the fading whispers and replacing them with a disturbing stillness. Suddenly, the door burst open, and a young woman stumbled in, disheveled, with wild hair and torn clothes. Demetria leaped to her feet, alarmed. *The loop has changed. Could it be because of Eva?* she wondered.

"Are you okay?" she asked.

The woman's gaze met Demetria and Eva; her eyes filled with terror. "Please," she pleaded, her voice trembling. "You must help me. There's someone after me."

Concerned, Demetria asked, "Who? What are you talking about? Who is after you?"

"They're coming. Help me! Help me, I beg of you!"

Demetria studied her for a moment. With fear etched on her face, Eva turned to Demetria and whispered, "What should we do now?"

"We'll help," she said to Eva, then turned to the terrified woman. "Tell us what happened?"

The woman shook her head, tears streaming down her face. "I was in the next compartment and heard a scream. When I checked, I found several people lying dead on the floor." Demetria and Eva were shocked. They hadn't heard any screams, but they should have, based on what the woman said.

"Did you see anyone?" Eva asked.

The woman shook her head. "No, but I heard footsteps. I ran out and locked the door, but I'm afraid they'll come after me."

"Okay. Stay calm. Wait here," Demetria said.

"Okay," the woman said nervously.

Demetria and Eva needed to know what was happening since their lives might be at risk, too. "Come with me," Demetria said to the woman.

"Yes." She took the woman by the arm and led her out of the compartment.

"Are you sure about this, Demetria?" Eva asked.

"No, but why not since she came to us?" As they walked down the corridor, they passed other passengers who were smiling and chatting as if nothing was wrong. "Can you believe this?" Demetria said to Eva in a whisper. "Where's the conductor?"

"We are getting off this train when it gets to the next stop," Eva replied.

As if appearing from thin air, Elias appeared. With the same sly smile, he inquired, "What has happened? What is all this about?"

"There have been several murders. People are dead," Demetria told him.

"Nonsense! It would be wise for you, ladies, to return to your compartment. As for this one, she's coming with me," he declared.

"Didn't you hear what my sister just said?" Eva snapped, her frustration evident.

"Impossible! There has been no such incident on this train, I can guarantee you that," he coldly responded, his piercing stare fixed on the woman whenever Demetria and Eva glanced at the passengers.

"Tell him what you told us," Demetria said to the scared woman. Shaking and a bit reluctant, she told him.

"Come with me," he said to Demetria, Eva, and the woman.

"I'm sorry, but I believe my stop is coming up soon," Demetria said.

"We passed your stop a long time ago. Evansville, right?"

That's impossible, Demetria thought. *How could that be? I just got on the train.*

"Demetria, I think it would be in your best interest for you and Eva to come with me."

"Wait! How do you know our names?" the sisters asked in unison.

"Come with me, and you'll learn everything," he replied with a smile, leading the way back to Compartment 13.

"Why are we going back?" Demetria said as Elias opened the door. Ignoring her words, he walked to the back of the compartment, knocked twice, and the door opened. Demetria and Eva were stunned as two men appeared and grabbed the woman. "What the fuck is this?" Demetria demanded.

Without warning, a perfectly dressed woman appeared as if from thin air, drawing everyone's attention with her graceful presence. Her face was strikingly beautiful, and her every move showed a strong sense of authority. "We have been waiting for you," the woman said.

"Who are you?" Demetria asked. "And I'm guessing you know our names too?"

"I am called Abby, but you can call me Lady for now. And yes, I do know your names."

"It's strange how you and the conductor know our names, but we don't know anything about you. Why is that?"

"Please, his name is Elias. Don't worry, you'll find out soon enough."

"Lady, or whatever your name is, we need to get off this train," Eva said, with a worried look. "It hasn't stopped since we boarded."

"This might sound a bit crazy, but you're with family and friends. You're a lot like me; you just haven't realized it yet."

"What is she talking about?" Eva whispered to Demetria.

"I have no idea, but we need to get off this damn train," Demetria replied. "It's getting creepier by the minute."

"It looks like you have something else to say, do you?" Lady asked.

"That woman said she saw dead people, and those men took her away screaming. Why?" Demetria asked.

"Come," she said, leading them to where the woman was. There, Demetria and Eva saw the bodies the woman had mentioned. The woman was shackled to a gurney, awaiting her fate. Demetria and Eva were stunned as they thought about what kind of evil this could be.

"You can't do this," Eva said aloud.

"Stop this fucking train. We want to get off," Demetria added in a frantic voice.

"You won't be able to get off until I say so," Lady replied.

"Why are you doing this to us? What about the passengers?" Demetria demanded.

"Haven't you noticed by now? We're all one big family."

"We're not your family. We don't know you. Who are you? The train, the passengers, everything is a mystery. Are you even real?" Demetria asked.

Eva's voice trembled as she pleaded, "Stop the train. Let us go. Why are you doing this to us?"

"Rest assured, you will be fine. The woman and the bodies that you saw are the enemies of our bloodline. They aren't worthy to be amongst the living or the spirits."

"Our bloodline?" Demetria asked, glancing at the compartment walls, which seemed to react to every word Lady spoke.

Lady levitated, spinning several times as the compartment's roof seemed to expand with her movements. "Let me tell you about family. You've heard the stories about Kramden, like all the other townspeople. It's on this train that the townspeople dumped the mutilated bodies of my bloodline, my family, and yours, after savagely killing them for generations. I was buried alive. My siblings, my mother, and my father were buried alongside me. Yet the ancient blood of our lineage carried me into the embrace of the abyss, where our blood rules and dominates," Lady said in a stoic voice.

Demetria and Eva froze, exchanging glances, their minds reeling from the revelation. Escaping the train suddenly seemed less important than the horrifying truth Lady had just shared.

"So, the stories we have heard about the train yard and the Aldan Circle are true?" Eva asked.

"Yes, they are. Let me continue. The passengers who ride with us are families that share the same fate. The Barrs, Siobhan, and Wicks are three of the oldest and most powerful families around. Aren't you, Siobhans?"

Demetria and Eva stuttered before replying, "Yes, we are."

Lady gave a satisfied smile before continuing. "The concrete barricade behind Aldan Circle was erected after the townspeople reported seeing the dead, and indeed, they had. To calm their fears, they built the barricade, cutting off access to Compartment 13, and created Aldan Circle. Thirteen families lived here at the time, including yours and mine.

Renegade Jones, you're familiar with the name, aren't you? Well, he and the other families share a dark connection: their ancestors did this to ours. That bastard Renegade Jones is a relative of Gerome Wick. Talk to your parents; they'll tell you everything. Again, this woman is from one of the families that attacked us. One by one, we bring them to the train and exact our revenge. What you've seen on the platform these past weeks is the Compartment train. Unfortunately for Renegade Jones and the others, they see it as the Aldan Circle train. We'll continue to ravage the town with their blood."

Demetria was speechless, struggling to believe what she had just heard. It seemed too bizarre to be real, but the woman, the bodies, and Lady's presence made it undeniable. Why was this happening to them? She glanced at her sister, realizing they needed to get home right away to talk to their parents about what they'd witnessed.

Eva's voice trembled with anxiety as she said, "We missed our stop. We just want to go home."

Lady reassured them calmly, "There's no need to be nervous. Don't worry; the next stop is where you get off." As the train approached the Aldan Circle stop, Lady, Elias, and the passengers waved and smiled at the sisters. "Remember, we'll be waiting, and don't forget our conversation," Lady reminded them before the sisters stepped off the train.

8

Answers

"It's night," Eva said, shocked, turning to Demetria. "It can't be."

"I don't know what to say," Demetria replied.

"We weren't on that train for long . . . That's impossible," Eva exclaimed. How? Did we really see and hear those things?"

"I know, it felt like minutes."

"Demetria, we got on the train in the morning."

"Eva, it's real. We experienced it. I thought something was wrong with me, too, the first time it happened to me."

"I'm glad I went with you, though. But you know what stood out to me?"

"What?" Demetria asked, hoping Eva would say what she was thinking, and she did.

"She said they killed members of our family, and hers, and that the Barrs, Siobhan, and Wick are three of the oldest families," Eva continued.

"Mother and Father will have to explain," Demetria said.

"They always do," Eva added. They exchanged a glance, wondering what other secrets their family might hold, and whether what Lady said was really true.

Demetria and Eva hurried through the streets, their minds still reeling from the encounter. Every hateful stare they met only deepened the growing animosity inside them. Eva's expression mirrored Demetria's as they held hands, the sound of gravel echoing in the night with each step toward their home.

As they reached the front door of their home, they took deep breaths and opened it. Their parents, sensing something was wrong, asked, "What happened to you two? You've been gone all day."

"You both look shaken," Alias said.

"Where is Mattie?" Demetria asked.

"She's in the room," Doris replied.

"Go get her," Demetria said to Eva. "She needs to hear this."

"You still haven't answered me," Alias said, as Eva returned with Mattie.

"What's happening?" Mattie asked, a curious look on her face.

Demetria sat down at the table, her voice trembling as she recounted the train ride and the shocking appearance of Lady. Shocked was an understatement as Doris and Alias stared at her and Eva, a look of disbelief on their faces when she mentioned the names of the murdered families.

"Father, she mentioned our surname along with the Wicks. She's a Barr. She told us everything. She's dead. Why didn't you tell us that Renegade Jones's ancestors murdered our family?" Demetria said.

"Wait, what? Who did what?" Mattie asked.

"You said she's dead?" Alias asked calmly.

"Yes, Father," Eva replied.

Doris turned to Alias, an apprehensive look on her face. "Alias, it's time to tell them," she whispered to him.

Alias nodded in agreement, his eyes reflecting the past.

It was time for Demetria, Eva, and Mattie to learn the truth about their family's dark bloodline. The girls, sensing the gravity of the moment, exchanged curious glances. Alias took a deep breath, summoning the courage to delve into a tale buried beneath layers of secrecy for generations. He began to speak, his voice calm yet filled with regret. It was a burden he carried for not sharing this important part of their family's history sooner.

"Girls, there is a darkness that has haunted our bloodline for centuries. Our bloodline is an ancient one from the Old Country," Alias began, his voice trembling slightly. "It all began with the Barrs, a powerful and influential family with whom we share blood. And the woman you met, Lady, is Abby. She was chosen by the ancient ones before she was born."

"He said her name," Eva whispered to Demetria, who bit her lip to signal her sister that she understood.

The sisters were all ears as they listened, captivated by their father's words. "What did they do, Father? What happened in the town of Kramden?" Demetria asked as Alias finished up.

"She led the family, and they killed with impunity before settling in Kramden. Even here, they killed, and our family," he stuttered, "we joined forces with them. It was a bloodbath."

"Our ancestors?" Eva asked.

"Yes," Doris replied. "Our family. It was done for a reason."

"And what reason was that?" Mattie asked.

Alias continued, his gaze fixed on his daughters. "The Wicks family was one of the founders of Kramden. They declared war against us alongside several other families, and we were ready to fight, which is why we joined forces. Initially, there were 13 families with connections to the Old Country. But the Wicks called upon several demons, chanting incantations, wiping out most of them. They abused their power, succumbing to their desires and wielding them without restraint. They brought pain and suffering to the people of Kramden, terrorizing the town with their evil."

"So, we never sided with the Wicks, ever?" Demetria asked.

"No, they were just one of the three oldest families in these parts," Alias answered.

Doris interjected softly, her voice filled with remorse. "But there were those who rose against us, including members of our bloodline. There was darkness in our line, and we had to rid ourselves of those forces. At the same time, we had to oppose the Wicks' reign of terror."

"Your mother is correct; it was the start of a generational bloodbath that thrives to this day. After they killed Abby, the chosen one, her spirit and the spirits of our murdered family members return every few years. This has been happening ever since and will continue after your mother and I are no longer here. So yes, Renegade Jones and his allies are our enemies, and people will continue to die because Abby's spirit reigns over Kramden. She wants vengeance."

Doris added. "The three of you are heirs to one of the most powerful bloodlines. On the night you were born, a crescent moon rose, marking you with a force given only to the chosen of our line."

The sisters stared in disbelief at their parents.

"So . . . this bloodline . . . it's ours?" Demetria asked in almost a whisper.

Alias nodded. "Yes. Everything you are, every unrealized gift you have, comes from the legacy of our blood. You are heirs to something far older and more powerful than you realized. Abby knows this."

"The crescent moon welcomed you, and the spirits rejoice. You carry the ancestors' gifts in your bones," Doris exclaimed.

"And when will we see and understand these gifts?" Eva asked.

"Yes, when?" Mattie said.

"You will know when it happens. Neither your mother nor I can say, but it will happen," Alias said.

As they spoke, the names of the families who had risen against the Siobhans became clearer to the sisters. They were some of the main instigators who not only stared at the sisters but also muttered under their breath whenever they saw them.

"So, our bloodline is tainted with evil?" Demetria asked.

Alias reached out, gently holding his daughter's hands, his eyes filled with compassion. "It is true that darkness once coursed through our veins, but our ancestors fought valiantly to redeem our family's name. They severed their ties with the Barrs and other families after Abby's death, forging a path of peace and using their powers to protect and restore balance."

"Why would they do such a thing, knowing what Gerome and his bloodline did?" Demetria continued.

"It was a truce that didn't last long."

"I'm sure Renegade Jones and his followers didn't think it would last," Demetria said, glancing at her sisters.

"I'm sure he didn't," Mattie said.

Alias knit his brows. "I understand. But we can't think like him now."

"Lady made it seem like there's still a connection between her family and us, is there?" Eva asked.

"Maybe I misspoke about that. But we're the same. There is a connection, but your mother and I never talk about it."

"Who do you think is responsible for the recent deaths?" Demetria asked, turning to her mother. "A woman passenger . . . she was murdered on the train. There were other bodies as well. Lady said her ancestors were with those who killed her family. And that, her ancestors will pay the penalty just as she did."

"Yes, it's the curse. It must be done. She tells the truth," Doris responded.

"Mother, shouldn't they be afraid after hearing all this?" Mattie asked.

"Who, Mattie?"

"Demetria and Eva," she replied.

"No, my dear. You and your sisters will be okay."

"Can I go now?"

"Sure, Mattie," Doris said. She turned to Demetria and Eva as Alias watched, nodding. "The sins of our bloodline are behind us. But by you seeing Abby, then there's more coming; it's just the beginning, and you will see her again until it's time for her to rest."

It got quiet for a moment, but Demetria and Eva, though shaken by what they had learned, felt they owed it to their ancestors to follow their paths, but at the same time were worried.

9

Questions, Answers, And Results

After leaving their parents in the kitchen, the sisters went to their room to discuss what they had heard.

"Now that we know who we are and where our bloodline descends from, we have to do something, and we need to start with the good people of Kramden. They need to know the truth. We can't keep pretending everything's fine in this town. The evil bloodlines deserve what's happening to them, and much more," Demetria said to her sisters.

"Are you sure there are good people here?" Mattie asked, jokingly.

"I would hope so," Demetria responded with a half-smile.

"Am I thinking what you're thinking?" Eva asked, staring at Demetria.

"What is that?" Mattie wanted to know.

"I'll answer that easily for both of you. Yes. I agree with Abby. The ancestors of those evil people should all be killed for what they did to our family," Demetria said angrily.

"But from what you two said, she's a spirit, right? So how can we follow a spirit? Can I see her?" Mattie asked.

"Mattie, she's real, and you heard what Mother and Father said. Don't worry, I'll take you. Kramden might seem nice on the surface, but this place has a lot of hidden secrets. Some of the people here are capable of terrible things, especially Renegade Jones. Abby has come to take revenge. It's the right thing to do to make them pay for what they've done. Look at how they treat us, the three of us?"

Mattie's face turned pale as she glanced between her older sisters. "But . . . but what if our parents are against it?"

"Against it? Are you serious? You heard what Mother said. Abby told us the truth, and neither she nor Father said we shouldn't do anything. We were chosen," Demetria replied.

"And she said we will be okay," Eva added.

"It doesn't matter what they think now that they're older. Some people in this town need to be taught a lesson," Demetria said.

Eva and Demetria exchanged a knowing look that Mattie didn't notice.

"Mattie, we don't know everything, but our parents know a lot more than we do," Eva said.

"But you just said it doesn't matter what they think, and they're old," Mattie responded.

"Sure, but not in the way you think. They only want to protect us. That's why they say the things they do. But this time, they're right. You can't always see the truth, but Demetria and I can. Got it?"

Demetria, trying to provide some assurance, added. "We've seen things that make us believe, Mattie. You've seen some of it. We can't stand by and let this shit continue."

"We are telling you this because the time has come for us to pay them back for our ancestors, our bloodline. It's not like you don't know the world around you. We will do everything we can to keep you safe, but we need you to trust us and understand why we support Abby.

We will take you with us next time, isn't that right, Demetria?" Eva said to Mattie.

Mattie listened, trying to make sense of the truths she had just learned. None of them knew that their journey would test their bond and challenge everything they thought they knew about good and evil.

****

Later that night, as the family slept, Demetria and Eva huddled together in the living room. Demetria whispered, her voice barely audible, "Eva, we can't let this go on any longer. Are you with me?"

Eva, her heart pounding. "You're right, Demetria. We owe it to our ancestors. It's time to turn up the heat and reveal the secrets that have haunted us for far too long. I knew something was behind the feelings that would eat at me."

"Me too," Demetria added. "I felt the stares and the walks were preparing us for something that we were born for. And when the train rides began, I wasn't so sure, but now, I'm convinced more than ever."

Walking back to their room, Demetria and Eva glanced at Mattie, who was already asleep. They couldn't let her grow up in a world filled with Renegade Joneses. "Yes, our bloodline matters," Eva said.

The next morning, as the sun began to rise, Demetria and Eva woke Mattie. She rubbed her eyes, a curious look on her face.

"Are we really going?" Mattie asked.

"Yes, we are," Demetria replied. "Now go clean up!"

Mattie had a look of excitement and uncertainty on her face. "But our parents say she's a spirit."

"You're a Siobhan, and if Abby is a spirit, then so are we," Eva stated.

"There's a long list of families responsible for our family's downfall, and we won't let those involved escape," Demetria added.

Eva knelt, embracing Mattie gently. "There are some things we need to talk to Abby about that concern all of us. We believe she holds the key to Kramden's dark secrets."

Mattie looked at Demetria and then at Eva. "Okay. If you think it's important, then I want to know the truth too."

As they headed out, they were caught in the mist. Mattie was surprised by what she was seeing. As Demetria and Eva guided her through the eerie fog, they tightly locked their arms, forming a protective circle. Mattie's wide eyes darted around, fear etched on her face. She peppered them with a flurry of questions.

"Is it safe? What's happening? Why is it so spooky?" Mattie's voice trembled.

Demetria squeezed her hand gently, "Don't worry. We're right here with you, and everything will be fine. We're just passing through a mist, that's all. We'll be all right." Mattie's fear faded. Once they reached the train station, the train whistle pierced the air.

"Hold on," Eva said to her. They stepped aboard, feeling the vibrations beneath their feet as the engine roared to life. Elias approached, his gaze on Mattie.

"Why is he staring at me like that?" Mattie asked.

"Don't worry. Let him look," Demetria reassured her. Extending his hand in the direction of Compartment 13, the three followed. As they settled into their seats, Mattie stood frozen as Lady's ethereal form materialized before her, draped in a flowing gown, her face a mask of haunting paleness.

"Stay calm, Mattie," Demetria whispered. "This is Lady, the restless spirit of the Barr family."

Mattie's heart raced as she glanced at the ghostly figure before her.

"You must be Mattie," Lady said. "There's no need to be afraid. I'm sure your sisters have told you everything. And if you're here, your parents must have, too. That's why you've come, isn't it?"

Mattie stammered, not realizing she had ignored Lady's question. "What happened to your family?"

The ghostly form of Lady floated closer, her voice carrying a mournful tone. "The same thing that happened to yours, murdered. We're linked by this, and that will never change." Turning to Demetria and Eva, she added, "I told you we'd be waiting, and now it's time."

"Time for what?" Mattie asked, glancing at her sisters, who didn't seem to know what Lady was talking about.

"I am bound to this earthly realm, cursed to wander until our family's story is told. It's time for revenge. The descendants of George Wick and his followers will feel our wrath. The Old Country agrees. Our bloodline is in agreement."

"But, Lady, how can we help?" Demetria asked.

"Don't worry. Greta and Anne, relatives of both yours and mine, will help."

"Relatives? Here?" Eva asked. "No one's ever mentioned them. Where are they, and who are they?"

"Your parents never mentioned them?"

"No."

"It's understandable. No need to worry. They live on the outskirts of town. Their last name is Whitlocks. They'll be waiting for you."

"And these people are real?" Mattie asked, a curious look on her face.

Lady's gaze softened. "As real as you and your sisters. The Wicks have long evaded the consequences of their wicked deeds. I appeal to you; we will find the truth and restore honor to our families' names."

Demetria and Eva nodded in agreement. "We will do everything in our power, Lady," Eva vowed.

With a flash, Lady began to fade, her voice softening as it echoed in the confined space. "Follow the directions I gave you."

As Lady disappeared, the sisters exchanged glances. Mattie absorbed every word Lady spoke, and from the look on her sisters' faces, she knew they were all in. The remaining families had to be dealt with, and Mattie was ready to act.

As the train pulled into the Aldan Circle stop, the sisters stepped off with a shared sense of purpose. They had a plan: to eliminate one member of each bloodline over time.

"It all feels so surreal," Mattie confessed.

Eva chuckled softly, understanding her sister's sentiment. "You mean the train rides and the mist, don't you?"

Mattie nodded. "Yes, everything. It's like stepping into another world, another existence altogether."

Demetria placed a reassuring hand on Mattie's shoulder. "You see, Mattie, the mist and the train create an out-of-body experience. They let us see and communicate with Lady. But once we step off the train, the mist disappears, and we return to our normal selves. The train and its compartments exist in a realm beyond our own."

Mattie took in the information, her mind trying to understand the strange situation. "So, the people who board the train with us, they're all. . . ?"

"They're all dead, Mattie, spirits. They are relatives of the families that were murdered by the Wicks and their followers." A heavy feeling washed over Mattie as she thought about what her sisters would do next. As the youngest of the sisters, she knew they were stepping into dangerous territory, but she also understood it was necessary.

"We must be careful and strategic," Demetria said. "We can't let anyone suspect our true intentions. We have to act when the time is right."

10

The Evil Four

It was a short drive to Greta and Anne's farmhouse. The two women greeted them. The sisters were surprised when they discovered they were also sisters. Demetria and Eva felt an instant connection, but not so much Mattie, who felt somewhat uneasy. After going over what Lady told them, there was an eagerness to please her. They were prepared to give the evil bloodline of Kramden a warm welcome. First on the list was Milton Jackson.

"It's time," Demetria said to the others.

"We are more than ready," Greta said.

Minutes later, the group got into Anne's truck for the ride to Milton Jackson's home. His place was on the far end of town. Demetria did most of the talking as they drove, oblivious to the changing looks on the others' faces.

"There have been many strange deaths along this road," Greta said. "Strange deaths for decades until we realized why it was happening, and who was doing it."

"Was it Lady?" Eva asked.

"Yes, but it wasn't just her. The dead and living ancestors of George Wick and several other families were killing anyone they suspected had ties to ours. Many strangers died, simply for being in the wrong place at the wrong time," Anne said.

It wasn't long before the truck turned onto a dusty road lined with several dilapidated homes in desperate need of repair. The rotting fence posts leaned to the right at an angle and were held up by loose barbed wire. As the truck came to a stop in front of a shabby house, Greta said it was the place. The truck pulled into a driveway that had seen better days.

"Wait here," Greta said to the others as she and Demetria walked to the door.

There was a knock on the door. "Who is it?" responds a gruff voice.

"It's the police, but not to be alarmed, we are investigating the theft of several cars from the community, and we would like to ask you a few questions, sir," Greta said.

"Okay. Give me a minute."

An unshaven old man opened the door. An old woman wearing glasses was sitting on a battered couch watching television. "Milton, tell them we don't know anything about any cars being stolen around here," the old woman said, in an agitated voice.

"We got to respect the law," the old man said.

"Milton Jackson?" Demetria asked.

"Yes."

"We would like to talk to you," she said, shoving him inside.

"What is this? You're not the police. Who are you, people? Get the fuck off my property!"

"Get out of our home!" the old woman yelled.

"Calm down now, Mr. Jackson. Don't you know who I am?"

"No! Who the hell are you and what do you want?"

"You do know me."

"No, he doesn't. Now get out!" the old woman continued.

"I'm Demetria Siobhan, and this is Greta Barr."

Scratching what was left of the shaggy gray hair on his head, he said, "Siobhan and Barr, hmm! Abby sent you. We know about her. They say she's been dead for a long time; either way, my family did what they had to."

"So, I guess you're ready to meet your ancestors?" Demetria asked. Just then, Eva, Mattie, and Anne stepped into the house.

As he looked at Demetria, for a moment, he saw Abby instead. Fear gripped him as he mumbled, "It can't be you . . . you . . . are young." The figure before him wasn't Demetria anymore. It was Lady. Milton Jackson shuddered in terror.

"What the fuck is going on, Milton?" the old woman asked.

"It's Abby Barr."

"Abby Barr? The whore who died generations ago, way before I was born. So what the fuck are you talking about?"

"Be quiet," Mr. Jackson said. "What do you want?" he paused, then added, regaining his composure.

"We already told you," Demetria responded.

The couple was quickly bound to their chairs, watching in fear as they screamed and hollered, but no one heard their cries. The women wielded scalpels with chilling precision, slashing the couple's throats and leaving behind a horrifying scene of blood. A spell seemed to overtake them as they cleaned up, shutting the door behind them before walking to the truck and driving off.

How did it go? a whispery voice asked.

"It went well. They weren't glad to see us. The old woman had nothing nice to say. But she said enough to recall you," Demetria responded.

Well, this is a notice to all of them.

"We'll take care of everything," Demetria declared with confidence. In an instant, the mist that had filled the truck dispersed, returning everyone to their normal state.

"We're fully aware," Eva acknowledged. "We heard every word. You are Lady's chosen medium," she said to Demetria.

"Yes, and we still have a lot to take care of," Demetria said. "It's going to be a long day, you do know that?"

"Yes. And I have no problem with it. I'm just glad the time has come because they were wrong for doing what they did," Anne stated. "My sister and I have been waiting for this moment. And what Lady has said must be done in a certain amount of time."

"What do you mean?" Mattie asked.

"We don't have an answer, but we know that there are times when she shows up and times when she doesn't. It can be years that she doesn't show up. We were told this from we were children. So, everything must be done on time. The Jacksons are the start of what is to come."

"So, what about the train, does it run when she doesn't show up?" Eva asked the sisters.

"It doesn't," Greta answered.

"So how do you communicate with her when this happens?" Eva continued.

"There's a way, and it's beyond the Aldan Circle. The old Compartment 13 stop is still there, and though it may not be visible to some, our parents told us that whoever the medium is for Lady, they can talk to her. So, you see, Eva, we can still get the job done on these bastards."

"Hmm! We will do whatever it takes," Eva smiled.

"I'm glad you feel this way because they will see our faces before nightfall," Greta said as the truck drove down the dusty road to a modest-looking ranch house.

"Stay put," Demetria said to Mattie as they exited the truck and knocked on Eugene Dimple's door. He opened it, scowling, cursing, and yelling, not realizing it wasn't the person he thought it was.

"Whoever the fuck you are, I have nothing to give. I don't read the bible, and I'm not a Christian," he snarled.

"Eugene, why are you so angry? And what a way to greet friends," Demetria said.

"I said, get the fuck away from here! And how the fuck do you know my name? I don't have any fucking friends. Maybe this shotgun will change your mind," he snarled, reaching for it. Before his fingers touched the weapon, he was tackled and subdued.

"Anyone else here with you?" Eva asked, looking over the filthy living room.

"No one else is here. You do know I'm going to report this to the sheriff?"

"You're going to do no such thing. You don't remember us?" Greta and Anne asked.

"Why the fuck would I remember you when I don't even know you?"

"What about me? Do you remember me? Look closely, you son of a bitch! You don't recognize me?" Demetria demanded. But the person he was staring at wasn't Demetria. It was a vision of Lady.

"What the fuck! You died. You're dead," he yelled.

"I have come to pay you a visit. You should know why I'm here, don't you?"

"I had nothing to do with it. It was my bloodline. I heard the stories of how they stood there and watched. Why come after me?"

"You'll know soon enough," the vision of Lady said before slipping away from Demetria's body.

"What about the recent murders?" Greta asked.

"I was there, but I didn't do anything. A lot of people were there. They stood and watched just like I did. It . . . it was Milton and those two women," Eugene said, his voice trembling.

"You mean like your ancestors did to our families?"

"No, no!" Eugene said, his eyes glancing at the women.

"So, you and your ancestors are still killing even to this day? And what two women are you talking about?" Demetria asked before Greta could respond.

"Lizzie and Suzan. They were behind it."

"Is that so?" Demetria smiled. "What if I were to tell you that Milton Jackson and his wife are dead?"

"Dead? No, I saw him earlier today."

"He's dead."

"Who did it?"

"We did. And you're about to meet him in hell," Demetria said, a disgusted look on her face.

While Mattie waited in the truck, the four women moved without hesitation. Seconds later, it was done. His private parts were removed and stuffed in his mouth. His eyes were gouged out, and his neck was sliced from ear to ear, and several markings were left on his body.

"What did he say, if anything?" Mattie asked when they got back to the truck.

"That he wasn't involved in the recent killings," Greta exclaimed. "And that Suzan and Lizzie are related and are from the Asher family."

"Andy Asher's family? But didn't he stand up for us against Renegade Jones?" Mattie asked, turning to her sisters.

"It doesn't matter, Mattie, his bloodline is our enemy, and they must be killed," Eva remarked.

Suzan and Lizzie were on the sisters' minds as the truck sped toward Suzan's house. As it came to a stop, they noticed two cars parked in the driveway. "Looks like she has company," Greta said.

Mattie rose from her seat and made it clear to everyone that she wasn't staying in the truck. "I'm coming," she said.

"There's no need for that," Demetria responded.

"Do you think that I don't know what I'm doing? I may be your baby sister," she stated, "but I'm not a fool. I won't take no for an answer. I'm coming."

"Demetria, she's coming. Mattie, it's okay," Eva said, glancing at Greta and Anne, whose expressions seemed to say, *leave us out of it*, as the women approached the front door.

The house was noticeably in better condition than the other two. Greta rang the doorbell. To her surprise, it was Lizzie who answered the door. Surprised as well, Lizzie didn't know what to make of the others. She greeted Anne before calling for Suzan.

"Well, if it isn't Ms. Greta and her sister Anne. To what do I owe the pleasure of your visit? And may I ask who your friends are?" Suzan asked.

"We're just making our presence known in the community . . ." Greta stated before being cut off.

"No, come on in," Suzan said, ushering them in, "please, sit down."

"Thank you," Greta responded with a smirk that went unnoticed.

"It's fine. You were saying, Greta?"

"I was saying that we're here to make our presence known."

"How so?"

"We're here to kill you and Lizzie," Mattie said with a scowl.

Stuttering, Suzan asked, "Is this some kind of a joke?"

"No, it's not," the others said in unison as they lunged at her. Lizzie screamed as Suzan's eyes were gouged out and her body sliced to pieces.

"No! You can't do this. I'm begging you. Please don't do this."

"It's a little too late for that," Eva responded.

"Please," Lizzie begged. It was over in an instant as Eva and Mattie tore into her.

Dusk had settled upon the landscape, casting long shadows as Demetria, Eva, Mattie, Greta, and Anne quietly exited the house, their faces masked with an eerie satisfaction. They climbed into the truck, their hearts still racing from the unimaginable horrors they had unleashed upon the last unsuspecting victims.

As the engine roared to life, they drove back to Greta and Anne's home. There was an eerie silence in the truck, broken only by the faint sound of their breathing and the occasional sigh of satisfaction.

Finally, they arrived at the house, hidden from prying eyes. The women stepped out of the truck and walked to the back of the house, where they entered. They entered the living room, which was dimly lit, and it cast an ethereal glow upon their faces.

Demetria stood tall and proud as she spoke. "We did it. We shattered their world, leaving nothing but bodies in our wake."

Mattie, her voice laced with a twisted glee, chimed in. "Oh, the fear in their eyes. It was as if we held the power of the ancestors."

Eva, her eyes glinting with a sinister delight, added, "Their feeble attempts to fight back were mere entertainment. We were unstoppable, like a force of nature."

Greta and Anne shared a knowing glance. Anne's voice dripped with chilling delight. "Their screams of agony still echo in my mind, reverberating with the sweet melody of our victory. They all got what they deserved."

Greta nodded, her expression twisted with pleasure and madness. "And the blood. Oh, the rivers of crimson that flowed under our hands. It was like art, an exquisite masterpiece we painted with every life we extinguished. Lady will be proud of us."

As they reveled in their wicked triumph, their twisted tales grew ghastlier, revealing the depths of their depravity. "I loved that their pleas for mercy fell upon deaf ears. With one swift motion, we silenced them forever," Demetria smiled.

Waiting for a pause in their conversation, Greta takes a deep breath. "So, you three experienced the mist and the train rides?"

"We did. But what I want to know is why she chose us?" Demetria said.

"We thought the same thing, but as time went on, we knew that our family's namesake wasn't going to be buried by the townspeople in this damn town. And when we found out that she shows up at certain times, we were more than willing to be chosen." As darkness loomed over the living room, they knew they were united by blood and Lady.

//

Sisters

"You think we're foolish to what the three of you have been up to?" Alias asked. "We know what you were doing outside the house, and we know who you've been traveling with."

"So, are you against what we're doing?" Demetria asked him.

"No. But why couldn't you tell us?"

"Pay no attention to him," Doris said. "I wanted you to do this. Because I couldn't do it." The sisters were taken aback as they listened to their mother's words. "But when you told us about Abby, I realized that it was time to take revenge. I was relieved. I knew it was possible. And with you in charge, Demetria, I was pleased."

"Mother, why didn't you say something? Why didn't you get involved back in your day?" Eva asked.

"Your father objected to my involvement." Alias only glanced at his wife.

"I never wanted her to take part in what we were doing. I wanted to bring her along slowly. Maybe I should have told you a lot more than I did," Alias said to his daughters.

"I was hoping you would," Demetria said. "But it's okay. I'm more in awe of what you did than ever before, and for making sure that mother was always safe."

"We only have each other. Our estranged family should never know about this," Alias added.

"Our estranged family?" Mattie asked.

"We were told to leave the past behind. But some of us just couldn't. We stayed. But some fled to other parts of Kramden . . . and beyond."

"They ran. They fled. Yes, they did!" Doris interjected.

"Greta and Anne, their family moved to the outskirts of town, and they have done their part in getting revenge. No one was angry at them because they did what they had to. But those who ran, we don't know what happened to them. But those of us that stayed never gave up. Greta and Anne's grandparents were our leaders here, and we reached out to them. It's been a constant battle. On the other hand, our estranged family is off-limits. If you cross paths on the outskirts of town or in one of the other cities, make sure to keep your distance. Understood?" Alias said.

"Yes," they said in unison before excusing themselves after the conversation.

****

"It feels good knowing that our parents were involved more than we thought, and having their support is a good thing," Eva said.

"We're all together in this. It's better they know now rather than later," Demetria added.

"The gall of these people and the way they are treating some of the town folks," Mattie said. "I'm glad that Greta and Anne took matters into their own hands."

"We are going to put an end to this bullshit. Those who make the laws around here will wish they were somewhere else when it's all said and done, especially that fucker, Renegade Jones," Demetria remarked.

"It has to be done," Eva added. The sisters nodded.

"What about our estranged family members that Father mentioned?" Mattie asked.

"What about them?" Demetria asked. "Like he said, we'll keep our distance, but if we cross paths, I'm smart enough to convince them to join us. If not, we'll get rid of them like the others, and especially if Lady agrees."

Mattie raised an eyebrow. "Are you serious?" she asked, glancing at her sisters.

"Very much so."

"And I second it," Eva added.

12

All Aboard

The next day, the three sisters were aboard the train. Elias smiled as he led them to the compartment, where Greta and Anne awaited. Demetria clasped her hands as a misty apparition appeared before her and the others as Lady's ghostly image took form. "We followed your instructions, and the evil four and the others are with their ancestors," she said as Lady appeared.

Ah, yes, excellent, and there's still a lot more to be done. They waited eagerly to hear what else she had to say as the train chugged along.

"Please, guide us further in our quest to continue the killings in Kramden," Greta added.

Lady speaking softly, *I sense your dedication, my dear ones. I am here, speak, and I shall listen.*

"We did as you asked," Anne interjected. "We went to the abandoned house and found the keys to the old library like you said."

One of the keys unlocks the entrance to the ancient church. Beneath lies the library, where, within its neglected archives, you'll uncover a tale long forgotten. It's a part of our existence and who we are.

"If it's a part of who we are, why is it cursed?" Mattie asked.

It is something that has echoed through our family for generations. I could tell you the reasons, but it would not change what it is, a part of who we are. Tell me, Mattie, do you consider yourself cursed? Answer that, and you will have your answer.

"No, I don't," she replied.

Good! Let's continue. It speaks of a cursed Artifact hidden deep within the town, feeding the darkness that has befallen Kramden. You will use the second key to retrieve the Artifact. Bring it to me. The sisters had a surprised look on their faces as they tried to make sense of what they had heard.

Lady nodded. *The Artifact holds the spirits of several powerful malevolent entities, which can be rebellious, drawing power from fear and chaos. To locate it, you must seek the chamber of forgotten relics, hidden beneath the ruins of the old chapel. But beware, for the spirit guarding the Artifact is relentless and will do anything to protect its power. I need it.*

"How can we confront such a powerful spirit?" Eva asked in a worried voice. "We're just ordinary individuals."

Remember, my dear ones, strength lies not in physical prowess but in the purity of your intentions. Unite your hearts and minds, for together, you possess a force that can overcome even the darkest of adversaries. Seek the sacred talismans scattered throughout the town. They hold ancient powers that will aid you in your battle. And think of me, and our ancestors, our voices will guide you.

Demetria braced herself. "We will gather the talismans you spoke of and confront the spirit within the old chapel. We will get it safely to you."

Once you have gathered the talismans, they shall guide you in harnessing that power. It's what we need. It's to guide you when I'm not around. It will allow you to banish the darkness and evil forces that have plagued us and shatter the cursed spirits that fight us. Evil versus evil!

A grateful Greta responded, "We are forever indebted to your guidance and wisdom. Thank you for believing in us and leading us on this path."

Eva responded, "We won't fail, Lady. We'll honor our legacy and rid Kramden of this evil."

May the spirit of our ancestors watch over you. We are the darkest of the dark, and we will prevail. Go forth, my dear ones, Lady said, her image fading away. Despite the challenges waiting in the old chapel, the sisters felt a deep sense of duty.

Duty Calls

"Why does Lady switch her voice when she talks to us. Don't you notice it?" Mattie asked as the Sisters' truck pulled up in front of the town's ancient church, the building looming silently as if waiting for them.

"Some things are best left alone, Mattie. And it's not for us to question," Anne said.

"Anne's right," Demetria stated.

As they approached, a ominous feeling settled over them, and they exchanged uneasy glances. A dilapidated door loomed ahead. They used one of the two keys to unlock it. Once inside, they walked down the creaking, worn stairs, paying close attention to each step. Turning on the lantern they brought with them, they noticed several bookshelves. They began searching for clues among the dusty old books and scrolls.

Eva whispered, "Demetria, there's a passage."

"Where?"

"There," she pointed.

"Mattie, bring the lantern," Demetria said. They entered, making their way through the debris on the floor and cobwebs.

"Look, there's a door," Eva exclaimed.

"Mattie, shine it over there," Demetria said. "Give me the keys." Mattie handed them to her. She unlocked the door.

"We need to find it," Eva stated. A dusty table held stacks of books and shredded fragments of what looked like old manuscripts.

"Is this an archive? It looks like a piece of shit," Mattie remarked, as they laughed.

"I thought the same thing," Demetria said.

They began rifling through the books and manuscripts. It wasn't long before they found the answer to what they were looking for. "We have to find the other passages that lead beneath the ruins," Demetria said.

"It says to go this way," Mattie said.

"Display the sacred talismans. Remember what Lady said?" Greta stated.

Demetria, closing her eyes, said, "You're right. Let's focus."

As the Sisters continued looking, a subtle warmth came over them. Voices stirred from deep within their blood, startling them as they echoed in their minds, urging them toward a hidden section of the archives. Anne froze. "Lady said we'd be guided," she whispered.

Following the clues, they navigated secret passages and deciphered cryptic symbols. Finally, beneath the church, they discovered an ancient chamber, and after several fumbles with the second key, they opened it.

There in front of them was a cryptic casket, and hidden inside was the Artifact. Shaken by the sight of it, the Sisters clung to their talismans, their only shield against the deadly force radiating from the Artifact. Without the talismans, the force would have been fatal. Yet their power held, letting the Sisters see it, and allowing Demetria, chosen by blood, to lift it.

Demetria carefully handled the Artifact. "We have to take this to Lady. She'll know how to neutralize its dark powers."

"Be careful with it," Anne said, eyeing it warily. "We don't know what else it's capable of."

"Hurry," Greta said, glancing over her shoulder. "I don't think we're alone."

The Sisters moved quickly, carrying the Artifact to a hidden place known only to them. They secured it, taking no chances, before vanishing into the dark. In hushed tones, they agreed on when and where to meet Lady. They knew the artifact was dangerous, and leaving it unguarded was not an option.

_13_

The Exchange

The train idled at the station, almost as if it had been waiting for the Sisters. Without hesitation, they stepped onto the platform and boarded. Demetria held the mysterious Artifact tightly. As the rhythmic clatter of wheels against the rails filled the air, they made their way to Lady's compartment.

"Welcome," Lady greeted them, standing before Elias and a woman the Sisters had never seen before. The woman, introduced only by her presence, appeared human, just like Elias, but she was one of them, an ethereal being bound to the unseen.

"You're speaking to us differently again," Demetria said, noticing the change.

"Don't worry, you'll get used to it," Lady replied.

Demetria handed the Artifact to Lady, who examined it carefully. "Ah, the key to unlocking the power we need to rid ourselves of our enemies." Lady's fingers glided over the intricate patterns on the surface, and it began to glow.

Mattie hesitated before speaking, "But Lady, is it safe to use such dark magic? Won't it bring consequences?"

Lady chuckled softly, but there was an eeriness to it. "My sweet Mattie, power is a double-edged sword. It's how we wield it that matters. This Artifact has been a part of our lineage for centuries; it's in our blood. Soon, you will understand."

As the train sped through the countryside, Lady began instructing the Sisters on the incantations needed to harness the Artifact's power. The air inside the compartment crackled with energy as the Sisters absorbed the knowledge, their eyes steady and alert. The Artifact, resting between them, pulsed faintly as if acknowledging their growing connection. Shadows danced along the cabin walls, shifting unnaturally with each whispered word.

The woman chanted alongside them, her voice calm and controlled, seamlessly intertwining with the Sisters' words. Then, the temperature in the compartment dropped. A gust of wind that shouldn't have existed inside the sealed train whipped through, carrying whispers that weren't meant for the living. The voices weren't eerie or threatening they were familiar, layered with the strength of those who had come before.

Mattie stiffened as the whispers grew clearer, a tightness forming in her chest. She wasn't afraid of the voices themselves, but the force behind them unsettled her. It felt like the past itself was bleeding into the present. Anne placed a firm hand on her shoulder, and Greta leaned in, whispering, "They're with us, Mattie. Just listen." Demetria and Eva nodded in agreement.

The Artifact pulsed again, harder this time, and a spark of something, an image, a memory, rippled across its surface like water disturbed by a stone. A burning house. Screams swallowed by the night. A name spoken in a voice that hadn't been heard in decades. The vision gripped Mattie, but the Sisters stayed close. Then, as suddenly as it began, the vision faded, leaving behind only the rhythmic hum of the train and the pounding of their hearts.

Lady's voice cut through the silence. She turned to face the Sisters, the dim light bouncing off her features as she spoke.

"You heard them," she said, her eyes glinting in the shadows, "the voices of those who were lost, those whose lives were taken in the Old Country and in Kramden. Their echoes were never meant to fade; they've been waiting, lingering, feeding on the resentment, the unfinished business. What you saw, what you heard, that's not just history. It's still alive, it's part of us." She paused, letting her words sink in, watching the Sisters exchange glances. "Those whispers, those memories, they connect all of us," Lady continued, her voice dropping to a near whisper.

"The Artifact, it's more than a relic. The power we wield, it's theirs, and it's ours. It's a curse and a gift. A reminder that we are not just sisters bound by blood, but by a legacy forged in fire and bloodshed. You felt it, how the Artifact stirred in your hands, how the voices rose inside you. They will remain with you from now on." Lady's gaze turned cold as she looked out the window, and her voice dropped. "Kramden deserves this," she said as her nostrils flared. "The town, the people, the ones who were complicit in the death and destruction. They will face the reckoning. Those who think they can ignore the past, bury it beneath lies and silence, they're wrong. They've never been more wrong. We will make them remember what they've forgotten. We will make them hear the whispers of the past. The Artifact will tear through the fabric of their world. It will break them, just as it was meant to."

Lady's eyes swept back to the Sisters. "The voices, they won't be quiet now. They'll keep calling, and the power we hold will bring it all crashing down. We are the storm they've been waiting for. And we will show them that what they deserve is long overdue."

14

A Debt In Blood

As the train rumbled through the outskirts of Kramden, a ghostly omen in the night, the sisters sat in silence, their faces expressionless. Lady's voice still lingered, curling through their minds like smoke as the train reached their stop: *The voices, they won't be quiet now. We are the storm they've been waiting for. And so, the storm came.* The Sisters stepped off, blending into the quiet of their town. They were prepared and unconcerned if anyone suspected them. They were about to give several of the townspeople a rude awakening. They moved like they always did, slipping through the familiar streets, giving no hint of what was to come. But tonight, something different walked with them. The past. The blood. The reckoning.

They split into two groups, gliding toward the homes that had been marked long ago. The families who had taken everything from them, who had let their ancestors suffer and die in brutal ways. The names were never forgotten, only buried beneath forced smiles and quiet grief. They knew the town's weaknesses, strengths, and every escape route.

Doors creaked open without a knock. The Sisters knew every floorboard that wouldn't groan beneath their weight. Their movements were guided by silent calculation, blades slipping into soft flesh before a breath could be drawn to scream. Old debts were paid in red as they moved from house to house. One by one, the homes fell silent.

A woman woke to a shadow at the foot of her bed, a face both familiar and off, eyes too empty, too knowing. The last sound she heard was a low, final whisper. "Now you understand," Greta said.

Eva's lips curled slightly. "I cornered à woman in the back. She ran, but there was nowhere to go. I let her think she had a chance; that was the best part. Then I ended it."

"Come, we must go now," Demetria said as they left in a hurry.

By the time the first flames crackled in the dark, the Sisters were already home, back in their beds, back to their quiet lives.

Morning couldn't come any sooner. Kramden would wake to bloodied doorsteps and homes turned to tombs. Neighbors would clutch their rosaries, whispering of devils and curses, of vengeance and sins that refused to die. Suspicion would fester, but no one would ever know. The Sisters would walk among them, their hands washed clean, their faces solemn. This would not be the end. This would only be the beginning.

****

Later that morning, Demetria, Eva, and Mattie approached their parents. The look on their faces was enough for Alias to know something had happened. The sisters realized they hadn't heard the news.

"What happened?" Alias asked with some concern.

Demetria spoke first, in a calm voice, almost emotionless. "We followed Lady's orders, Greta, Anne, Mattie, Eva, and I. We did what needed to be done."

Alias and Doris exchanged a glance before Alias, his voice filled with pride, uttered, "It was about time. Those not of our bloodline needed to be taught a lesson. You've done the right thing."

"Hmm," Doris nodded, a look of satisfaction on her face. "It's only a matter of time before we get rid of those sons-of-bitches. And that Renegade Jones, he's been a thorn in our side for far too long. When the time comes, you'll handle him just as you did with the others. Show him no mercy."

"That's not all. Lady's orders were clear: Renegade Jones and the other bloodlines, their time is coming. They and their dark spirits from the pits are the last ones standing in our way. Once they're gone, everything will fall into place," Eva said. "And with Greta, Anne, and our bloodline, we'll see it done."

Demetria's gaze was on her sisters. "We will. Kramden will be a distant memory for them and their generation. It'll be ours and Lady's."

Alias shook his head before asking, "What about the Artifact? Did that go well?"

Eva, her eyes gleaming with satisfaction, nodded. "Yes. We gave it to Lady, just like we said we would. It's in her hands now."

Mattie grinned. "We took care of them all, every last one of those pieces of trash. Kramden's safer now. There's still more to do, there always will be." She glanced at her parents. There was an edge of respect in Mattie's voice. Her parents glanced at one another. They realized that she was no longer the naive baby of the family.

15

The past weeks had passed without issues for Demetria and Eva as they went to and from work. No one suspected anything beyond the usual chatter about the killings. Demetria and her sisters didn't lose sight of the stares and whispers; they had long been part of their walks to and from work. Greta and Anne experienced the same stares, though in such a rural area, it wasn't unusual for the townspeople to eye each other suspiciously. As if that wasn't enough, Renegade Jones's stares turned their stomachs. His ugly, menacing looks didn't help either. He would glare at the Sisters, giving them the evil eye, and they would stare right back. They weren't going to let him intimidate them.

By the time Demetria got home one evening after another of those stare-downs, she was pissed. The usual small-town whispers and Renegade's unsettling gaze had drained her. She was exhausted, both from the walk and the tension in the air. She hadn't realized how much it had taken out of her until she stepped through the door, eager for a moment of peace.

She heard the splattering of rain on the roof and looked out the window. An evening mist had cast a shadow over the town, giving everything a somber feel. After a quick shower, she sat down for dinner with the family, hoping the meal would bring some comfort. But just as they started, a knock on the door interrupted the moment. It was an old family friend of her parents. The woman called them aside, and from the look on her face, it was clear this was serious. Though they couldn't hear what was being said, they knew something terrible had happened.

"The Woods' daughter was attacked and raped last night. Her body was cut to pieces in one of the back alleys near the warehouse behind the mill, and a circle of blood was around the flesh," Doris said after the neighbor left. The sisters were speechless, gazing at each other in disbelief as they processed Doris's words. "Several families were also murdered, and their bodies mutilated."

After a long pause, Mattie finally spoke. "Lady is right. The evil in this town runs deeper than we thought."

Doris raised her eyebrows as she looked at her daughters. "There are spirits in high places working with demonic forces to punish this town, and Lady showing up now couldn't have come at a better time. The sad truth is, the Woods and the others talked about leaving Kramden with their family."

Alias calmly looked at everyone and said, "They should have never thought about leaving Kramden. This is home, and they should have seen it as such. Now, girls, Lady has given you, along with Greta and Anne, the means to rid Kramden of the evil that besieges us. Do it! Do it with a smile, just like they did to our family."

"Father is right," Demetria said. "We will meet with Greta and Anne soon."

"If any of those bastards set foot in our home, it will be the last place they will ever enter," Eva added.

Mattie tapped her fork against the plate. "We already know who's behind this. They think no one will dare stand against them, but they're wrong. It's time to put an end to this."

Doris nodded. "We don't just stop them, we wipe them out. Every last one of them."

"We're not waiting," Demetria said. "They made their move. Now we make ours."

Eva's eyes met her sisters, and she gave a slow nod of approval. The sisters exchanged a look. No fear. No hesitation.

Alias and Doris leaned back in their chairs. Rain kept tapping the windows, steady as a heartbeat. The family sat in silence, not out of fear but focus. What came next had to be done right.

****

Later that night, under the cover of mist and dark clouds, Demetria,

Eva and Mattie moved through the narrow streets. Dressed in black, hoods pulled over their heads, they met Greta and Anne behind the old bakery. The alley stank of wet brick and trash, but none of them flinched. They had outgrown fear.

"You heard what happened?" Mattie said.

Greta nodded. "Yes, and we're ready."

"No more warnings," Demetria added. "We do this clean."

"The warehouse behind the mill," Eva said. "That's where they've been hiding the bodies. Where the butchers sleep."

Greta lit a dried sage bundle and blew the smoke low. "Then we don't leave till it's ash and silence."

They split into pairs, slipping through the back streets like shadows ready to sin. Anne and Eva took the left flank, covering the rear exit. Mattie and Greta headed for the entrance while Demetria made her way to the front. They didn't knock. They pressed their hands against the door, whispering the words of the Erethal, the Tongue of the High Spirits, spoken by those who ruled from the high places Lady told them about. They knew its power, the price it demanded, and they were ready. The lock rusted in seconds. The hinges groaned open. Inside, the stink of rot hit them. Blood still stained the floorboards in the back room, where shrines and symbols etched in strange letters and numbers gave the place an eerie feel. Chains hung from iron bolts. Bones piled in crates. This wasn't just a slaughterhouse; it was a shrine to something vile.

Suddenly, from the shadows, a figure emerged, tall, hulking, with a presence that seemed to swallow the light. Burt stepped into the dim glow; his eyes were no longer human, cold, and distant. Behind him, several figures loomed, their faces twisted with the same unnatural hunger.

"Well, well…" he snarled. "The little witches think they're gonna clean house."

"Fuck you, Burt!" Demetria snapped, stepping forward, her hand outstretched as Burt attacked. But before he could reach her, a sudden glow surged from her palm. It wasn't fire. It wasn't light. It was a presence, something older. Something that knew his name. A force that moved like breath from the grave.

It struck Burt. His body staggered, limbs shuddering. His mouth opened, and a gargled sound came from his throat. And then the twisting began.

He tried to regain control, but the force of the curse held him in place, his body writhing as if something was tearing him apart. The glow slammed into him again, sending him stumbling backward. His limbs twitched, like something deep inside had been shaken loose. His mouth opened again, but there were no words. Just the sound of something unraveling. And then the twisting became more violent.

Greta and Mattie moved swiftly as the men lunged, their twisted forms now fully revealed. The first man came at Greta, his face contorted with rage, and though his hands were empty, the hunger in his eyes was as deadly as any blade. But she didn't flinch as she pounced on him with daggers of fire.

Mattie was already moving before the man could strike. She threw herself into him, using his momentum to slam him into a nearby post. He stumbled back, grinning, his teeth yellow and sharp. A hiss came from his mouth. Mattie didn't hesitate. She drew a blade from her hip, its edges covered in blue flame, and in one motion, drove it through his chest. The grin on his face vanished as he sagged like burnt paper, leaving only ash and a settled hush where the hiss had been.

"They're not men anymore," Greta spat, barely avoiding a clawed swipe.

Meanwhile, Anne raised a piece of mirror and whispered the spirit's words. The man in front of her broke down, sobbing uncontrollably as his body crumpled. He gasped for air, but it was already gone, ripped from him by the force of the curse. He collapsed in a twisted heap, still and silent.

Another man turned and bolted for the door, his movements quick and desperate. But Eva was faster. She reached out, her fingers brushing the edge of his shoulder. His body folded, his bones turned to dust. He collapsed into a heap.

The last of the three men let out a feral scream, but before any of them could move, Demetria stepped in. With a flick of her hands, a burst of wind sent all three sprawling backward into the flames already spreading across the floorboards. Their bodies writhed in pain, and one by one, the demons in them screamed and fled as the fire devoured them. But unlike the fleeing spirits, no screams escaped their lips, only the crackle of burning flesh and the hush of death that followed.

Once the area was secured, the five women moved methodically through the warehouse, pouring oil and sprinkling salt to keep the fire burning, just as Lady had instructed. The fire devoured the walls, and the building's old timbers creaked and groaned under the weight of the flames. The evil within it burned like dry wood, feeding the fire with all the hatred and darkness it had collected.

As they watched the fire from a distant hilltop, the rain having finally stopped, the sky was painted red and black with smoke. In the silence that followed, they could hear the wail of sirens, local fire trucks closing in on what remained. And just as suddenly as the rain had stopped, it began again, drenching them as they made their way down the hill and away from those coming to see what had happened.

Alias and Doris were waiting for them at the edge of their property. They didn't need to speak as he opened the door and stepped aside, letting them pass into the warmth of the house. Inside, the rain still tapped against the windows. The fire down the hill was just a glow now, lighting up the fog as it moved like the eye of something ancient.

"Welcome home," Alias said, a faint smile tugging at his lips.

Doris followed, a glint of warmth in her eyes as she added, "It's good to have you all back safe." The women exchanged glances.

"It's wonderful seeing you," Greta and Anne said together.

"It's always good seeing family," Alias replied.

"I'm guessing you took care of business?" Doris asked, glancing at them.

Demetria, rain dripping from her coat and face, said, "We're not done."

"No, but tonight was a start," Greta added quietly.

"Good," Alias and Doris said in unison, gesturing toward the fireplace. "Get out of those wet clothes before you catch a cold."

Kramden wouldn't speak of what happened in that warehouse, but the town would feel it, in the spiritual warfare, in the dreams that never returned. The spirits that once ruled from the high places had been dragged down, screaming, momentarily. But Renegade and his minions wouldn't take it lying down.

<h1 style="text-align:center">16</h1>

Echoes Of Revenge

Renegade stood before his followers, his hands clenched in a tight fist, a scowl on his face. The commanding presence they had always feared gave way to something far worse: a man burning with rage. Upset at what happened to Burt, and several of his followers didn't sit well with him. Something deeper, darker, had been at work, and Renegade could feel it in his bones.

"Who did this?" Renegade's voice was low, like a growl, and his eyes scanned the open barn. His followers shifted uneasily. None of them had answers. Pacing the room, he shouted, "Speak up."

One of his followers hesitated, then spoke up, "We don't know, Renegade. No one's seen anything . . . But this wasn't just a simple killing. It's . . . It's spiritual. I can feel it," he stammered.

"You can feel it?" Renegade nodded coldly. He knew this was something far more dangerous than a rogue spirit or a misguided summoning. "Whoever is behind this isn't just playing at the edges of dark forces. They've summoned something powerful, something ancient. And only a few families in Kramden are capable of calling on such powers."

"So, we kill the families who aren't of our bloodline; that will solve everything," a voice shouted from the back of the room.

"We've been playing with fire," another follower muttered, looking at the others. "Could be the Siobhan girls, sure. Or maybe the two sisters, Greta and Anne? Their family also has a history like the Siobhan's. They've always been tangled up in things they shouldn't be. Hell, it could even be someone else we haven't crossed paths with yet."

All valid points. However, Greta and Anne are of Siobhan's bloodline, skilled, dangerous, and far too unpredictable for anyone's good. They aren't amateurs. They and the other bloodlines in town are capable of much more. If they're involved . . . " Renegade voice grew colder, darker, as an eerie smile spread across his face.

"We have to do something. We can't stand still!" several voices roared.

"Hmm! As for the Siobhan family, they have been quiet for too long," Renegade muttered, pacing slowly, his mind working as he thought of all the families who dabbled in the spiritual realm, those who summoned spirits and sought to control the eternal dark. But none of them were as skilled as he and his ancestors, or so he thought. None of them had the raw power and control that they commanded.

"Is he giving us a speech?" a follower muttered to another.

"Sounds like it, and I'd advise you to shut the fuck up!" The follower didn't hesitate.

"Someone thinks they can challenge me, thinks they can pull the strings of the dead without consequence. We'll make them regret ever thinking they could challenge me. We'll drag them out of the shadows, tear apart every secret, and burn and bury them to the ground if we have to. And if they've summoned something they can't control? We'll turn it against them. We'll punish Kramden," Renegade said. "And we'll reach out to the Exuis when the time comes. We'll rid this place of everything hiding in the dark."

Then Sox, newly second-in-command, who had been listening to the whole exchange and had said little, stepped forward. "But what about the souls and bloodlines the Exuis have kept prisoners all these years? You think they will come to our aid?" Sox said, keeping his eyes on Renegade. "You think they'll be allowed to leave their abyss . . . just to fight our fight?" The others glanced at one another, unsure, waiting.

Renegade turned slowly, eyes locking on Sox. "Is that a question?"

Sox didn't flinch, but he didn't answer either. He knew better. Renegade scanned the group. "The Exuis, they're not strangers. They're not a fantasy. They're ours. Blood of our blood. They worship the same spirits we do. And they haven't forgotten." He stepped closer to Sox, his voice low. "They'll come." Then louder, to the rest: "Sox, send word." Sox gave a nod, but he knew getting rid of the Siobhans and the other families wouldn't be easy.

****

Sox turned and walked into the dark, his boots pressing down on the wet grass. He approached the shed, a small, half-sagging building near the barn where Renegade and his group waited. Old and worn, it held what it needed to hold. The relics had been waiting, waiting to be called. Inside, he struck a match and lit the oil lamp hanging from a crooked beam. Its spark revealed the old sigils etched into the planks: some scorched in by heat, others carved deep with bone.

He dropped to one knee at the ring in the dirt and opened the box buried beneath the floorboards. The contents were simple. Bone, cloth, a vial sealed with wax so dark it looked like dried blood. The words came out in a tongue that didn't belong in the present. The floor groaned, and a cold passed through like breath from a sealed grave. It was not meant for soft ears. It cracked the air. It twisted the flame.

When the chant ended, the temperature dropped, not like a breeze; this was cold. Deep and ancient. A silence came after, as if something had stirred beneath the ground and was now listening. And then it responded. Sox bit his lips. His chest tightened. They had heard. He closed the box, stood up, and snuffed the lamp.

Back outside, he found Renegade standing alone at the fence line, staring in the direction of the old railroad yard. Rain soaked his coat, darkening the fabric with each drop. He didn't turn when Sox approached.

"They heard," Sox said.

Renegade gave a slow nod. "And?"

"They'll come. Ohn Landis will lead them himself."

"Good," Renegade said. Neither of them said it aloud, but they both knew what it meant: it wouldn't just be a reckoning. It would be a purge.

From The Depths Of The Exuis

The Exuis was known to the old bloodlines of the Old World, and to those who carried that bloodline, it was a name that brought terror. They were born out of fire and rejection by the ancients, forged in the days when the bloodlines of the thirteen families still sat in high places, blessing themselves with stolen power and watching entire bloodlines rot beneath them.

Ohn Landis didn't rise to lead the Exuis by chance. He was chosen, groomed in silence, raised beneath the old rites, and brought forward by the ancestors who believed the world could be remade, but only if the weaker bloodlines, the rival families, and the outsiders were killed. The New World gave him that chance. He wears no crown. He signs no decrees. But every word from his mouth shapes the course of the Exuis. They are not rebels. They are not prophets. They are the abyss. The evil that lives.

When the Burrs, Siobhan, and the other families began twisting sacred rites to stretch their lives, and seize what they called "divine blood," and build ethereal prisons for the living and the undead who refused to kneel, it was the Exuis who answered back. Quietly at first. Then with fire.

****

"They're coming," Renegade had said. "Our people, the Exuis. To finish what was started." To some, it sounded like madness. They trembled. To others, prophecy. But those who understood what Ohn Landis had been building felt it like thunder in their bones. The Exuis had waited in the cracks of the dark pits, training, preserving, growing stronger with each year, while some from the thirteen family bloodlines grew weaker, more desperate, and more afraid of death. And now the call had gone out.

The blood that built the Exuis runs in Renegade, too. His ancestors may be ash, but the blood never forgets. When he called for them to rise, it wasn't a plea. It was a summons. And Ohn Landis heard it. What the Exuis despised wasn't just the Burrs and Siobhans' rule; it was their arrogance. Their comfort. The way they treated power like something to be eaten instead of honored. The Exuis had been hunted, branded dangerous, and locked away for holding to their truth. Now, they were free. And they were coming to Kramden, not as saviors. Not as saints. But as vengeance incarnate.

The storm didn't break, but the air shifted. Something had cracked open, and Demetria felt it in her chest like pressure building under her ribs. She wasn't the only one. Eva stood at the window, staring at nothing, arms folded tight. Mattie had gone quiet. Not her usual kind of quiet, but the kind that made even the walls feel tense.

"Did either of you feel that?" Demetria asked.

Eva nodded without looking back. "Something's coming."

They didn't wait. Within an hour, the three of them were standing in their parents' living room. Doris sat knitting, but the thread had dropped to her lap, forgotten. Alias stood near the fireplace, staring into the cold ash.

"You felt it too," Mattie said. Neither parent denied it.

Alias finally spoke. "Something's been waking up for a while now. But tonight . . . it stirred." Alias looked at his daughters. "The Exuis," he said. "They're close. They are coming."

The room sank into silence. Demetria stared. "What are you talking about?"

Alias stepped forward. "They were a force the Old World tried to bury. And if they're stirring, it means someone called them. It could have been that they were called because of the killings."

Eva frowned. "Father, are you saying those bastards meant something to them?"

Strumming his fingers on the tabletop, Alias replied, "You can never underestimate Renegade, his followers, or the families with them."

"We aren't afraid of him," Mattie added.

"None of us are . . . but . . ."

Cutting her father off, respectfully, Eva said, "Why are we just hearing about them now? You told us everything else, the bloodlines, the rites, the Siobhan legacy. Why not this?"

Doris answered, "Because we didn't think you'd need to know. We thought they were gone, faded into the ash with the others. We thought the old warnings had passed with the old wars. And some things . . . some things are hard to say out loud."

"But you still knew about them, mother," Mattie said, in a low voice. "And you didn't think that maybe we should too?"

Alias responded. "We made a choice. Maybe the wrong one. And not everything was ours to tell."

Demetria folded her arms. "And Lady? Why didn't she mention them?"

"That's a hard one to figure out, Demetria," Eva said. "Maybe, Anne and Greta know."

"Sure, it won't hurt to ask," Demetria replied.

Getting up from where she sat, Doris said, "Maybe she wasn't ready. Or maybe she hoped it would never rise again."

For a moment, the sisters said nothing. Then Demetria spoke. "We need to talk to Anne and Greta. And then we're going to see Lady," she said, reaching for her coat.

"Wait," Alias warned. "The Exuis aren't a storm, they're the silence before it. If they're moving, then so is Ohn Landis. And if he's awake . . . the old war is no longer history."

Demetria pulled her coat tight. "If the Exuis are coming, then we need to know if it's because of the killings, and if so, why now."

The sisters didn't speak again until they were outside, walking toward the outskirts of town. They were prepared as they headed to where Anne and Greta lived. Rain drizzled in sheets across the rooftops, and the streets were quieter than they should've been.

The wind had picked up again, moving low and nasty across the land, and none of them liked how it felt as they made their way through the tall, whispering grass to Anne and Greta's home.

Eva knocked once on the back door. Anne answered, giving them a look. "That's the kind of knock that comes with news."

Demetria stepped forward. "Yes, we need to talk."

Inside, they all gathered near the woodstove. Greta poured tea out of habit, but no one reached for a cup.

"You two ever hear of something called the Exuis?" Demetria asked. Anne paused, her eyes shifting to her sister.

"And someone named Ohn Landis?" Eva added. Greta froze with the kettle in her hand. Anne didn't speak right away.

"So . . . you have heard of them," Demetria said quietly.

Greta set the kettle down. "We've heard the names. Whispers, mostly. Nothing anyone wanted to explain. The older folks used to mention them, but it always felt like something they didn't want passed down. Still . . . we don't know if it's real."

"Greta is right," Anne said. "But if you ask me, I think they're real."

Demetria hesitated. "Something's moving. Our parents felt it too. They started telling us things, things they hadn't before."

Eva glanced between them. "We've spent years learning about the old fights, the bloodlines, everything. But no one ever mentioned this."

Anne let out a breath. "It wasn't something we meant to leave out. Honestly, it never felt close enough to matter . . . until now."

Greta nodded. "It always sounded more like a story. Like something buried."

Eva cast a glance at everyone. "And Lady? She knows. So why hasn't she said anything?"

Anne met her eyes. "If she hasn't, it's because she doesn't need to. Lady doesn't speak until the dead start stirring."

Mattie frowned. "They're stirring now."

Demetria nodded. "We don't know exactly what's coming . . . but it's tied to the name Ohn Landis."

Greta looked at them all. "Then we need to talk to Lady."

Anne's voice was quiet. "Yeah. Before whatever this is comes any closer."

18

Lady The Talk

The rain had let up, but the streets still glistened. Kramden was quiet, too quiet, for a town that never fully slept. The women moved in silence, glancing back now and then, fully aware Renegade's people could come out of the dark at any moment. Although the Aldan Circle was familiar ground, at night it felt different. No one ever confused the ghost train with the local routes. The sound of it cut deeper, low and haunting; it came from a time Kramden tried to forget.

The women stayed close to the shadows as they moved, coats pulled tight, eyes on every corner. The station stood in plain view now, a solid, brick structure that had weathered the years, a reminder of the past that still served the town. As the wind blew, the streetlamps near the station cast a weak orange glow, flickering as if they wanted no part of what was about to happen.

They stopped at the platform's edge. Anne stepped forward and took a breath. Then she let out the call. It wasn't a song. More like a low chant that belonged to the ground. Her voice didn't rise, but it pulled, dragging something across the veil.

Greta closed her eyes as curtains stirred in town and old men shifted uneasily in their chairs. The whistle echoed, and the people of

Kramden knew. The tracks started to tremble. Then came the sound. Not the clean whistle of the local trains. This one groaned, deep, drawn-out, full of memory and warning. Metal crying through the dark. Kramden knew that sound. It meant something was happening. What, they never wanted to know.

The rain had settled to a mist, clinging to the sisters' coats as they stood at the platform, waiting. Then the train arrived, its wheels silent, windows glowing, steam crawling like something alive. Its presence wrapped around the station like a breath held too long. A single door creaked open. Lady didn't step onto the platform. She never did, unless the order she ruled over was disturbed. Instead, her figure stood still in the doorway, framed by the pale light of the train, as the familiar smile of Elias welcomed them. Lady's voice carried across the night as she spoke. Her long coat drifted behind her, eyes lit with that strange fire only the dead carried.

The Sisters followed Lady down the corridor, the train humming beneath their feet. She walked with purpose, her coat brushing the walls as she moved. At the last door, she stopped. She looked at each of them. They followed her in. The door closed behind them. She moved gracefully to her seat by the window.

"You called. So, speak," Lady said.

Demetria took the lead and spoke in a calm voice. "We need to know about the Exuis, and who Ohn Landis is. What are they, and who is he?"

Eva followed up with a bit more urgency in her tone before Lady could answer, but Lady didn't mind. Elias glanced at Eva. "Anne and Greta told us just enough to know this isn't just some old legend."

Demetria, Anne, Greta, and Mattie stayed quiet, their gazes fixed on Lady, waiting for the answers.

Lady exhaled slowly. "The Exuis were never meant to rise. They were bound, not killed. Bound. Didn't your parents share this with you?" Lady asked, looking at the three sisters. "Anne and Greta, were you aware of this?"

"They said something," Mattie said.

"We heard things as children, but no one ever said it was real," Greta answered.

Lady's eyes darkened, that fire behind them burning colder than before. "The Exuis weren't always demons, though they've worn those skins before. They became what they are through betrayal, one they still deny. Our ancestors buried them deep, bound in the lowest pit they could find. But Ohn Landis . . . he wanted them free. Said his bloodline was cursed, said the Siobhans and the Barrs sealed his kin in fire and ash. So, he swore, one day, he'd tear open the gates and let their screams rise again. And now it seems he has."

Unknown to the Sisters, Lady was never just the Queen of the Dead. She wasn't some simple spirit bound to the past, guarding the line between life and death. No. She came from the same dark forces that birthed the Exuis, only she chose silence, order, and waiting. That was her destiny. While they feasted on betrayal and grief, Lady learned to watch, bide her time, and let the world grind down to dust around her. They were born of chaos. She was forged from the aftermath. And now, the Exuis had awoken, and Lady would rise with them and be ready.

"It seems they didn't bury them deep enough," Demetria said with raised eyebrows.

Lady didn't blink. Her voice carried a chill only the dead could bear. "He went looking for the old rites. The forbidden ones. Dug up bones, spoke names that should've stayed forgotten. Each step he took brought him closer to the mouth of the pit. And when he found it . . ." Her words trailed off, like even she didn't want to say what came next. Elias shifted behind her, hat low over his eyes. Lady's gaze swept across the women. "They heard him. The Exuis don't need a key. Just an invitation. And he gave them one wrapped in blood and vengeance. They're not fully through yet, but the cracks are spreading."

Anne whispered, "So what do they want?"

Lady looked at her. "To finish what was started. Burn the bloodlines that buried them. And if you're not ready, they'll do just that." Lady nodded slowly. "This is the work of Renegade. I'd bet the last of the old ash on it." The Sisters stayed still. Lady went on, "You killed his right hand just as I ordered. That wasn't just a loss. That was a message. And Renegade, he doesn't take messages. He answers them. Blood for blood. Which was my intention all along." She glanced toward the window, though nothing moved beyond it. "Calling on Ohn Landis wasn't out of desperation. It was revenge. A summoning like that . . . it's ancient, foul, and not meant for the living. But he did it. Dug up the old rites, offered what needed offering, and cracked open what's been sealed for centuries."

Eva swallowed hard. "And now the Exuis are coming?"

"They are, but we'll be here to greet them," Lady said. She stepped closer, the hem of her coat brushing the compartment floor. "You've all done what you thought was enough," she said. "But enough won't close the wound now."

Demetria glanced at her. "Then what will?"

"You kill, Renegade," Lady said flatly. "Renegade and the families who still carry the curse in their veins. No more hiding. No more waiting for them to strike. You go to the place where Ohn Landis has anchored his pit of rot with the living and drag him out. The place went dead quiet.

"You're sending us after all of them?" Demetria asked.

Lady nodded once. "Yes. You tear them out by the root."

Greta spoke carefully. "And the Exuis?"

Lady's eyes darkened for a second, "You won't be alone. When the time comes, I'll be there, and so will our ancestors and all the dead they couldn't bury properly. The Exuis won't walk through Kramden unchallenged."

"Why didn't you say that before?" Mattie's voice cracked, almost childlike in its innocence. Elias looked at her, his expression unreadable.

Lady smiled; she understood the innocence in Mattie's words. She answered her in a motherly voice. "Because you weren't ready." She then lifted her hand, and in her palm rested a small Black Stone, rough, cold, like carved stone soaked in shadow. "This is the key to the Old Craft, ancient, cruel, and buried for a reason. It's what you'll need to reach Ohn and close that door for good." Her gaze swept over the group, then settled on Greta and Anne. "The other half of this Artifact is with you," she said, holding it up. "You've held it before, but it never revealed its true nature." She paused, letting that sink in. "And when the time comes, we'll get rid of Ohn Landis and the Exuis."

Greta's hand closed around the Black Stone. "You trusted us once," she said. "This time, we finish it."

Anne stepped beside Greta, her eyes on Lady. "Just tell us where to go and what to do."

Lady gave the faintest smile. "You'll know. The Old Craft remembers the way. This fight won't be loud. It'll come in dreams, in silence, in things that don't make sense until it's too late. The Exuis feed on forgetting. So your power will come from memory. Use the Artifact and the Black Stone."

Demetria didn't blink. "Then we won't forget."

"Don't. If you do, Kramden won't be the only thing they take." The train began to slow, though nothing shifted beneath their feet. The lights sank to a low glow. "When the doors open . . . you'll be exactly what this town needs. And remember, take the old dirt road home."

Lady remained in her seat, silent, as the Sisters stood up. They waved to her as they turned and exited the compartment. As they walked the corridors, the passengers sat where they always had, lining the other compartments in silence.

When the door slid open, the platform was there, just as it had been when they boarded, like the train had never moved at all. "I thought we were moving," Mattie said under her breath.

"We were." But the train hadn't gone anywhere. "It just felt like it had," Eva said.

"So you're saying we never left?" Mattie asked. "No . . . I felt it moving."

"Not in the way you think," Eva said. "That was Lady's doing, or the ancestors'. They carried us where we needed to be."

"Don't worry, Mattie," Demetria said quietly. "Even though you joined us in the killings, in time, you'll understand things more clearly. There's more to all this than blood."

Elias, with his usual expression on his face, gave a small nod as the Sisters walked along the platform. He smiled gently. "Thank you," he said. "We'll be waiting. Good night."

As the Sisters walked off into the night, the town was quiet. It was just the sound of their footsteps hitting the ground as they remembered Lady's last words: *Take the old dirt road home. Stay off the main roads. Stay out of the light.* And they did. Their boots kicked up dust along the cracked, narrow path, the night clinging to them like a second skin. No cars. No porch lights. Just the sound of the wind scraping over the fields and the dry whisper of gravel under their feet.

Every few steps, one of them would glance over a shoulder. No one spoke. The town lights were far behind them now, and home awaited. But something else waited too. They could feel it, just out of sight, just out of reach, pacing the edges of the night, waiting for the moment the dark would call them by name.

The three sisters stepped into the house, the familiar creak of the floorboards greeting them like an old companion. Alias and Doris were already waiting, calm, as if they'd known this night would come.

Mattie, Eva, and Demetria spoke openly about Lady, the Exuis, Ohn Landis, and the Black Stone Lady had given Greta and Anne to guard. Alias and Doris listened, calm and composed, carrying the long memory of the old ways without fear or regret.

Across town, Greta and Anne moved quietly through the house. Greta went straight to the hidden space under the floorboards where the Artifact lay. She knelt, drew it out, and placed the Black Stone beside it. A faint hum, like a slow heartbeat, rippled through the room, carrying a presence they could not see. The hairs on their arms stood up, but they felt no fear, only an ancient recognition as they exchanged a glance. Greta closed the floorboards, sealing the two relics together, just as they were meant to be.

19

The Gathering

Ohn Landis moved like a shadow among his followers, his presence a cold, oppressive force that rippled through the forest. The group traveled in the dark, their footsteps light on the earth but unmistakable — six figures, each with a purpose, each marked by the darkness that lingered around them. The child with them, seemingly innocent, was older than anyone could guess. To the human eye, he looked no older than thirteen, but his eyes, ancient, knowing, spoke of a soul born of an era long before Kramden's beginning. He was their silent observer, their key to the power they sought.

Behind them, bodies lay scattered. The villages they passed had been ravaged by the violence of their passing. There were no survivors, just the remains of human life, the charred remains of homes, the broken, bloodied earth where communities once thrived. It was part of the journey. They took what they needed, leaving only destruction in their wake. Ohn saw it all clearly, the vision of a world remade, the Old World erased, and a new order rising from its ashes. The Exuis were not dreams; they were his instruments, ready to do his will. Yet he had never asked the child for permission. Ohn's brashness would matter in the endgame.

A convoy of trucks reached the meeting place just as the first light of dawn began to push the darkness back. It was a secluded location, far from the eyes of Kramden's citizens, and hidden well enough to avoid suspicion. Renegade waited for them, accompanied by members of his bloodline. They stood in a tense circle, eyes locked on Ohn and his group as they approached.

Renegade's sharp eyes scanned the faces of the strangers, taking in the sight of the strange child and the eerie presence that followed Ohn. The air felt colder as the two stood in uneasy silence.

"Where is the one called Sox?" Ohn asked, expecting an answer. "He's the one who reached out. The one who opened your door to us."

"He's gone to the Old Country," Renegade said. "He said he needed answers to questions from the old guards. He'll return soon."

Ohn tilted his head slightly. "The Old Country . . . Strange timing," he repeated.

Renegade replied quickly. "If he were here, I know he'd stand with us." He said nothing of the argument the two had, and how Sox walked out on him, and the words said in anger. He kept the truth buried.

"Now let's get down to business," Ohn said in a firm voice.

Renegade replied, "You brought your toys, Landis?"

Ohn smiled, almost mocking. "Toys?" he said. "We are the builders of the New World. And I don't think you're in a position to question anything."

Renegade's eyes turned toward the child. "I don't deal in things I don't understand. Who's this?"

Ohn's gaze shifted to the child, who remained still and silent, eyes hidden beneath a curtain of dark hair. "The key," Ohn said. "He is part of the old blood. You don't need to understand. Just know that we're on the same side, and what you see here is all powerful," he said, glancing at the child.

"Seems Renegade doesn't know his place," the child said in a language known only to him and the others.

"Maybe, he needs a lesson," Ohn replied.

Renegade leaned back, folding his arms. Without warning, the child met his gaze and chanted a string of unintelligible words. For a few tense seconds, Renegade felt himself slip out of his own body, hovering above and staring down at the shell he'd become, before he snapped back into control.

"I wasn't here just now. What happened?" he demanded.

"Be very careful as to how you speak. What are you talking about? Nothing happened," Ohn said, a sly smile tugging at his lips, as the child's eyes were fixed on Renegade. "Now, what is it you want?"

"It's an offer to shake up Kramden. I have lost several members of my bloodline, or should I say our bloodline, to an unknown power. I seek revenge. I want to reshape Kramden and join you in reshaping the world."

"I'm listening." But there was a pause before Ohn spoke again. "There are things to consider before we move forward, Renegade. Talk amongst the spirits tells me we can't overlook one thing."

"What are you talking about?"

"Abby Barr. The whispers say she might be building something of her own, an army. No one knows where she is, but the Exuis . . . they are on the lookout. The power she commands is unknown, and even the Exuis aren't invulnerable."

Renegade smirked, a look of disbelief crossing his face. "Abby? You think she's a threat to us?" He scoffed. "She's nothing but a whisper in the dark."

Ohn didn't blink; his voice grew cold. "There's something you don't understand, Renegade. The Exuis may be our tools, and they are formidable. But there are forces at play, things older than even the Exuis. The Exuis heard something . . . older than us. Older than fear. And Abby's name isn't spoken lightly anymore. We have to be smart because not every war should be fought in the open. Some victories are earned by letting your enemies think they have hope . . . before you rip it away. You think we're the only ones controlling the darkness? We're not. There are other forces, things the spirits fear. And Abby may be one of them."

Renegade wasn't convinced. "It's not just Abby. It's the bloodlines. The ones that kept the Barrs and the Siobhans alive when they should've been wiped out. Families like the Ashers, too, all of them tied to the old ways. That's where the rot starts. They've been playing both sides, and it's time to call them out. You know who they are. And then there's the old train yard, Aldan Circle. We both know the blood that was spilled there, the bodies that were buried. But there are still whispers of the train moving through the night. The people hear it. They talk. That can't be ignored." The silence that followed Renegade's words was filled with old sins and the echoes of what had been buried but never forgotten.

Ohn didn't respond right away; his attention instead shifted to Maera, the woman at his right hand. Her expression was unreadable, but there was a quiet authority in the way she held herself. She spoke in a clear voice, cutting through the tension. "Kramden's days are numbered," she said. "It's already rotting from within. We're just speeding up the fall."

Renegade turned to her. He studied her for a moment, then gave a small nod, his mouth tightening. "That's what I needed to hear."

Maera's gray eyes glanced toward Renegade, studying him. "Kramden is a nest of old blood and old mistakes. It should've been leveled long ago. Now it festers. It's time we strike before it breeds something worse."

Renegade held her stare for a moment, then shifted his attention back to Ohn. "I like the direction in which our conversation has taken. We're ready for this, and for what comes after?" he said. "So, what's next?"

Ohn smiled; there was something cold behind his expression. "Kramden's fate was sealed long before tonight. We're just giving the old souls what they want." Ohn's gaze turned to the child who had not moved during the entire exchange. He was watching, his dark eyes calculating, his ancient soul understanding things the others couldn't.

Ohn gestured toward the darkness beyond, and for Renegade and his followers to follow, where a hidden underground base lay in wait. "Come," he said. "We have work to do. You and your followers will see what we've built. And perhaps, you'll understand why we are the ones who will reshape the world."

"The child, who is he? We know of Maera. But we were never told about a child in our bloodline," Renegade whispered to Ohn, eyeing the boy's strange, detached demeanor.

Ohn smiled faintly. "In due time, you'll know his name. And those not of our bloodline will know his wrath."

"But . . ."

"Enough," Ohn cut him off as the child turned his gaze on them, silent and unblinking. With that, they began their descent into the darkness, into the world beneath the surface, where the child, Ohn, and their bloodline had imprisoned their enemies and offered them in ritual to the dark powers they served.

The child walked beside Ohn, his steps light on the earth, his presence an eerie reminder of the ancient forces still ruling the shadows. Renegade followed behind, his mind already alive with thoughts of power and betrayal. The Exuis would return. And Kramden would burn. But in the quiet of the underground, where the abyss seemed to breathe, one truth remained: neither Ohn nor Renegade could ever control the darkness.

20

The Hidden Entrance And The Exuis Sounds

The trees whispered in the wind, but beneath them, in the deep shadows, something far darker stirred. The child whispered in Ohn's ear as he gestured for silence as they walked the long, dark passageway that led to the concealed entrance of The Petra. Hidden beneath layers of stone and twisted overgrowth, the door was nothing more than a faint outline in the earth. With a slight touch from his hand, Ohn pressed a stone hidden in the rocks, causing the ground to tremble slightly. A low rumble vibrated through the soil, and the massive stone slab shifted, grinding open with a sound like the groan of an ancient beast awakening. Legend had it that it was carved out long before Teveras rose to power. Most of it was quiet, sealed off, or used for rituals.

"Welcome to The Petra," Ohn said, as Renegade and his followers stepped forward, the air heavy with the scent of damp earth and decay. The passage before them was narrow, winding, and suffocating, a forgotten tube leading to a forgotten place. The walls, slick with moisture, held whispers of the past. And deeper still, as they descended further, there was a low, almost indiscernible sound, a distant, unsettling hum. It was faint, but unmistakable.

Renegade felt it first, like a shiver running through his spine. He stopped, motioning for the others to halt. His eyes found Ohn, who had not slowed, his face unreadable. "Do you hear that?" Renegade asked, his voice barely a murmur, swallowed by the vastness of the underground.

"The welcome from the Exuis is such a beautiful sound. Wouldn't you say so, Renegade?" Ohn said, his voice barely more than a whisper. "They're restless. But they won't show themselves just yet."

Renegade, his eyes scanning the shadows as did his followers, replied, "Why pull them back?"

Ohn said nothing more. Instead, he continued leading the group deeper, his pace deliberate. The air grew colder, the walls narrower, and the sound of the Exuis grew, a rumbling that seemed to vibrate within Renegade and his followers' bones. Renegade and his followers glanced at one another as they tried to act unfazed by the unnatural silence one minute, and then the roar of the Exuis. The child glanced at Ohn and Maera. He had seen the unease on the faces of Renegade's people, and it pleased him in a quiet way, a distant way, because they were threading in a place they barely understood.

Ahead, the passage widened into a cavernous chamber, the ceiling high and lost in darkness. The walls were covered in strange symbols, etched into the stone with what seemed like old hands. At the far end of the chamber, torchlight revealed an altar of blackened stone, its surface stained with old dried blood. Around it were several iron cages, some empty, others filled with the remnants of those who had once been prisoners in The Petra. As they continued, the hum of the Exuis was unbearable.

Ohn stopped and turned to face Renegade. It was a look that demanded obedience from him and his followers.

"This is where they are kept," Ohn said, his hand sweeping upward toward the cages high above them. "This is where the rituals are carried out. The Exuis feed on the blood of our enemies and the innocent. And we give them what they want."

Renegade's gaze swept over the cages, "This, this is exactly what we've been waiting for. It's time to bring our ancestors' spirits to Kramden and rid ourselves of the forces that have plotted and killed our ancestors."

Ohn's lips twisted into a cold, subtle smile, his voice a low growl as he stepped forward. "Kramden will be the crucible, Renegade. We will cleanse it in blood and ashes. The Exuis aren't just here to kill; they'll burn it to the ground. And when the smoke clears, the true bloodlines will rise, and their old bones and souls will be crushed by what's coming. Let the shadows come alive once more."

A chilling laugh echoed from the darkness, drawing Renegade's attention. It was Maera; there was a cold chill in her dark eyes. "The Exuis will show themselves when the time is right, just as Ohn said earlier," she said. "But until then, we feed them. We give them what they need to keep them hungry."

Renegade could feel the ancient power stirring beneath the surface as she spoke. It was a force he knew could either break them all or lead them to unimaginable power.

"Let's move forward," Ohn said in a commanding voice. "There is more to be done."

****

While Renegade and his followers waited in one of the chambers, the child addressed Ohn, Maera, the Exuis, and the rest of their bloodline. He told them he'd received word from the Old Country: the Glorious One, Shadan, had been attacked and killed on his way to the New World.

"Where was he attacked?" Ohn asked.

"Crossing the waters," the child replied.

"As powerful as he is, couldn't he have fought them off? It had to be more than one ghoul," Maera said.

"Do we know who did it?" Ohn pressed.

"I asked," the child said, arms folded across his chest. "I was told no one knows. Whoever got wind of him coming moved first."

"But who could that be?" Maera said. "We have enemies here and in the Old Country."

"True," the child said. "But I will find out. When I do, we will take our revenge. Shadan mentored me as a child; I'll see this paid back," he snarled.

"It was he who took us under his wing," Ohn reminded Maera.

"Very much so. Revenge will be ours," Maera agreed.

The child glanced at everyone in the chamber. "We'll discuss Shadan later. Right now, we deal with Renegade, that bastard who should never have been of our bloodline, and with our enemies in Kramden and along the coast. We will not bow. We will show no mercy." He turned and walked into the dark.

21

The Sisters And The Rituals Of Power

While Renegade and the bloodline with him were scheming with Ohn, Meara, and the child in the Petra, the leadership left behind wasn't aware of what was about to hit them. The Sisters were preparing to strike again. This time, their target was the unsuspecting families of Renegade's bloodline, those who had aided in perpetrating the suffering, lies, and deaths of many townspeople. Their complacency had kept his power alive. But their time had come, and no one left behind would be spared.

The Stone and the Artifact had given the names, and now the punishment would be exacted. And as they moved through the streets of Kramden, the voices of their ancestors whispered in their ears. Their eyes glowed, knowing what had to be done, even if it meant staining their hands with more blood. The air trembled around them, and the darkness welcomed their arrival. The victims would soon be swallowed by the inevitable purge.

They had no sympathy for the families they would drag to the train.

"We should hurry," Greta murmured.

Demetria nodded. "We're close. We have to move quickly."

Greta's grip tightened around the Stone. Its power surged within her, filling her with an almost unbearable intensity. The names they had gathered, the whispers of corruption — they all led to the homes of the doomed.

In the dead hours of the night, they struck, rounding up the marked families with a brutal efficiency that left no time for questions. The families fought back with words, not weapons, pleading, bargaining, and making promises no one intended to keep. They knew the powers of the occult had marked them.

"You don't understand," a man stammered. "We weren't involved. We kept to ourselves."

The Sisters didn't answer. Instead, he was shoved forward like livestock.

A woman in a panicked voice cried out, "We can make this right! You don't have to do this."

Still, no response. Only the crunch of boots on gravel as the Sisters drove them forward, the train yard looming like a grave.

A boy no older than seventeen tried to fall back, his hands raised in surrender. "Please, I'm not one of them! I'm not like them!"

Demetria brushed past him without a glance, as if he were nothing more than part of the night air. Anne gave a cold tug on the binding around his wrists and kept moving. Their silence was more brutal than any weapon. To the Sisters, these people were already dead. Their pleas, their protests, even their cries, were all noise and meaningless.

They reached the train yard without anyone noticing. The old twisted tracks, twisted from years of neglect, stirred at their presence as the distant clanging of train wheels and the sound of the whistle drew near. It was a whistle they were used to hearing, and the stories behind the train sent shivers down their spines. As the vessel for the damned hissed, growled, and came to a stop, several of the condemned tried again to speak, to reason, to plead for mercy.

The train, Lady's train, pulled to a stop. It loomed like a dark specter against the night sky, its engines quiet but alert, its windows dark and empty, as though it were waiting for the next passengers.

The train door creaked open, and Elias nodded to the Sisters. A chilling smile appeared on his face as he surveyed the doomed group as they were pushed in one by one, their movements sluggish by the sudden realization of what was happening. Fear was in their eyes, only to be met with the cold, penetrating gaze of the passengers. Unlike when the Sisters had boarded, these faces were twisted with pure malice, eyes burning with a cruel satisfaction, hungry for retribution. They clapped in unison as their cold gaze continued.

Suddenly, Lady appeared, her dark eyes scanning the group. There was no warmth in her eyes or demeanor, only the cruel finality of what was to come, as she levitated above them.

"You've brought them," she said to the Sisters. "It's time."

The condemned were herded toward Compartment 13, and at its rear, hidden behind an unassuming wooden partition, lay a door that few had seen. It was a passage known only to those who had witnessed the true horrors aboard the train. A heavy iron door led into a section where the rituals were performed. This space, darker and colder than the rest of the train, was where the transformation of souls took place.

The atmosphere inside was suffocating; it was filled with the scent of metal, smoke, and the stench of burnt incense and blood. There were no windows in this compartment, only cold walls. Dim lights cast erratic shadows, their faint glow barely cutting through the darkness.

The doomed faces were etched with terror, and they began to struggle. The ritual was set into motion. Elias stood at the entrance, his eyes glinting with the dark knowledge of what was to come. The compartment door slammed shut behind them. The sound was the death knell of their fate.

Breathing shakily, an old woman started chanting in a tongue known to Lady and Elias. "She won't help you now," Lady scoffed.

"You fucking bitch, come down here and face me!" a man yelled. Lady granted his wish. Her eyes locked on him as she descended, and with both hands raised, a violent gust ripped him to shreds.

"Please, please," the others pleaded. But it was to no avail. Forced forward, they were dragged to tables lined with cold metal instruments. Each was strapped to a gurney, the leather restraints biting into their skin, unable to move as their screams filled the sectioned-off compartment. Their eyes were wide with terror, the fear of the unknown clawing at their minds. The scent of their sweat, the terror on their faces, was soon replaced by the stench of blood.

Without hesitation, the Sisters tore the clothes from their bodies, leaving them exposed and vulnerable to the horrors that awaited. Flesh was peeled back with brutal precision as knives and cold hands worked swiftly to remove organs, eyes, everything that was once human. There were cries from those who waited for their turn. The cries of the condemned were drowned out by the chants coming from the Sisters. It was in a language older than time itself. The Sisters moved in unison, their hands running over the Stone and Artifact, rubbing them with an almost reverent touch as they recited the forbidden verses that had been passed down through bloodlines steeped in dark history.

The Stone, pulsing with an unholy glow, began to vibrate in their hands. The Artifact, too, came alive as the demonic energy was being summoned.

Lady floated above them, suspended in the air, as she called upon the names of the ancient ones. Her form, which was a dark silhouette, was now as fire. The power of the forces she commanded washed over the sectioned-off compartment. Her arms outstretched, she called forth the dark entities that had waited, imprisoned within the Stone and Artifact for centuries, their hunger now awakened.

The chants grew louder, more urgent, each word carrying with it the weight of ancient evil. The doomed struggled, but it was futile. Their blood spilled freely, soaking into the gurneys, the floor beneath them, as if the earth itself thirsted for it. The air grew colder as Elias opened the door. The chants from the passengers echoed as the temperature dropped, a bitter chill creeping over the doomed, making their skin crawl.

The Sisters, now in a trance-like state, moved faster, more urgently. Their eyes were wide and unblinking, their voices blending with the passengers into one harmonious call to the abyss. As the last of the screams faded, the shadows in the corners of the sectioned-off area seemed to stir. There was a whisper, then a low, guttural growl. The ancient demonic forces of their bloodline answered the ritual's call, a cacophony of dark, foreboding chants mingling with the dissonant whispers of the demonic forces. Lady's laughter, low and chilling, rang out above it all, her eyes glowing with sadistic pleasure.

As the chants rose, the car trembled. Blood pooled into unnatural shapes, turning black before the demonic forces ripped the souls free, screaming into the void. The bodies twisted, then melted into the train itself, the walls pulsing as if drawing breath, the floor groaning under the feast. The compartment was alive, fed by death, its hunger endless. Within its walls, the last echoes of the victims' cries faded into nothing, and the door slammed shut.

22

Revenge In The Mist

The Sisters stood in the blood-soaked ritual compartment, their robes clinging to them. The compartment door creaked open, and Elias stepped inside, his white gloves clapping slowly, his smile wide and sinister. From the rows of seats beyond the compartment, the passengers remained where they always sat, yet somehow the sound of their hollow, mocking applause filled the corridor, rattling through the train like a storm.

Lady descended from where she had been hovering above the ritual, her bare feet touching the floor without a sound, and a look of satisfaction on her face. Her voice carried through the compartment as she spoke. "You have done well, my beautiful daughters," her mouth curving into a smile that did not reach her cold eyes. "You have fed the abyss. You have honored the old blood." The Sisters bowed their heads slightly. Lady's eyes gleamed as she glanced toward the corridor where the clapping still echoed.

Demetria, her face still splattered with blood, replied. "We live to serve you, Lady."

"Indeed. Our ancestors are satisfied for the moment," she said. "And soon," her voice a silken thread of promise, "Renegade and his followers will return. They will see the fruits of our labor . . . and they will understand."

Elias stepped forward, tipping his cap toward Lady and the Sisters with a wide, unsettling grin. "They won't just understand," he said. "They'll kneel."

Lady's laughter was eerie. "Let them try to resist," she murmured. "The train is always hungry." The train shuddered beneath them, almost in approval, as the final cries of the damned faded into the living walls.

Meanwhile . . .

Renegade's convoy rolled into Kramden, engines growling as they screeched to a halt. One by one, his followers jumped down from the trucks, dust and mud clinging to their boots. There was something in the air, as if the town itself was bleeding. As they made their way into the center of town, they were met by panicked faces and frantic voices.

People rushed to them, breathless and pale, speaking over each other.

"There was screaming," one woman cried. "We heard the screaming all night!"

"And the train!" a man added, eyes wide with terror. "We heard the old train yard come alive again, the whistle, the grinding wheels, it never stops!"

Another shouted, "It's the families! They're gone! Dragged off toward the yard!"

Renegade had a pissed look on his face, but he kept walking, brushing past the hysterical townspeople. His followers exchanged nervous glances, unease settling in their ranks. One of them muttered, just loud enough for Renegade to hear, "We should have waited.

Shouldn't have left without the Exuis. Ohn said they would reveal themselves when the time was right, but . . ."

Another of his followers said, "This is the second consecutive time that our bloodline has been slaughtered. The pits of evil are hungry."

Renegade whirled around and stared at the two who spoke with a glare that could've cut through steel. "Shut your fucking mouth!" he growled. "The time is still ours to decide." He studied them for a moment before walking off, his followers falling in line behind him. His plan was simple: find the families he believed had betrayed them and wipe them from the face of the earth.

Renegade stalked the town with a viciousness that left no stone unturned. With his bloodline moving at his command, the families he accused of betrayal were ripped from their homes. He didn't kill them quickly; he made it a ritual. Symbols were carved into the dirt with broken glass, the families forced to kneel before him as he whispered curses under his breath. One by one, they were slaughtered, their blood soaking into the dirt as offerings to the darkness he served. The town watched in horror, powerless to stop it. The ground shifted beneath the bodies, dragging them under as ethereal spirits reached from the abyss to claim what was theirs.

Without saying a word, he turned his wrath toward his true targets, the Siobhan. But as he neared the property, he staggered to a halt. A force, intense and unnatural, pressed against his chest, as if the very ground itself was warning him to turn back.

"What the fuck is that?" one of the followers whispered, staring at the house.

Renegade didn't answer. He squinted his eyes, rage burning behind them. He could feel it, the power radiating from within the home was powerful and ancient.

Inside the house, Demetria, with a scowl on her face, assured her parents, who felt the shift in the air, that everything was okay. They weren't the slightest bit afraid. "He's here," she murmured, her voice barely above a whisper.

Mattie moved to the window but didn't pull the curtain back. "He won't come in. Not yet."

Eva's fingers brushed the amulet at her throat, a faint shimmer of dark energy swirling around it. "Lady said to wait," she said. "Let him see. Let him rage." They stood together in the dim light, the house breathing around them, alive with ancient power, watching as Renegade and his men lingered on the edges.

Renegade's men shifted nervously. One muttered under his breath, "We shouldn't be here . . . this place ain't right."

Another wiped sweat from his forehead, glancing back the way they came. "Feels like the ground's waiting to swallow us."

Renegade ignored them, pulling a blade from his belt. He muttered a few chants, and the blade began to glow with a fiery red light.

"Demetria! Eva! Mattie! Doris! Alias!" he roared into the darkness. "Come out and face me!"

The house answered with a groan that seemed to rise from the very bones of the structure. Shadows twisted along the walls, not following any natural light. Whispers of unintelligible words circled the house, and panic spread across the followers' faces at the sound. Suddenly, a gust of cold wind blasted through the house, extinguishing the dim light from a cracked bulb above. In that instant, Renegade saw them, not the sisters, but towering figures, their forms blurred and writhing.

He staggered backward, spinning on his heel as his coat whipped around him. He shoved the blade back into his waist. "Hurry, let's get the fuck outta here!" he barked to his followers as they fled. "The ancient spirits are awake!"

While he fled, Renegade believed he had a better chance with Anne and Greta, whose home wasn't far. He was hell-bent on leaving pieces of them in the dirt before the night was done, or so he thought. A chill settled in as their house came into view, and something in the air told him he wasn't alone. Compared to the suffocating darkness and voices around the sisters' home, Anne and Greta's place pulsed with something sharp and cold, a barrier they couldn't see but could feel digging under their skin.

Renegade and his followers slowed near the property. The house stood silent as if it were watching them. "They're in there," he muttered.

One of his men stood beside him. "This feels strange. We shouldn't be here either." Renegade felt it too, and he knew he was right.

Inside that house, the Artifact and the Black Stone stirred restlessly, the energies leaking into the night.

Renegade stepped forward, but the second his foot crossed onto the front walk, a crackle of unseen energy snapped through the air, knocking him back a step. He caught himself, snarling under his breath. From inside the house, a faint black pulse lit the windows, slow and steady like a heartbeat.

One of the men stumbled to a halt. "We can't go in there," he whispered hoarsely. "That place . . . it's worse."

"They're protected," a follower whispered.

They stood frozen, staring at the house. From within, they heard it, a slow, scraping sound, like something sharp being dragged across wood. Then, there was a rattling whisper; it was as if the house itself was breathing words they couldn't understand. No one dared move closer. Something was waiting inside.

Renegade's mouth twisted into something between a snarl and a grim smile. "Not for long," he remarked. Still, he gave the order to fall back. This wasn't the night.

From an upstairs window, Anne and Greta watched the dark shapes fade into the distance. But as Greta held the Black Stone in her palm, it grew hotter, warning her that the men were coming back. Anne clutched the Archive to her chest, her heart pounding. "They're coming back," Anne said quietly.

"Let them," Greta answered, in a cold voice.

Walking a few paces behind his men, his boots crunching in the dirt, Renegade suddenly turned around and cast one last look over his shoulder at Anne and Greta's house, as the Black Stone pulsed in the windows like a dare.

His voice was low enough for his men to hear. "Next time," he growled, "we tear it down brick by brick, and burn what's left." No one dared answer him. They followed him into the dark, leaving behind the two homes that had pushed back harder than they expected, for now.

23

A Town On The Edge

Inside the house, Demetria, Eva, and Mattie stood in a circle with their parents. It was tense, right up until Alias finally spoke. "They know they can't touch us, not yet."

Doris tightened her shawl around her shoulders, casting a wary glance toward the window where Renegade and his men had vanished into the night. "They'll be back," she said in a calm voice. "Next time, they'll come harder."

Demetria smiled at her parents. "Let them."

Alias gave a grim nod. "You three . . . you're stronger now. And you're not alone. Abby and the ancestors are with you now."

Eva let out a slow breath, her hands clenching and unclenching at her sides. "We need to move fast. Before they get desperate."

Demetria responded. "Tomorrow. First light. We meet with Anne and Greta."

Their parents exchanged a look, a silent agreement between them. "If you go," Alias said, "be ready. Don't trust the streets. Don't trust the town. Trust yourselves. The eyes and ears are open."

"We will," Mattie said to her father.

The Next Day

The morning broke under a grim, gray sky. The three sisters set out with hoods pulled low over their faces, remembering what their father had said as they took the backstreets. Every window held the possibility of a pair of eyes. They moved quickly, silently.

As they neared the outskirts where Anne and Greta lived, Eva muttered under her breath, "Feels like we're being watched."

Demetria's hand brushed against the hidden dagger tucked into her coat. "We are. He's still out there. I can feel him."

Mattie's eyes scanned the surroundings. "He's afraid, though."

They didn't speak again until they reached the house. The porch creaked as they climbed it, every step loud against the silent morning. Before they could knock, the door opened.

Anne stood there, clutching the Artifact, Greta just behind her, the Black Stone resting on the table. Greta stepped aside. "Get in. Before you're seen."

The sisters hurried inside, the door shutting behind them like a final lock against the world. The house smelled of old wood and something deeper; it was the strange, electric scent that clung to the Artifact and the Black Stone. Anne led them to the back room, where maps and strange symbols were spread across a heavy oak table.

"They were here," Anne said in a calm voice. "So, I'm guessing they were by your place."

"They were, but we gave them a glimpse of what is to come," Demetria responded.

"So did we," Greta replied. "He'll come again. Next time, he won't just lurk outside."

Eva nodded. "And next time, we'll be ready."

Demetria placed her hands on the table. "We're done waiting. Whatever we're going to do, we do it now."

Mattie responded. "Yes, before he tears this town apart."

Greta looked at Anne, then back at the sisters. "We've already started something he can't stop," she said. "He just doesn't know it yet."

Unbeknownst to the Sisters, outside, beyond the cover of trees, Renegade crouched in the brush, watching the house from a distance.

One of his men shifted uneasily beside him. "Do we move or wait?"

Renegade didn't answer right away. His eyes stayed locked on the house, on the threat pulsing from it like a heartbeat he couldn't ignore. Finally, he grunted in a low voice. "We wait for now. But the next move's ours." Secretly, though, a small seed of doubt twisted in his gut. He had faced fear before, and he knew this was war. The Sisters watched in silence as several trucks rumbled off in the distance.

24

The Evil

Renegade and several of his most loyal bloodlines drove out at dawn, their trucks kicking up dirt as they rolled down the old road, passing unkept cemeteries on their way to meet with Ohn. Ohn stood at the base of the ridge, watching from a distance as Renegade and his followers stepped out of their trucks and made their way toward him. The stone slab, already removed, welcomed Renegade and his team as they followed behind Ohn. The men descended the narrow spiral staircase into the dark of The Petra, a place they were never meant to see until now.

At the bottom, Maera waited with several grotesque followers. The child was seated on a worn throne of bone and stone nearby. His eyes were bright and cold. His long fingers, which seemed to appear out of nowhere, were stroking a small, twitching creature he held by the neck.

"You returned," the child said in an eerie voice.

A look of surprise spread over Renegade's face. The child had never spoken before, and seeing Ohn and Maera at his side, quickly told him who was in charge.

"I want power," Renegade said. "They've grown stronger, those Sisters, and the bloodline moving with them. You said the Exuis would rise."

The child glanced at Ohn. "They are rising," Ohn said.

Maera looked at Renegade. "We sent several of our messengers to contact Lady and her followers in the abyss. They'll be waiting there for us."

Shaken, Renegade and his men swallowed hard, exchanging uneasy glances. "Do we need to be there?" Renegade asked.

"Don't you?" the child replied.

"Sure . . . sure," Renegade said.

****

They gathered at the sunken abyss, a rotting pit where the walls bled shadow, and the air shivered with whispers. The wails of spirits and the cries of the undead rose around them, echoing through the blackened void. The abyss stretched before them, like a living wound in the earth deeper than any human could measure. The black winds howled with voices no one could understand, and the place was neither part of Kramden nor anywhere else. It simply existed.

Suddenly, Lady appeared with Elias and the ancestors at the far edge, surrounded by shadows that twisted like veils in a storm. Her face was calm, and her eyes burned like flames. On the opposite side, Ohn emerged from the dark with the Exuis and Maera, at his side, the child leading them. The unintelligible voices of the ghouls on both sides fell silent, the creatures slowing as they scampered and twitched, sensing something greater in the atmosphere.

Seeing the Exuis, Lady, and the ancestors, Renegade and his men stayed hidden, their eyes filled with curiosity and fear. They crouched in the deeper shadows beyond the gathering, unwilling to reveal themselves yet unwilling to leave, watching as the dark forces conversed in whispers and veiled threats.

The abyss trembled, not with a meeting of equals, but with the presence of deceit. Lady stood cloaked in her shadows, Elias and the ancestors arrayed at her back. The Exuis clustered around them, silent but restless, like wolves waiting for a signal.

The child's voice rang out, piercing the silence like a knife. "Abby, it's been a long time, hasn't it?"

"Long time, huh? Why the sudden request to talk after such a long time, as you put it?"

"I'm sure you've heard about Shadan, haven't you?"

"The Glorious One? Like you, I heard he met his end. So yeah, I've heard. Is that why you wanted to speak?"

"No, no, I just wanted to see if you knew."

"Well, now I do. So what's the real reason?"

"We come seeking peace," he said, lying through his teeth. "We know the Sisters, Anne, Greta, Demetria, Eva, and Mattie, have grown strong with the Black Stone and the Artifact you gave them. But they're not loyal to you, Abby. They'll deceive you. Betray you in the end."

"It's funny you say this, Teveras, you wretched sorcerer, hiding in a child's skin when you're older than the stones beneath our feet. Perhaps you should concern yourself with Renegade and his kind turning on you, as his ancestors did, remember? This game you're playing, trying to distract me with stories of the Sisters, is nothing but smoke and mirrors. You and I both know what's really at stake."

"You make fun of me, Abby, but the balance is bound to shift. Too many eyes are watching. Too many hands reaching for what lies beneath."

Lady tilted her head. "Speak clearly, little mouth."

Teveras snarled. "You've been warned, Abby. Kramden will belong to us, as will the soul of your ancestors."

A cold smile appeared on Lady's face. "I will not be threatened by a worm pretending to be a serpent. Remember this night, Teveras. When the wind turns black, and the earth splits beneath your feet, it will be your own doing that brings it down."

Maera hissed, stepping closer to Teveras. "You should listen, Abby. You and your line will fall," she said.

Ohn's voice joined hers, low and seething. "Your ancestors couldn't stop us before. They won't stop us now." The Exuis murmured behind them, their whispers swirling like smoke.

"You play with fires older than the world, Teveras. Fires that will consume all of you," Lady grinned.

"We'll see, Abby. Just remember, you've been warned," Teveras said mockingly.

"You sent your messengers for this? You're a waste of time," she scoffed.

"Beware, Lady," Ohn said.

Without saying another word, Lady turned, her form melting into the shadows as Elias and the ancestors followed.

Teveras laughed, "Run while you can."

The darkness around Teveras, Ohn, Maera, and the Exuis collapsed inward, pulling them into a swirling void. An ear-splitting shriek tore through the abyss, neither human nor beast. Black tendrils lashed out, striking the ground and trees, sending icy winds flying and screaming. At that moment, Renegade and his men, crouched nearby, were caught by the tendrils. The shadows wrapped around them like cold chains, yanking them off their feet. Their hearts pounded in terror as the air shimmered with dark energy, and then, the world twisted and the abyss vanished.

When the shadows receded, Renegade and his men found themselves in The Petra. Ohn, Maera, Teveras, and the Exuis stood before them.

Teveras gave them a twisted smile. "Return to Kramden. Wait for my word."

Ohn's voice rumbled low. "Speak of this to no one."

Renegade's throat was dry as he nodded, signaling his men to obey. They turned to leave The Petra, shaken to their core but relieved to be breathing. The shadows behind them moved in sync as they headed for the woods, Teveras' faint laughter echoing in the dark.

"This is the Abby the ancestors spoke of?" a follower asked.

"Yes," Renegade said, a screw face twisting his features. "She's the evil that's haunted our bloodline for generations. If we get rid of her, Kramden and the New World will belong to us, just like that little motherfucker said."

"You call him a motherfucker?" another follower asked. "Aren't you afraid he might hear you?"

"It doesn't matter. They need us," Renegade said, a trace of doubt in his voice.

"I knew there was something off about him," the follower walking beside Renegade muttered.

Renegade bit his lip. "He's the one they spoke of. None of us even knew his name. I never . . ." He trailed off.

"He could've sent us to the pits," another said quietly.

"Enough!" Renegade snapped, pushing forward through the woods.

25

The Return To Kramden

The night air in Kramden felt colder than when they had left. Renegade and his men stumbled back into the outskirts of the village, their breath fogging in the dim light of the half-moon. They huddled together, still reeling from the force that had whisked them from the hollow to Teveras's lair and then sent them back again.

Renegade's voice cracked in the silence. "Did that just happen?"

One of his men, trembling, muttered, "I thought we were dead. But what about our trucks? Are we going back for them?"

"We aren't dead, and I don't think we should," another of Renegade's men said.

Another rasped, "After what I saw, it's too soon to go back."

Renegade exhaled slowly, as the shadows that had coiled around them still felt etched into his skin, like invisible bruises. He scanned the quiet houses and the narrow alleys of Kramden's outer edge. "Keep it together," he said, though his voice lacked its usual force. "We're alive. That's what matters. We do as Teveras said, wait for his word, and don't breathe a word of this to anyone."

One of his younger followers, his face pale, shook his head. "What the hell did we get ourselves into?"

Renegade glanced at him. "Something bigger than us. But we've seen what happens to those who cross them." He paused, feeling the weight of those shadows still clawing at him. "Whatever's coming . . . it's already started."

They crept back toward their hidden meeting place in the old brewery cellar, away from prying eyes. The thick stone walls and the musty air of the cellar gave them a small measure of security, but the fear clung to them like wet clothes. Renegade paced for a long time in silence, the others glancing at one another but too scared to speak. Finally, he stopped, "We stay sharp," he said. "Keep our heads down. And when Teveras sends for us, we'll be ready."

No one said a word. They all knew, deep down, that the spirits with Lady in the sunken abyss hadn't just sent them back; they had marked them. Outside, the wind picked up, a sharp, whispering wind that rattled the base of Kramden's crooked houses. The moon hung low, painted with an odd rust-red glow that hadn't been there before. Renegade's men sat huddled in the brewery cellar, but it wasn't long before they heard the sounds, soft, scraping noises, like nails dragging against stone, coming from the walls.

"What the fuck is that?" one of his men whispered, his voice barely audible.

Renegade crept closer to the stone wall and pressed his ear against it. There were voices on the other side, soft, whispering voices, speaking words he didn't recognize. He took several deep breaths as he realized the stone itself was vibrating, as though something were scratching its way from the other side.

"I thought the child, Teveras, or whatever his name is, was supposed to protect us," the follower closest to Renegade muttered.

Then a faint, wet sound, like something heavy sliding through a narrow passage, caught their attention. Renegade stepped back, his skin crawling. "We need to get out of here," he yelled. "Now!"

They scrambled out of the cellar. Outside, the streets of Kramden were eerily silent. No night birds, no dogs barking, just the sound of their footsteps and the strange rustling of unseen things moving through the dark. They passed by the old churchyard, and it was there they saw it: a faint glow, pulsing from the ground as though something beneath the earth were stirring.

"Something's waking up," one of the men murmured, in a hoarse voice.

Renegade grabbed the man by the collar. "Don't look back," he ordered. "Whatever's coming . . . it's powerful and not for us to fight. Keep it moving. Let's go!"

As they hurried through the streets, a foul scent, rotting earth, old blood, and damp ash followed them like a curse. And behind them, in the depths of Kramden's oldest graves, something shifted. A crack echoed from the old cemetery as the graves shifted and split. Without warning, skeletal hands burst from the crumbling soil, clawing at legs and boots, dragging down any who wasn't quick enough to escape.

One of Renegade's men gave a strangled cry as bony fingers wrapped around his ankle and yanked him into a collapsing grave. Another tried to pull him free, but skeletal arms clawed up his chest and dragged him down with a sickening crunch.

Renegade's eyes flared. "Back! Get out of here!" he shouted, his voice cutting through the rising shrieks of the dead. The remaining men scrambled back, daggers and knives of fire flashing in trembling hands as more graves split open around them. One of the men let out a rasping cry as the earth beneath him gave way, as another set of skeletal arms erupted from the shifting soil, clawing at his legs. He tried to twist free, but the jagged bones locked around him like a trap. Another man lunged to help, but the ground split open further, spilling a writhing mass of limbs that swallowed them both. A sickening snap echoed from below as the earth closed over them.

Renegade grabbed one of the younger men, shoving him away from the graves. "Run! Get outta here!" he snarled. "Go! Get word to Ohn, Maera, and the child, Teveras, whatever the fuck his name is."

The man hesitated, his face pale with terror. "But the dead . . ."

"They're coming for all of us if you don't move!" Renegade barked.

Reluctantly, the man fled into the night, followed by a handful of others, while Renegade turned, face pale and sweat-slicked, staring back at the graves still shuddering and splitting apart. The moans of the newly risen dead filled the air, crawling through the night like a bitter wind.

"We'll hold what ground we can," he muttered under his breath. "If the bloodline of Abby and the other families wants Kramden, they'll have to take it from us, bone by bone," he said aloud as they ran toward the underground tunnels beneath the town.

26

The Gathering

Lady, Elias, and her followers moved through the dense fog that had risen from the earth, her form barely visible against the swirling shadows. She had left the sunken abyss behind, leaving Teveras and the others in their self-congratulatory silence, unaware of the true depth of her reach. She hadn't merely retreated; she had set her will upon the land, and it had responded.

"It seems Teveras has no idea it was us who rid the world of that devil Shadan," Elias said, a look of satisfaction on his face.

"That's true. Knowing that slimy ghoul, he would've mentioned it. They all have a history with him," Lady replied.

An old female spirit among the followers spoke up. "It was he, along with others, who first came to the New World. But he was cruel, and what came to him was long overdue." They all murmured in agreement.

"Will you tell him next time?" Elias asked. "We're bound to cross paths again."

"In due time," Lady said in a cold voice. "Let him wonder a little longer."

The night air curled around them like a living thing. The cold was not a threat but a loyal companion, wrapping around their shoulders as they walked. They could feel the pull of the earth, the old bones shifting beneath Kramden, the spirits they had loosed feasting on those who had dared to cross their bloodline. They were theirs to call, and theirs to dismiss. As they continued, Lady pressed her hand to the midnight sky, her voice a whisper that rippled through the night air.

Anne and Greta were home and felt the familiar pull of Lady's dark energy. From where the Stone and Artifact lay hidden, a low, rhythmic thrumming rose, like a heartbeat reverberating through the walls.

"She's calling," Anne said to her sister.

"Answer her, but we'll bring the others," Greta said. They exchanged a glance, knowing what came next. Greta gave a small nod. "Let's go."

They arrived at Demetria's house in near silence. She opened the door before they even knocked, as if she'd felt the pulse of Lady's calling herself.

"Lady wants us," Anne said simply.

Demetria's eyes turned to Mattie and Eva, already gathering their things. "Let's not keep her waiting." The air beat like a drum faintly behind them as they headed to the train station.

As they made their way through the streets, a group of townspeople stood at a distance, watching them in eerie silence.

"Who are they?" Mattie whispered.

"Keep moving," Demetria said. "Don't give them a reason to follow."

The Sisters entered the train station, trying not to glance back. Once aboard the train, Elias led them to Lady's compartment. They sat in silence, waiting. The train doors slid shut with a metallic clunk, and the carriage rattled to life, pulling out of the station. Seconds later, Lady stepped from the corner of the car, accompanied by a man they had never seen before. Beside him stood the woman they had met before. Lady gestured toward the two. "Her name is Elowen," Lady said, then nodded to the man beside her. "And this is Bolshan." The Sisters nodded.

Demetria spoke first, "We came straight from the house. But people were watching us. We didn't stop to find out who they were."

Lady's voice remained calm. "Good. Keep your focus on me. She let the weight of her words settle before adding, "While you were unaware, I called on the old powers." Her eyes gleamed. "We're no longer dealing with whispers in the dark. There's a child, Teveras. He's not what he appears, and he's not alone. We know him quite well. He stands with Ohn and Maera, and the Exuis, forces from the past that are here to wage war amongst the living and the undead.

The graves answered my call. The ground has begun to wake, and Kramden will feel its breath before long. Renegade's men trespassed on ground that was never meant for them. I reminded them of that. Some of them won't be coming back. They will make their move against Kramden. But we are not finished."

The Sisters stiffened, glancing at one another. "You mean . . . this is it?" Eva said softly.

"It's time. We'll need the Stone and the Artifact soon. Tonight was only the beginning." The Sisters braced themselves for what was to come as their grips tightened on the backs of the train seats.

"This isn't just a matter of waiting and watching," Lady continued. "The stakes are high, and Kramden is in their sights. You have all been loyal. But now I ask more. The Exuis remember what was taken from them and who took it. And Teveras, as I said, he's one of the oldest and most vicious."

Bolshan shifted his body, his arms crossed. "They've already breached the Veil in two places," he said. "Strange things had stirred in Ashlow Ridge, Vermont, graves unsettled, wind howling through trees that didn't bend to it. In Millbrooke, Connecticut, the dead along the river had begun whispering again, dragging fog through the streets. And down in Weld's Hollow, along the Rhode Island coast, the sea was colder than it should be, and louder."

"And this has taken place recently?" Greta asked.

Lady confirmed it. "What awakens in those places spreads. And I had to respond along with the others. You think the past is buried. But it never is. Not on this soil."

Elowen then spoke. "Rumors of people vanishing, lights in the woods, and ancestral shrines being disturbed in Ashlow Ridge speak of death. And not too far from here, near the river bend, by the old millhouse, the ground has become shallow. They're testing how far they can push."

Anne felt the chill coil around her chest. "And the Stone . . . will it hold them back?"

"Not alone," Lady said. "We need the Artifact. The two were never meant to be kept apart, and not for long."

Demetria looked up. "Then we'll go for them. Tonight."

"No," Lady said, holding up a hand. "Not yet. You'll be watched. We must wait until the third sign is given. Then the path to the Sanctum will open again. Not before."

"The third sign?" Eva asked.

Bolshan answered this time. "Fire. Where it shouldn't burn. You'll know."

The train gave a sudden lurch, slowing as the outskirts outside turned to shadowed woods. Mattie peered out the window. "We're not heading to the Circle anymore, are we?"

"No," Elias said. "We're going to the Threshold. Where the first line was drawn."

"It's time you remembered the oaths made there," Lady added.

Demetria glanced at everyone. "That place is cursed."

Lady nodded slowly. "So are we. You'll feel it when we cross over," she murmured. "It's not just memory. It's an inheritance." As if in answer, the trees outside bent in unison, windless, and the faint scent of ash filtered into the compartment. "We're getting close," she said, her eyes meeting the Sisters. "Once we pass through, there's no turning back." The train shrieked against the rails as it veered onto a hidden track. Ahead, the forest opened like a wound, swallowing the light. Behind them, Kramden pulsed, unaware, for now.

There was a brief silence between the Sisters, broken only by the rhythm of the tracks. Lady lifted one hand, her fingers barely moving. The compartment's lights dimmed, and the glass of the window shimmered like water under moonlight. "Look closely," she said.

The Sisters turned toward the window. What once reflected their faces now revealed the train's other passengers, rows of silent figures sitting perfectly still. Men, women, even children. Their eyes glowed faintly, all fixed forward as if they were waiting for a signal only Lady could give. Obedient. Loyal.

Still carrying a trace of innocence despite the blood on her hands, Mattie finally asked what none of them had dared: who were the passengers?

"They are not like others," Lady said. "They remember what was done and who did it." A chill settled in the compartment as cold crept through as the train sped deeper into the dark. The world outside the windows twisted. Shapes moved beyond the glass, not reflections, not passengers, but figures drifting between the trees, too tall, too thin, their faces blurred as though smeared by unseen hands.

The Sisters watched in silence as pale eyes blinked from the branches, lids closing sideways like something reptilian, ancient. What little light there was seemed to fold inward, devoured by the weight of things long buried.

Still, none of them spoke of fear, nor did they glance at each other. They belonged to this now. The old bloodlines had led them here, not just to fight, but to remember. To take back what was stolen. And as the train carved deeper into the unknown, none of the Sisters turned away from the window. They met the gaze of what stared back, steady and unflinching. Lady and the others exchanged faint smiles as the Sisters stood in a trance-like state, their lips moving with unintelligible words, words only Lady and her companions could understand. Just as suddenly, the trance broke. The Sisters blinked, just as the train gave a low hiss and slowed to a stop at their station. After a brief exchange with Lady and the others, they stepped off, passing the smiling passengers who lifted their hands in silent farewell.

27

Reprisal

The Sisters exchanged quiet goodbyes before making their way home. As for Anne and Greta, it was eerily quiet as Anne closed the door behind them with a soft click. The house felt colder than usual, as a low, dragging hum pulsed through the wooden floor, as if it carried a secret. Subtle at first, almost like a distant heartbeat, the sound grew stronger with each second as it vibrated through the walls. It was the Artifact and the Stone, giving off a pulse of energy that the sisters first thought came from Lady, but the unease on their faces told another story.

"What's going on?" Greta said, looking at her sister.

Before Anne could speak, the rug was swept aside and the loose floorboard pried up. The Artifact and Stone lay side by side, their surfaces faintly glowing in the dim light. The hum twisted sharply and deep, filling the room. And then, the voice came, not from a person, but from the aura around the relics. Soft, frayed with fear, but unmistakable.

Ashlow Ridge . . . the Whitlocks . . . it's begun . . .

Anne stepped closer, "Aunt Eleanor warned us," she said under her breath.

Greta bit her lip. "She did. Didn't Bolshan say strange things were happening in Ashlow Ridge?"

"He did," Anne responded.

"We thought they'd stayed safe, but…"

Anne swallowed hard as Greta's hand brushed against the cool surface, as the whispers began once again: *Teveras, Ohn, and Maera have awakened their bloodline, and Renegade's. They're coming for the Whitlocks.*

Greta nodded slowly, "This isn't a warning. It's a summoning."

Unbeknownst to Anne and Greta, as the voice faded into the low hum of the Artifact and Stone, the sound carried like an omen, and what followed was far worse than words could ever describe. At the Whitlock estate, a home that had held their bloodline for generations, the ground itself betrayed them.

It began as a low tremor beneath the foundation stones; it was subtle to the ears of the younger ones, but the old ones in the family knew better. The scent of ash hung in the air, bells tolled, but there was no church nearby. Then the sound came: a long, dragging pull, like the world itself was inhaling through broken teeth. From the woods bordering the estate, grave markers cracked open as clawed, filth-caked hands burst from the earth. Figures crawled free like soldiers rising on command. Their skin sloughed, their eyes hollow, their jaws hanging loose with the weight of the curse that had pulled them back from rest. These were not strangers. They were ancestors long thought gone, risen to collect an unpaid debt.

And there, standing like a conductor before an orchestra of the damned, Teveras raised his arms. His incantations rose across the churned earth, his face pale and carved with vicious intent. His voice rose once again, not a scream, but clear like something spoken in the marrow of old bones.

I call you back, he hissed. *The Forgotten Blood. The Broken Tongues. Come take what was promised.*

The ghouls moved at his command, not lumbering, but stalking, with mouths wide and teeth long, their claws curling like hooks. The ground split open in deliberate seams, black roots coiling upward, sinewed tendrils slick with rot, grasping for the ancient stones beneath the home, dragging down timbers, and hearthstones. The old beams groaned like something alive.

Inside the estate, the Whitlocks didn't scream. They stood firm, Eleanor at the center, her eyes fixed on everyone, even as the first of the dead reached the porch. They had heard the old stories. They had known this was coming. But knowing wasn't enough. She led the incantations, each word growing louder until the sound filled the rooms.

Teveras' smile deepened as the ghouls swarmed, not like beasts, but like ancient executioners returning to finish a sentence long overdue — as fleshtore and bones snapped.

Eleanor spoke as the others continued the incantations, which were loud enough to carry over the roar of breaking stone. "Coward!" she spat. "Sorcerer hiding behind old bones! You will choke on what you summon."

The others joined in, old aunts, uncles, cousins, children, lifting their voices in unison, their words not pleading, but condemning: "May your blood rot before your heart stops. You will drown in the names you've forgotten. You are nothing but bones wearing bones."

Teveras' smile didn't falter. If anything, it widened, the glare of his teeth unnatural, erroneous against the hollow cast of his face. *I am not forgotten*, he said softly. *You are.*

There was a loud shriek as Teveras' ghouls broke through the walls, their bodies filled with the stench of decay. Eleanor's bloodline stood their ground, chanting the old words through trembling lips. Faint spectral figures to defend them, answering the call of blood and memory. For a moment, the house blazed with light, the ghouls staggering back under its force. But the light faltered, their voices cracking as fear set in. One by one, the defenders were dragged down, their cries swallowed by the roars of the abyss. The last echo of Eleanor's voice clung to the air before it, too, was consumed.

And as the last light vanished beneath claw and soil, Teveras lifted his arms and let out a scream, the sound twisting into a guttural chant spoken in the tongue of his bloodline. The ghouls paused, their mouths slick with blood, before turning one by one, dragging themselves back into the broken earth. As the smoke swirled and cleared, Teveras vanished with it, fully satisfied.

****

Anne and Greta couldn't believe their eyes when they reached the estate. The private road was littered with debris, and the iron gates were bent and scorched. Windows hung shattered, the roof partially collapsed, and smoke curled from the ruins like ghostly fingers. Inside, the halls and rooms were dark and empty, the floors streaked with soot and ash, and the lingering scent of blood hung heavy in the air. What had once been a place of memories and warmth was now a shell of destruction. What had once been their aunt's sanctuary was now a ruin of silence and death, the faint sound of whispers drifting through the scorched estate.

Saddened as they made it back home, something overtook them. They began speaking in an unintelligible language, not to each other, but to the Artifact and the Stone. There was a response, Lady's voice. Greta and Anne had told her everything without realizing it. But Lady already knew. She'd felt the aftermath the moment the carnage ended. "Bring the Artifact and the Stone tomorrow," she commanded. Moments later, Anne and Greta snapped out of the trance, clear on what had to be done. Tomorrow, they would find Demetria, Eva, and Mattie. The others needed to know.

28

Blood For Blood

Anne and Greta left before dawn, carrying the Artifact and the Stone in a satchel between them. Their boots echoed on the narrow pathway leading to their truck as they moved with urgency. The raw memory of what they had seen the night before was on their minds.

Their first stop was the Siobhan's home. Greta knocked. Alias opened the door. "They're not here," he said before they could ask. "Left early this morning. Didn't say where they were going."

Anne glanced at Greta. They both knew what the other was thinking. Without wasting another breath, the two turned from the door and made for the station. The train was there when they arrived. The platform was empty except for a hunched conductor farther down the way, his face lost beneath the brim of his cap. Greta and Anne had never seen him before and wondered who he was. Greta tightened her grip on the satchel, and together they boarded. Elias greeted them with a smile as the train pulled away from the station.

"Who is the conductor?" Greta asked

"Yeah, is he new?" Anne added.

"No, he's not new. He's of our bloodline. Nothing to worry about," Elias said.

Elias led them to the compartment where Demetria, Eva, and Mattie were talking to Lady, Bolshan, and Elowen. Demetria glanced up first, a surprised look on her face, which didn't last long. Demetria would later tell Anne and Greta that Lady had summoned them.

"We've been waiting," Lady said.

Anne and Greta slid into the seats across from them. They handed the satchel, carrying the Artifact and the Stone, to Bolshan. Without saying a word, he took it to a closed-off section of the compartment.

"We know what happened," Eva said, her eyes locked on Anne and Greta.

"You felt it too?" Greta asked Eva.

"No. None of us did, but we sensed something was wrong."

"We saw everything," Anne added.

No more words were needed as Lady said, "Teveras and his minions are ready. Retribution has started, but it will not end with what took place at Ashlow Ridge."

Anne's hand twitched slightly. "Good. Because neither will theirs."

Lady stared at her for a moment. Then the faintest smile curled the edge of her lips. "Be careful how far you reach. Even bloodlines thin over time. I'm aware of the things you did on your own." The Sisters glanced at each other and smiled. Lady smiled in return before continuing, "We move forward. But on my orders. The energy from the ancestors will watch over you and guide you."

"Thank you," the Sisters said as the train came to a stop. They stepped onto the platform, watching in silence as the train vanished into the thin morning mist.

"We saw it all. Teveras did it, Ohn, Maera, their whole bloodline is behind it. The ground itself gave way, and the dead rose for them. There's nothing left of our family now," Anne said.

"They're gone," Greta said quietly. Demetria, Eva, and Mattie met her gaze, vengeance burning in their eyes.

****

Meanwhile, on the far edge of Kramden, opposite where Anne and Greta lived, the Aldric family, descendants of a bloodline bound to Renegade's ancestors-believed the blood that protected them would always keep them safe. They never imagined it would be the very thing that marked them for death. Among them was J.T. Aldric, one of Renegade's closest allies.

Aldric's family owned a spread of farmland, barns, silos, and machinery, all of it rusting in the fields like the skeletons of a failed industry. And soon, two things would happen: one by design, the other by something far older than revenge.

Later that night, it was Greta who spotted the perfect opportunity. J.T.'s son and his family had started working on one of the old silos two days earlier, trying to dismantle it. The framework was brittle, rusted, and ready to collapse with just the right nudge. Nightfall brought the sisters to the edge of the property, hidden in the shadows, watching as J.T.'s son's children helped their father near the base of the silo. Anne and Greta cautiously approached. Demetria, Eva, and Mattie circled to the far side, unseen.

They didn't speak. It took only one gesture of Anne's hand, two fingers brushing along the ancient sigils carved into a discarded piece of machinery nearby. The symbols pulsed faintly as the rust weakened, a long-forgotten spell echoing through the metal's decay. A sharp groan echoed through the night as bolts and rivets strained. The family looked up, confused, as the entire structure gave a sudden shudder, then began to tilt before collapsing in on itself. The silo came down in a roar of iron and dust, the shrieks of twisting metal drowning out the screams beneath it.

Seconds later, the estate was in flames. It wasn't a towering inferno, nothing so obvious. A frayed oil lamp was left near old, dry curtains. And a stable door was mysteriously unlatched. A slow, creeping blaze spread just enough to collapse one section of the home, killing three members of the Aldric line before help arrived.

When word reached Renegade and J.T., his followers whispered that it was tragic. Accidental. But one of Renegade's lieutenants stepped closer, glanced between them, and said what they were both thinking: "That was no accident."

But Renegade stood still as stone, staring at nothing before muttering. "They've made their move," as something deeper stirred in his eyes. "They think they're clever. They want a blood war . . . fine."

One of his men shifted nervously. "You think it was really them?"

Renegade's smile was thin and humorless. "Accidents don't happen to allies of mine. Not out here. Not now. This is them. This is a message." He spat into the dirt. "Message received." Behind him, the wind shifted strangely, curling in from the woods, carrying with it the faintest scent of ash and something older, something watching.

29

The Weight Of Vengeance

Doris sat at the table, hands folded tight, while Alias leaned against the counter. There was a moment of silence between them, broken only when the back door creaked open, and their daughters stepped in. Alias glanced at them. Demetria, Eva, and Mattie met their father's glance with quiet, half-smiles. They didn't have to say a word for their parents to know something had happened.

"Sit," Doris said quietly. "All of you." They exchanged a look, then did as she asked. They understood. Alias didn't move from the counter, but his eyes never left their faces.

It was Demetria who spoke first, "Anne and Greta's family. The Whitlocks. They're gone, killed."

Doris let out a soft gasp, one hand flying to her chest.

"Gone? Dead? What do you mean?" Alias asked, with raised eyebrows.

Eva answered. "Father, Lady told us. But Anne and Greta saw it. The Artifact and the Stone led them there. The house, the land, swallowed whole. By something old. Something ancient. Something from the other side."

Alias glanced at Doris, who responded, "Doesn't it sound familiar?"

"You think it's Teveras and the Exuis?" Alias replied.

"It's him, and the others," Doris said.

"So, you know of them?" Demetria asked.

"We do," Alias said. "Everything. They're behind it. Isn't that what Lady told you?"

"She did," Demetria replied.

Before Alias could speak again, Eva cut in. "We're more worried about you. We know they'll come for you."

"Us?" Doris smiled, "Don't worry about us. Alias and I know how to handle ourselves. "We've done a lot in our time, traveled near and far. Haven't we, Alias?" she said with a smile, and he returned it.

Noticing the look on Mattie's face, Alias asked, "What is it, Mattie?"

She swallowed. "They didn't just destroy it. They desecrated it."

Doris's eyes welled, not from sentiment alone but from deep-rooted evil that her and Alias's eyes have seen. "They've come to settle old oaths. That blood never stayed buried."

Alias sat down. "Tell me," he said, his eyes on Demetria. "What did you do? I can tell something else happened."

The girls didn't respond immediately. Demetria glanced at Eva, who nodded. "Along with Greta and Anne, we paid the Aldrics a visit," Demetria said.

"J.T.'s family?"

"Yes. We had to, Father. We hit back," Demetria said.

Mattie's voice cut in, barely above a whisper. "We made it look like an accident."

Alias exhaled, "You went against them without Lady's blessing?"

"Yes," Demetria admitted.

"Father, she has to know by now," Eva added. "They burned our blood. Did we need permission for that?"

Doris stood up slowly. She walked to the window and looked out, as if expecting the ground to open. "I understand. What is taking place is bigger than all of us."

"Mother, I agree. The line was crossed when they took out the Whitlocks," Eva said. "We just reminded them that we're not prey."

"The line was crossed before you were born," Doris said, smiling at her daughters.

Alias got up from the table. "This isn't just about them and us. The ancestors, ours and theirs, they're at war now." Alias kept their gaze; his eyes burned like fire. "And that doesn't end when the sun comes up. It ends when one bloodline is buried completely."

Doris turned from the window, "This isn't a simple family quarrel you can walk away from. This war beneath us isn't about mercy. It's demons and souls, blood and bone, shadow and spite — an endless torment neither side can escape. Teveras, Ohn, Maera, the Exuis, they are not just ancient names. They are the wrath of the dead, risen to settle scores written in agony and fire."

Alias spoke again. "Our ancestors fought them and theirs in the black depths long before any of us drew breath. The battle has already begun in the shadows, unseen but relentless. It doesn't matter who started it, only that it's here, and none of us will be untouched. The echoes of the past are waking, and the cost will be paid in souls."

"Teveras won't let this go. He'll call on the old ones," Doris added. It's the natural order of how things will go. Ohn and Maera will bring whatever's left from beneath the ground. And like your father warned, when they rise, they won't care who lit the fire. Only that someone has to burn." The sisters sat in silence. Each of them had known, in some quiet corner of their mind, what would come. But now it was spoken aloud.

Alias stepped closer, putting a hand on Demetria's shoulder. "If you're going to keep walking this path, know that it leads straight through the graveyard. Many have taken it and never returned. But the three of you were born for this, and I believe you'll make it through; your mother and I were told so by the ancestors."

Doris nodded, her eyes on Mattie. "Be smart. Be fast. And for the love of everything sacred, tell Lady what you did. Because when the ground starts splitting again, she needs to know where the cracks began."

"Mother, believe me, she knows," Eva said.

"It doesn't matter. You need to tell her!"

No one spoke after that. The sky outside had gone from purple to black, and the wind began to stir the trees like waves crashing to the shore.

30

Renegade's Wrath

Renegade's followers buzzed with energy, their faces etched with suspicion and bloodlust, gathered close, waiting on his command. Whispers rippled through the crowd: *an accident,* a cruel joke that no one but the foolish believed. J.T., flanked by two grim-faced cousins, paced beside Renegade, their fists clenched.

"Like I said before, Renegade, an entire structure collapsing? No. My bloodline doesn't go down in house fires," he muttered. "Someone planned this."

Renegade didn't say a word as his eyes scanned the circle of faces, loyalists, killers, seers, and saw what he expected: fear, yes, but something else. Anticipation. The crowd shifted restlessly. Some called for blood, for swift vengeance.

"Kill Alias and Doris," a burly man hissed, his voice filled with hatred. "Burn their home to the ground. Make them bleed like we have."

Another follower shouted, "Awake the ground! Call upon the ancient ones!"

Renegade's eyes swept over the faces, the hunger for violence in their eyes. "Not yet," Renegade said, lifting a hand. "We are no fools.

We strike when the time is right. Not in blind fury." J.T. scoffed but nodded, biting back the impatience that burned beneath his skin.

Far from the fire and fury, Alias and Doris stood on the porch of their house, the wind tugging at their coats like a warning. With it came a message: Renegade was coming, and he had made his threats clear. Demetria, Eva, and Mattie had already fled with Anne and Greta to safer ground under Lady's protection. The Sisters had no illusions about what awaited them, but for now, they were alive.

A shadow emerged from the darkness beyond Alias and Doris's property. It was Renegade. He stepped forward. Behind him, a handful of his most loyal followers lingered, their weapons catching the faint moonlight. Alias and Doris's eyes met Renegade's. A slight smile played on Alias's face — more a smirk than anything else.

"What brings you and your evil here?" Alias asked.

"Your daughters and the sisters from your bloodline," he said, with a sneer.

"How dare you, you fucking son of a bitch!" Doris snapped.

"Hmm! No answer, huh? You really think you're safe here? Your bloodline's been bleeding for centuries. I'm here to finish it," Renegade snarled.

Alias squared his shoulders, staring him down. "You'll find no fear here."

Doris's voice was cold. "We've faced darker threats than you. We've survived."

Renegade gave a cold smile. "Brave words. But words don't stop what's coming. I'll tear this town apart if I have to."

He turned to his followers. "Watch them closely. They're the last light before the darkness swallows all."

J.T. spat at the ground. "I say we end it now. Kill 'em both."

Something shifted in Renegade, as if the darkness itself had spoken. His voice dropped. "No. Not yet. We need them alive, for now."

Alias laughed mockingly. "You need us alive. Did you hear this, Doris?" she smiled.

"This isn't over. We'll meet again. And next time, you won't be so lucky," Renegade sneered. Without saying another word, he and his men vanished into the night, leaving behind only the bitter scent of danger.

****

Meanwhile, in a hidden grove shrouded by old spirits, the sisters gathered. Anne and Greta stood close. Beyond the train station, Lady, Bolshan, and Elowen appeared. They led the Sisters down an overgrown embankment, past the rusted bones of a freight line. At the edge of a crumbled retaining wall, Elowen uncovered a panel embedded in stone, not with modern tools, but with bare hands and memory. A silent click echoed through the brush as a hidden mechanism was released.

Lady moved her hand in a circular motion over the stone. The lift sank into the darkness. The earth sealed back above them, and all sound from the surface faded. They'd entered The Hollow, a centuries-old sanctuary Lady ancestors had used to evade demons, hunters, colonizers, and worse. Around them were massive carved stones, hidden wells, and a maze of narrow tunnels, which Lady had memorized since childhood. Only she and a handful of ancient souls from the Old World knew its every corner. Not even the spirits who roamed above could see beyond its boundary.

"You're safe here," Lady said, her voice leaving no room for doubt.

Mattie had a concerned look on her face. "They'll come."

"They will," Lady agreed. "But I've wrapped this place in zones. Nothing living or dead can enter."

Eva glanced toward the tunnels surrounding them, as shadows hovered over them. "We can't run forever."

"No," Lady said quietly. "But sometimes, retreat is the first step to victory."

Outside, the wind whispered through the branches, carrying with it the promise of war and the unyielding will of those who refused to bow.

****

The smoke from Renegade's ritual drifted east and stalled over Aldan Circle. The spirits weren't clear, but he felt it in his bones; the Sisters were near. Renegade and his men scoured the area, circling the old train yard. But the trail had gone cold. "They're down there. I know it," he growled, his eyes scanning the overgrowth. "The Hollow. I've heard the stories since I was a boy, but no one ever found the damn thing." They searched through the night. At one point, the Sisters heard boots thudding above them and the muffled cursing of Renegade and his followers. But no light breached the sanctuary's veil.

Furious, Renegade sent J.T. and a group of trusted followers to reach out to Teveras, Ohn, and Maera. Within minutes, the three showed up. Four women followed, barefoot, dressed in black, their skin marked with jagged symbols. Whatever they were, they weren't human anymore. Their smiles were slow, cruel, and wrong. Even the trees bent slightly away as they passed. It was as if death walked with them.

They gathered under the trees surrounding the suspected site. Ohn took the lead and whispered in tongues, casting spell after spell. "Something's buried here," he muttered, sweat on his brow. "But whatever Lady did, she sealed it tight. I can't see past her mark."

Symbols glowed briefly, then vanished into the dirt like they were never there. Teveras stepped forward with a low chant. "Renegade, step aside with your followers." With a frightened look on their faces, Renegade's men did as told.

The ground pulsed beneath Teveras, and the sky above dimmed unnaturally, as if light no longer belonged to this place. He lifted one hand, fingers trembling not from weakness, but from the sheer force he was channeling. Still, the veil around Lady's sanctuary held.

Behind them, the four women and Maera spread out in a slow, deliberate formation. They dropped to their knees, their mouths stretching open, as if unhinged. A deep black mist poured from within them, thick and wriggling. The grass beneath them shriveled into ash. Trees bent away. One of the women dug her fingers into the soil, blood dripped from her nails, not hers, but something else's. The mist crawled forward, slamming against an unseen wall, then screamed as it recoiled, scattering like smoke caught in a storm.

Teveras eyes were fixed on the rituals. His body jerked in violent spasms, small limbs twisting in ways they shouldn't, but Teveras never blinked; his eyes were fixed on the ritual's glow. Then he whispered the name of the Exuis. The wind stopped. A deep, guttural groan rose from beneath the ground, some distance from The Hollow. The very earth cracked, a thin line splitting outward from Teveras's feet. Shadows bled through it, thick and foul. The air reeked of sulfur and decay. Still, The Hollow held. Teveras stepped back, his chest rising and falling. Even he looked rattled.

"She's wrapped them in something old," he muttered. "Older than me. Older than any of us."

"How can we prevail?" the Exuis asked. The others echoed it like a chant, their voices overlapping, echoing, and rising. Renegade didn't flinch. But his followers exchanged anxious glances.

"If you have to ask how to prevail, you are already losing. Burn what must burn. Tear the rest apart," Teveras said.

Renegade lowered his head slightly. "Then guide us. If there's a way forward, I'll follow your lead."

Teveras turned toward the darkness. "The Sisters are buried under her protection, sealed by forces that should've stayed forgotten." He looked to the others, Ohn, Maera, the four women, and the Exuis still whispering in the shadows. "We'll deal with Lady."

Nothing else was said as one by one, they slipped into the night, their forms swallowed by the darkness.

Renegade watched them go. Then he turned to his followers. "Call it a night," he said quietly. "We've got things to handle come morning."

31

Echoes Of The Spirit War

It wasn't long after Teveras and his legions left that Lady and her followers descended into The Hollow. The Sisters stood waiting in the central chamber, a concerned look on their faces.

"We heard it," Demetria said, stepping forward. "Voices outside, moving around. They were close."

Eva glanced upward. "They were right above us. We thought they'd found us."

Lady moved past them without a word at first, her cloak trailing along the carved floor. She stopped at the altar near the back of the chamber, placing her hand on the cold stone surface. The faint hum of the Artifact stirred beneath her touch, as did the Stone. "I heard them, too," she said finally. Her voice was calm. "But like I told you before, you're safe here. What matters more right now . . . is what's happening beneath us."

"What do you mean?" Anne asked.

She turned and faced Anne, "There's a war unfolding far below this sanctuary. One older than our names. Our ancestors, and those of Teveras and Renegade, are clashing even now."

Bolshan glanced at the Sisters. "The spirit world was in full revolt. Old gods were awakened. Benevolent spirits are clashing with corrupted ones in underground channels the living can't see."

The chamber darkened as Lady laid both hands on the altar. The Artifact pulsed, its crimson glow spreading outward like veins. Beside it, the blackened Stone began to shift, its surface shimmering with unnatural light. Screams echoed through the veins of the stone, not human, not beast, but something older.

"Look," Lady whispered. The Sisters stepped closer. The surface of the Stone rippled like disturbed water, and then the vision came.

They saw a pit, endless and broken, filled with screeching winds and twisted terrain. Spirits tore into each other in savage bursts of violence: some cloaked in flames, others in skeletal armor, all screaming in voices that no longer belonged to the living. One lunged with a jaw stretched to its chest, ripping through a burning form with claws made of bone. Another spirit, bound in rusted chains and missing half its face, dragged a spiked weapon across the field, leaving trails of fire behind. A winged figure, faceless and enormous, split open and released a swarm of howling shadows that consumed everything in their path.

"These are our ancestors," Lady said. "And theirs." The vision glowed. A blackened spear impaled a screaming spirit and lifted it into the air, only for the body to explode into ash and rebuild itself mid-fall. "This is no longer about hiding," she said. "It's about which bloodline survives."

The Artifact let out a sharp crack of light, then dimmed. The Stone's surface stilled. The Sisters stood frozen, shaken by what they had seen. Lady stepped away from the altar, her words deliberate as she spoke. "If we lose . . ." she said, her eyes fixed on the Stone, "they'll rise. Not just Teveras, but his entire bloodline. All of them, and every twisted thing their blood ever fed. Spirits dragged from pits that should have stayed sealed. Creatures even the dark won't claim will rise." Her voice grew colder. "They won't come to rule. They'll come to consume. They'll rip The Hollow apart, if we allow it, then the land above it . . . and then everyone you've ever loved. It won't be done fast, but slowly. They'll rot the world alive." The Artifact let out a low, guttural pulse. "And when they're done here," she continued, "they'll go back . . . to the Old World. Where our ancestors rest. And they'll crush them. Strip them of name, memory, and meaning. They'll be erased from time itself." Lady's gaze was on them now. "That's what happens," she said softly, "if we lose."

Mattie broke the silence. "Can they really do that?" she asked quietly. "Wipe out our ancestors?"

Lady didn't hesitate. "If they break through, nothing sacred will remain, and I'm not saying they will, but . . ." She turned back to the altar, retrieving a cloth-wrapped bundle from a carved recess in the wall. Inside were several black stones, veined with silver and pulsing faintly. She removed five. "These will anchor you to The Hollow," she said, placing one in each sister's hand. "If the walls begin to fall, you'll feel it. If it comes to it, bleed on them. Call on the old power directly. Do you understand?" She looked at each of them.

"We do," the Sisters said in unison.

Elowen slowly approached the Sisters. "Keep in mind, even sanctuaries bleed when the war beneath turns. The spirits holding the line are your ancestors. If they fall, the protections above them begin to rot. And if that happens," she paused. "It will be a battle for the ages. Because they want our souls."

Demetria stepped forward, clutching the stone in her palm so tightly her knuckles whitened. "Then let them come," she said. "I won't run. Not while our ancestors bleed beneath us." She looked to her sisters and at Greta and Anne. "I swear on their names, if the walls fall, I'll bleed with them. I'll call the old power myself." Eva and Mattie moved beside her. Ann and Greta followed, their stones held close, fire in their eyes. "We stand," Demetria said again, her voice rising just enough to echo. "And if it ends her . . . then we end it fighting."

32

Beneath The Surface

Morning broke cold and gray; there was a light fog. The train station buzzed with commuters, but no one paid any attention to the sealed-off Compartment 13 stop, where creeping vines and overgrown weeds claimed the platform. Renegade stood at the edge of the clearing, his dark coat pulled tight against the chill. His eyes scanned the cracked pavement and twisted roots, searching for the slightest tremor, any sign of weakness in the earth below. Around him, his men moved quickly and quietly, each one knowing what was expected.

J.T. wiped sweat from his brow despite the cold and hesitantly approached Renegade. "We're digging blind," he said, his voice low. "Teveras already told us the Sisters are down there. What's the point in breaking our backs trying to find something he's already found?"

Renegade didn't respond immediately. He stared down at the cracked earth like it owed him an answer. "The traditional ways work sometimes. Not everything is left to the spirits."

"But . . . I thought . . ."

"Thought what?"

Upset, J.T. hid how he truly felt. "Nothing," he muttered.

"Listen, Teveras sees the abyss," Renegade said, his voice filled with contempt. "But I don't trust anything that swims in it." He turned to face J.T., with cold eyes. "You really think he told us everything? He's a shadow. A trickster who deals in secrets and lies." J.T. shifted uncomfortably. Renegade stepped closer, close enough for only J.T. to hear. "That thing walks with death on its tongue and a grin full of secrets. If the Sisters are beneath us, I want to be the one who cracks the stone and drags them out. Not him."

"I say we still kill that Alias and his wife. I want my revenge," J. T. said.

"We will when the time is right, and we all seek revenge. Don't you forget this," Renegade snapped. He gestured toward the men, who had stopped their work at the exchange. "Keep digging. Burn the brush if you have to. I'm not giving that little demon the final move."

As the men resumed their work, strange things began to stir around them. The ground pulsed faintly under their feet, like a slow, restless heartbeat. An uneasy chill crawled up their spines. Whispered murmurs seemed to rise from the cracked stones themselves, barely audible, slipping through the air like a ghost's breath.

A few of the men exchanged nervous glances but said nothing. They had learned long ago that fear was a luxury they couldn't afford, especially not with Renegade watching. The earth beneath them hummed with power, restless and watching. The fog swirled around their feet like something was alive. It curled between fingers and slithered up pant legs, ignoring the laws of wind or warmth.

Renegade stood back, watching the process unfold. He had a determined look on his face. Every scrape of a shovel, every shift in the soil fed his sense of where The Hollow might lie beneath their feet. J.T. approached from the far edge, where a patch of roots had refused to burn. "It's holding," he muttered. "Won't break. Won't even smoke."

Renegade's gaze fell to the untouched roots curling out of the earth like fingers. "It's not just soil," he said. "That's bloodline magic." He crouched down, touching the ground lightly. It pulsed barely, but enough. "She's clever," he murmured. "I'll give her that."

J.T. glanced back toward Renegade. "You think Lady knows we're this close?"

Renegade rose slowly, "Of course she knows," he said. "But I don't think she's worried."

"So why are we still doing this?" one of J.T.'s cousins said. "You called Teveras a trickster and a liar, but he's more powerful than us, and more powerful than most of our ancestors. Maybe we should just give this up and go after the sisters' parents . . . or the families of the other two, wherever they live."

Renegade turned with a look that could raise the dead. "So now you're questioning my authority? Have you given any thought that they might all be here?"

"No, I'm just saying . . ."

"Say nothing. And keep your fucking mouth shut. You think because Teveras is stronger than us, we stop trying?" he asked. "What, we sit around and move only when he speaks? And just so you know, the Whitlocks, the close bloodline of the other two, were sent to hell by Teveras."

The cousin opened his mouth, but nothing came out. Renegade stepped closer, his stale breath brushing the cousin's face. "We follow his blood because it's ours. Because it's written. But don't mistake that for surrender." He glanced at the others. "Teveras has his way. I have mine. The ancestors are also with me." He pointed at the ground. "And if the Sisters are beneath us, I'll be the one to drag them out, as I said before, not him."

J.T. moved quickly, grabbing his cousin's arm and pulling him back. "You've said enough," he muttered under his breath.

The fog pressed in, unusually still. Renegade crouched at the edge of a half-cleared trench. The soil there was darker, denser, and damp as if it had soaked in secrets. He pressed his hand into it and chanted several words. A faint pulse trembled beneath his fingers. He stood slowly. "This place wasn't overgrown by accident. The Hollow's bones are restless."

A low groan echoed from beneath the tracks, long, slow, and muffled. Something deep below had shifted. Several men froze. One gripped the charm around his neck.

J.T. muttered, "We've stirred something."

Renegade didn't flinch. "Good. We have done something Teveras, and the others didn't do," he said. "Let it come to the surface." The men froze. Even the fog seemed to pause. Then came the sound, scraping. Not from a tool, not from boots. This was something fingernail-thin, dragging against rock from beneath the soil. A patch of earth near the edge of the platform cracked, then split. Dirt crumbled inward as something pushed from below, slowly and deliberately.

Meanwhile, inside The Hollow, the Sisters heard the spirits and the earth cracking, even from deep underground.

"Did you hear that?" Anne said to the others.

"Yes," they said in unison.

"It's spirits, someone called them. But they can't reach us; we're too deep," Demetria said.

"But who could have called them?" Mattie asked.

"It's not our bloodline, so it must be our enemies," Greta said.

"Remember, Lady explained everything to us, it's them," Eva added.

"I know what Lady said, but why not engage them?" Mattie suggested.

"No, Mattie. Absolutely not. What's wrong with you? Lady's orders are orders," Demetria snapped.

"I was just saying," Mattie replied, as they looked at her with straight faces.

"We understand, Mattie. We're ready to fight, but we do it on Lady's command, okay?" Anne said.

"Sure, sure," Mattie said, nodding.

Back At The Upper Level

A pale hand broke the surface. Thin, gray, and shriveled, it clawed upward with twitchy, jerking movements. Its fingers were long, nails black and cracked. A rotting stench followed. Several of the men staggered back.

"No . . ." one of the men whispered. "That's, no. That's Dalo, the one they talked about."

"How do you know?" Renegade asked.

"The description. He fits it. It's him. He and several others were killed over a hundred years ago. Maybe two."

"It's true," J.T. added. "They were burned."

Their hands pressed down. And arms followed, then shoulders. The faces that rose next were hollowed and dry, like something dug up from a forgotten grave, only the eyes were still. Not dead. Not human. Just black. Black like tar. Black like nothingness.

Renegade didn't move. Dalo's mouth opened, silent and wide. His head twisted, joints cracking, skin tearing. Then, one by one, the others clawed their way up beside him. Then, as if recognizing the faces around them, they tilted their heads. They smiled, eerie and empty.

The cousin who had questioned Renegade took a step back. "We shouldn't be here," he said.

"No," Renegade muttered, stepping forward. "We're exactly where we need to be."

The ground beneath Dalo and the others shifted. Renegade stood silent, staring at the figures that had clawed their way out of the earth.

Dalo's voice was low and spine-chilling. "We know why you're here, blood of our blood. But not even the all-powerful Teveras and Exuis can reach them. Even we cannot reach them," he said. "The blood below is locked behind something older than us all."

Before Renegade could respond, a chilly breeze whipped across his face. It was suddenly cold. Dalo paused, his black eyes looking upward. The others tensed, heads tilting like animals, sensing a storm. Then it hit. An invisible force, thick and violent, ripped through the clearing like a scream with no sound. Dalo's form jerked once, violently, before splitting in half with a sound like cracking glass. The others followed, twisting, unraveling into ash and bone as if yanked back into whatever pit they had crawled from.

Renegade staggered back. "What the fuck was that?" he shouted, as Dalo and the evil with him were swallowed by the thickening fog. Renegade and his men turned and ran. Behind them, the ground closed, sealing itself without a trace. Whatever watched from beneath . . . wasn't done watching. Moments later, and unknown to Renegade and his followers, the thickening fog returned, and the ground opened, releasing Dalo and his followers. As they clawed their way from the pit that had swallowed them, their appearance began to change as they headed to The Petra.

33

Reckoning In The Dark

The morning mist hadn't yet lifted when J.T.'s two cousins broke off from the others without saying a word. They did this without Renegade's say-so. Along with four others, still enraged and arrogantly convinced they could handle what even Renegade had hesitated to act on: the big payback, which included Alias and Doris. After parking their truck, they cut through the backroads and wooded trails, under the impression that Alias and Doris would be easy prey. They moved through the tall brush behind the home, silent, armed, eyes ready for blood. The wind was light, the trees still. Everything around them felt as if it were sleeping, but something was awake. The first sign came as they neared the back porch. The second sign was the silence itself: no birds, no wind, just the soft crunch of leaves under their boots.

The cousin in front took the lead, weapon drawn, and gestured to the others. Just as he stepped forward, he froze. From the shadows between the porch columns, two faces emerged, pale, hollow-eyed, and half-formed in the dark. Alias's face stared out like the ghost of death itself. Beside him, Doris's lips curled into a slow, unnatural smile. The cousins felt the cold of dread pass through them. Their eyes bulged. The cousin who had taken the lead doubled over. The other staggered back, his hands trembling so violently that his weapon nearly slipped from his grasp.

Suddenly, something locked them in place. Whatever gripped them clawed at their souls. Before they could scream, their faces twisted and stretched, becoming something cold, merciless, and unholy. A force slammed the first cousin backward, his chest caving in as if crushed by invisible hands. The others screamed, but creeping shadows, like living roots, slithered between the porch columns and reached for them. The shadows whispered the names of Alias and Doris as they dragged the men down into the earth. One by one, five of the six men vanished into the dark, their final sounds lost to the hush that followed. The lone survivor fled blindly in panic, desperate to escape, but did he really?

Inside the Siobhan home, Doris set down a pan with a quiet clatter. Alias sat at the table, eyes distant but calm, a book open before him. The two eyes met, and a shared grin crept across their faces. No one would find the bodies. No one would even know they came. And Renegade? He'd find out much later, too late to change anything, and too shaken to ever be sure who, or what, answered the door first.

****

While the lone escapee ran for his life, sweat stinging his eyes and branches tearing at his clothes, he didn't look back; he couldn't. What he'd witnessed clawed at his mind, twisting it into madness. Suddenly, he lost his balance and stumbled into a clearing. From the darkness, three figures emerged: Teveras, Ohn, and Maera.

"Where are you going?" Teveras's voice cut through the night like a blade. It's like fear had stolen the escapee's voice. He opened his mouth to speak . . ., but his words were stuck in his throat.

Instead, his paranoia took hold of him. "The Siobhans, they took them."

"Took who?" Teveras asked.

He went on to explain what happened.

"So, Renegade is upset?"

"Yes . . . he's mad at you. Called you a trickster. Said you deal in secrets and lies. Said he doesn't think you told us everything."

Teveras didn't blink. His voice was calm, too calm. "A trickster? he repeated. "You repeat a fool's words and expect what, pity? Protection? Renegade speaks of lies while choking on his own. What I keep hidden is what keeps our bloodline from crumbling." He turned his head slightly, just enough to glance at Ohn. Without hesitation, Ohn moved toward the man. The man's scream barely began before a dark force crushed him mercilessly. Teveras turned and glanced at Ohn and Maera, their eyes locked on something only they could see.

****

Morning found Renegade surrounded by his most trusted followers, gathered in the stone chamber where they had long paid homage to the bloodline. Teveras and the others appeared like shadows rising from the far end of the chamber, where the torches barely reached.

Renegade braced himself. "What brings you here?" he asked, trying to keep calm. "Why the visit?"

He said nothing, only raised his hand and turned. The others followed. The silence was more chilling than any answer. He led them through a narrow stone passage, deeper into the earth, where the air grew colder and eerier. They reached the pit, a jagged maw in the ground, carved centuries ago. It breathed cold darkness and a rotting stench. From within came the echoes of torment: agonized wails, choked sobs, and the brittle snap of cursed bones.

Teveras raised a hand, and the shadows peeled back, revealing the pit's depths. Bodies hung suspended, half-living. Eyes hollow. Flesh warped by dark spells. "These are the ones who broke the vow," Teveras said in a harsh voice. "Those who defy the bloodline, who question what was never theirs to question, and who dare spit on the names of their leaders."

Renegade's breathing quickened. His men stirred, stricken with silent terror. He dropped to his knees. "Please," he begged. "We obey. We swear it. Just . . . please." The pit didn't care. It groaned beneath them.

Teveras stared down at him, unmoved. "Remember this moment," he said. "Because next time, the pit will call your name. It is your fate if you stray again." The cries surged again, rising until the stone passage trembled. Renegade and his men backed away, haunted by what they had seen, and could neither fight nor flee.

Teveras never mentioned the sixth man, nor the words he had spoken in fear. Whatever judgment had been passed, it remained between the bloodline and the pit. Renegade, J.T., and the others were left in the dark, for now. It wouldn't be until later, when the hours stretched on and no word came, that they would realize the cousins and four of their men were gone.

34

They Rode The Train

The Hollow fell quiet as Lady stepped forward, a solemn look on her face. "Your parents reached out to me," she said. "Something happened last night." The Sisters turned toward her. "Some of Renegade's men came to their home," Lady continued. "They didn't leave."

Demetria, with raised eyebrows, responded, "Wait . . . what do you mean they didn't leave?"

"Your parents dealt with them as they should," Lady said.

Mattie's mouth dropped. Eva took a step forward. "Handled them? Our parents?"

"Yes," Lady said. "They didn't just survive the attack. They ended it, except for one."

"But . . . they're just our parents," Mattie whispered.

Lady turned to them, Greta and Anne now just as transfixed as the sisters. "That's what you believe, even after everything they told you, they're just your parents?" Lady said. "Your parents are part of something older. Much older." Her voice dropped. She spoke more slowly now. "Our bloodline has always been linked to Compartment 13. Elias, Bolshan, and Elowen's parents were the original caretakers on our arrival from the old countries. It wasn't just a stop. It was a gateway. And our ancestors didn't run it, they ruled it."

Anne's eyes widened. "We've heard stories . . . but we never knew the names."

"The stories you heard," Lady said, "those stories are yours, ours. Alias and Doris once rode the train, not as travelers, but as enforcers. They left behind wreckage wherever the bloodline was crossed."

Demetria, her eyes fixed on Lady, said, "They shared a lot with us. We were told that we were chosen and destined for great things. But you're saying they can . . . call on the ancestors?"

"They were given that power," Lady said. "Just as Renegade and others in Kramden were. But your parents never used it for pride or vengeance. Only when it was needed. And they did what had to be done." Demetria, Eva, and Mattie stood speechless, the truth rewriting everything they thought they knew. Anne and Greta remained quiet; the weight of the revelation hit all five of them like a speeding train. "The bloodline," Lady said, "is no longer hiding. And neither should you."

"We welcome the bloodline," the Sisters responded.

The Hollow breathed low as the Sisters circled Lady. She called for Elias, surprising the sisters. She then raised her hands, and Bolshan and Elowen emerged from the darkened corners.

"Before you go," Lady said, "There's something you must take, an echo from the depths, long hidden, now awakening to claim you."

The Sisters stood in silence as Elias, Bolshan, and Elowen stepped forward. A faint hum rose from the altar. It wasn't music. It was a memory. Bolshan extended his hand over Demetria first, a shimmer of light pressing against her chest and sinking into her skin. She gasped, staggered slightly. One by one, the others received the same. Elowen's touch came colder, older, like being dipped into something buried centuries ago. When it reached Anne and Greta, their eyes fluttered; something in their blood remembered this. Elias let out several chants of an ancestral hymn, and the Sisters joined in, singing each word perfectly, a hymn they had never heard before.

When it was done, the circle was broken, and Lady stepped forward. "This power is not a weapon," she warned. "Not unless it must be. You do not wield it on anger or whim. You call on me first. Only then will it answer." She looked at each of them. "And if you reach for it out of pride or rage . . . it will consume you." No one spoke. They didn't have to.

The Return

The Sisters split at The Hollow's edge. Demetria, Eva, and Mattie turned down the path that led back to the old Barrs' house. Greta and Anne turned toward the woods that led to their homes, equally guarded, equally haunted.

Back at the edge of the Aldan Circle Station, the sealed-off track of Compartment 13 remained untouched. No one dared approach. But what had taken place with the Sisters was felt by the townspeople. They knew it was only a matter of time before strange things would begin to take place. Despite the prying eyes of those who passed the station, everyone knew it was sacred ground, not out of reverence, but out of fear, the kind passed down through muttered warnings.

35

The Blood We Carry

The soft overhead light cast a calm, steady glow across the Siobhan kitchen. Alias sat at the table, hands clasped, his expression unreadable. Doris leaned against the counter, arms crossed. Across from them, Demetria, Eva, and Mattie sat shoulder to shoulder.

Demetria finally spoke. "Lady told us everything." Alias didn't flinch.

"What exactly did she say?" Doris asked with a smile.

"She said you have power," Demetria replied. "That you were given it through the bloodline, and that you can call on the ancestors, and you did to get rid of some of Renegade's men."

"And don't forget the travels on the train," Mattie said.

Doris sighed, glancing at her husband before turning to face them. "She said that, huh?"

Eva leaned forward. "You're not denying it."

"Why should we? We just . . . didn't expect it to come out like this."

Eva turned to her father, "When were you going to tell us?"

Alias looked at her with calm eyes. "When the time was right."

"See," Mattie said. "That line again."

Eva raised an eyebrow. "What does that even mean? When exactly would it have been the right time?"

Doris shrugged. "Maybe around a nice, quiet Sunday dinner. When we're passing the mashed potatoes, oh, and by the way, we can summon the dead." Alias let out a laugh he clearly tried to stifle. The sisters broke out in laughter.

"It's not funny," Demetria said, trying to hold back her laughter.

"No," Doris said, "it's not. But it's true. We didn't want this for you. Not the secrets, not the spirits, none of it. We wanted you to grow up different. Free. But as we told you, the ancestors warned and gave us signs that you were chosen. It's your destiny."

Alias nodded. "We're not like some of the families in Kramden, chasing power they can't handle."

"So, you just kept it hidden?" Eva asked. "All of it?"

"Some, but not all," Doris said.

Alias looked each of them in their eyes. "This," he said, in a low voice. "The war outside. The blood calling. The truth is waking up in all of us. We knew it would come, and we're more than convinced that you can hold your own against the other bloodlines. Lady and the ancestors know this. Again, it's your destiny."

The sisters sat in silence, processing what they were hearing.

Finally, Mattie exhaled. "Well . . . next time you're keeping world-shaking ancestral powers from us, maybe give us a little warning before the spirits come calling."

Alias smiled. "Noted."

Doris chuckled. "We love you girls. That's why we stayed quiet. But now? No more secrets. Right, girls!"

Demetria glanced at her sisters before speaking. "There's something we need to tell you."

Eva nodded. "Lady gave us powers, too, but they're different from yours. Not as strong, but . . . enough."

Mattie added, "We didn't mean to keep it from you. Everything happened so fast, and we didn't know how you'd react."

Alias exchanged a knowing smile with Doris. "We know that all of you were given the gift by Lady."

"You knew?" Mattie asked.

"Aren't we all, Siobhan?" Doris smiled gently. "It's not the same gift, but it's a start. You've got your own path to walk."

Alias reached out, squeezing Demetria's hand. "We're proud of you, powers or not."

****

Things in Kramden had begun to shift. The whispers were spreading faster than facts. The relatives who died in the collapse and the fire were still fresh in everyone's minds. Yet no one mentioned the six missing men.

J.T.'s family ranch had become the subject of hushed talks and wary glances on the street corners. Some claimed the Barrs were behind it. Others whispered it was the Siobhans. A few even dared to say it was the old blood stirring again. Those of the old bloodlines, once silent and restrained, were now angry and were speaking openly with Renegade to act.

A meeting was held on the edge of the northern woods, behind a long-abandoned chapel. Twenty-seven men and women gathered beneath the rotted rafters. One stood up, Cloris Durn, her hands still stained from her last summoning. "They've ruled this place long enough," she snarled. "The Barrs. The Siobhans. The Whitlocks and their followers. That cursed train line. We let them crawl back into their holes, but now they're crawling back out. It's time we end this, before they remember how strong they really are." Murmurs of agreement rose as they began planning.

Back at the Siobhans, Demetria stood on the porch, her hand resting on the wooden rail. She looked toward the northern woods, where chimneys in the distance belched fire into the sky like warnings.

She could feel it. The Hollow still hummed beneath the earth. The compartment wasn't silent. And neither were the streets of Kramden. *It's coming,* Demetria said softly. Wondering where she was, Eva and Mattie approached. Demetria pointed to the sky above the northern woods. Eva and Mattie felt it too, a sudden chill that slid beneath their skin. The sisters joined hands, muttering something unintelligible, then turned and went inside. Across town, Greta and Anne stood by their doorstep and paused. Something cold and familiar clung to the air. They didn't need to speak; they both knew.

36

Train Bloodline Plot

Greta stared out the window as the last embers of daylight vanished beyond the rooftops. Anne paced behind her, uneasy. "We let too many things linger," Greta said.

"I agree. We should've done this sooner," Anne muttered. "We waited, and now look. Our family . . . J.T.'s cousins . . . all of it. Teveras started this. We need to get him."

Greta didn't respond at first. Then, quietly, she said, "We're not going after him. Not yet. We need to reach out to the others."

"Who are you talking about?"

"Our bloodline in Vermont."

Anne stopped pacing. "You think they'll help us?"

"They're blood. They'll at least tell us what we need to know."

That night, the incantations from Greta and Anne began. It wasn't long after that the response came; it came through a whisper carried by the wind. Their Vermont relatives never spoke with warmth, only with warning.

"If you want Teveras," the voice said, in a cold tone, "you start with his shadows, members of the Exuis, Ohn, or Maera, or the council of old ancestors that he sometimes listens to. Bring one of them down, and you send a message. But don't go straight for the hand before you cut the fingers." There was a low hiss, something ancient had exhaled, then it was gone.

By morning, Greta and Anne were standing before Lady, recounting the conversation. Demetria, Mattie, and Eva were nearby, listening. Lady's face remained unreadable until they finished. She turned toward the darkened corner of the room where the Artifact pulsed and Stone pulsed.

"I don't like it," Lady said. "You're not ready for Teveras. Not even close. But if one of his lieutenants can be drawn onto the train . . . then the train will decide."

"And if the train decides?" Anne asked.

Lady looked at them, a grim expression on her face. "Then they'll meet a fate worse than death. But you must get them on board willingly, or not at all. The train only takes passengers; it doesn't drag them."

Greta nodded. "Then we'll start with members of the Exuis."

Lady warned. "Be careful. Those members walked with the dark beneath their feet. Trickery won't work. You'll need something deeper, something they won't see coming."

Greta gave one final look at Lady, her mind already racing through the possibilities. "We understand," Greta said as the wind picked up outside.

Later that evening, the plans were put in motion. Demetria stood at the edge of a crumbling overlook near the train yard, watching the last light fade. Mattie and Eva were in town, laying the bait, quietly planting whispers in the right ears, whispers the Exuis were known to chase. In the distance, Greta and Anne slipped through the shadows of the old quarter, placing the final piece: a sealed letter wrapped in black twine, addressed in a language only those of the Exuis bloodline could read. It was left beneath the fractured arch of the clocktower ruins, where secrets were always found.

"They'll smell the trap," Anne said.

"Of course, they are who they are. They'll show up," Greta replied. "They always do, especially when they think they're in control."

Inside the compartment, the Artifact and Stone glowed heavily now, like they were listening. Lady sat still in the darkness, her hand resting on the Stone. "The train is ready," she whispered. "Because this time, it's not just taking passengers. It's taking vengeance." Elias, Elowen, Bolshan, and a terrifying group of twelve, faces veiled, bodies gaunt like living skeletons, smiled.

Two days later, the sealed letter beneath the clock tower was gone before dawn. No one saw who took it, but Greta and Anne knew. The writing, the twine, the place, every piece had been crafted to stir the Exuis's hunger for forbidden knowledge. Later that night, in the old derelict graveyards, the whispers were that the four had taken the bait. A male Exuis with the crescent brand under his eye read the letter aloud in a voice straight from hell. The words spoke of a power once buried, now stirred again beneath the tracks of the old train line. "A relic from the first blood," he murmured. "Said to consume even those it favors."

"They think they can lure us?" one of the female Exuis sneered, her smile crooked and cruel.

But it was another male, tall, silent, the one they all followed without question, who finally spoke. "We go. Midnight. The four of us. And not altogether. We show up one by one. The train line likes patterns; it also likes when they're broken."

"But what about Teveras?" the other woman asked.

The one they all followed said, "Teveras will be proud when he sees what we've brought, and how we plan to strike while they think we're asleep." So, they came to a spot near Compartment 13's edge, where Eva stood as planned, alone, barefoot, pale as chalk, whispering into the mist. Her voice wasn't hers. The first Exuis stepped forward, enchanted, his eyes darkened, pupils dilating as if caught in a spell. Eva's every movement rippled with a deadly sensuality that tangled with the shadows around her. He could see the firmness of her breast and the way the silk gown clung tightly to the curves of her body, tracing every secret on her as she swayed in a slow, hypnotic dance. He was drawn to her like moths to a flame, a raw hunger flickering beneath his mask.

The second male Exuis was caught in her web of beauty and sensuality as he turned toward his partner. The two women, unaware of what was happening, whispered their partners' names, but there was no response. One of the women's eyes flashed with suspicion, but it was already too late. Suddenly, a mist curled around their ankles like fingers pulling them forward. The whistle of a speeding train pierced the night.

The train materialized behind Eva, dark as the abyss itself, its windows alive with shifting shadows. The first Exuis vanished, no scream, no fight, just silence swallowing him whole. Still, the others came. Drawn by a force they couldn't deny, trapped by a game they couldn't win. One by one, the train claimed them. Their shadows were etched into the rusted platform for a moment, burned in by the force that claimed them. Then nothing remained.

Inside the Compartment, the Artifact and Stone wailed, long and mournful. Lady rose from her seat. "They've boarded," she said. "And they will never get off." She stepped into the aisle, her cloak dragging, as the door of the compartment slammed shut behind her.

The four Exuis froze, stunned, as the passengers cloaked in shadow and draped in rags that smelled of the grave, lifted their heads. Their eyes were sunken and gleaming with something far darker than hate. Their mouths sewn shut, yet they began to sing. It was low at first, as it crept out slowly, like breath from a sealed tomb. Then it grew louder and twisted, a hymn not of praise but of reckoning.

"Blood of the black root . . . tear their marrow free . . ."

"Hands that fed the serpent . . . now must feed the pit . . ."

"No god will hear you now . . . no bloodline will save you . . ."

The Exuis looked on in horror as the passengers rocked gently in their seats, their sewn lips parting impossibly wide to form the words. The chants clawed at their minds, memories of rituals long buried, ancestors burned for sins never spoken aloud. Each word was a blade against their soul.

The first Exuis stumbled back, his mouth opening in a silent scream. The second wept. The women clawed at the walls. From the ceiling, blood dripped, rich, old, and thick.

37

Train Bloodline Plot 2

The four Exuis stood twitching, their eyes wide, their heads darting back and forth like trapped animals. Then Lady appeared, and the four turned to face her. They watched in silence as the passengers bowed their heads, paying homage to her.

"You cross oceans of blood to serve Teveras," Lady said. "But what has he promised you? What is it you think he'll become?"

The first female Exuis hissed through clenched teeth. "A god."

Lady tilted her head. "Then let's see how gods are made. It's an honor to rid the world of four fewer Exuis."

Behind her, Elias, Bolshan, and Elowen emerged from the fog, their forms barely human now, elongated shadows, their faces veiled, their limbs twisting at grotesque angles, as if their bones had healed in the wrong places. Close behind them, Demetria, Eva, Mattie, Greta, and Anne stepped forward, their eyes burning with fire. Surrounding the group, the terrifying Veiled Twelve moved like phantoms, silent, relentless, their skeletal frames twisting with unnatural grace, a living nightmare ready to descend.

"You betrayed the balance," Lady said, her voice now deeper. "You dared awaken forces that should've slept. So, we'll give you what you wanted . . . eternity."

The compartment groaned. Chains snaked up from the floor, blackened, rusted things that moved with purpose. The four Exuis tried to run, but space itself had twisted; every direction led back to Lady. The chains struck like serpents, piercing skin, bone, spirit. They didn't bind bodies; they latched to something deeper.

The second male Exuis screamed as his eyes turned black, bleeding. The two women clawed at their own chests as something inside them was dragged out, something that was not meant to be touched.

"You'll know no rest," Lady whispered, raising a hand. Around her, the passengers, Elias, Bolshan, Elowen, and the Sisters began humming the words, their voices rising and falling in a haunting chorus as the Veiled Twelve moved in rhythmic unison. "You serve Teveras," Lady said, "then scream his name while you rot."

The walls of Compartment 13 shifted and groaned, twisting inward like iron jaws, yanking the four into the walls, which opened like mouths, gasping, and full of teeth as the singing continued. The doors slammed shut with a final, deafening clang, locking the four Exuis inside. For a moment, the space felt endless, as the walls closed in. Then, as if nothing had happened, the compartment's walls slid back into place, returning to the familiar, cramped interior-and then the train went quiet as the Artifact and the Stone pulsed calmly, now satisfied. The four Exuis were condemned to a torment reserved for those who believed power came without consequence.

As the train sped into the darkness, everyone aboard began singing. Lady moved past the passengers, followed by the others as the singing grew louder. Twisting into verses no human would understand, Lady joined in the singing. The train itself breathes in time with the rhythm. She stood in the center and raised her arms. "They called on the dead when they had no right to do so. Teveras and his bloodline will feel our wrath," she sang, "and their bloodline will sing for them, just as ours did in the past. The dead will sing for them."

The passengers rose to their feet. Still singing. Still smiling. "Chain the soul . . . break the name . . . let the dark remember them . . ." And as the train rolled on, its windows now glowing with images of agony, the Sisters knew they had arrived.

****

Inside the dark ancestral depths of The Petra, Teveras, Ohn, Maera, and the remaining Exuis gathered with Renegade, Cloris Durn, and other members of their bloodline, summoned for counsel. But Renegade and his followers, including Sox, recently returned from the Old Country, were unaware of one chilling presence among them: Dalo and his followers. It was Renegade's defiance, the same that led him near The Hollow, that stirred the ashes. Now, Dalo was here. His charred form still bore the scars of fire, but his eyes gleamed with something worse than death. Behind him, the once-dead followers moved with jagged grace, their bodies twisted by time and rage, silent sentinels of vengeance.

Ohn tensed up. Maera and the Exuis stepped back as Teveras spoke. "Dalo is not yours to summon," Teveras said, his voice calm but laced with authority. "He walks because you stirred The Hollow without knowing who still listens. He was burned a century ago, yes, but even fire bows to his name. Show respect, Renegade. You're standing in the shadow of one who was feared even by our ancestors." Teveras took a step forward, still talking in an authoritative voice. "And when were you going to tell me about the cousins of J.T., and those who followed them?"

"I wasn't aware of it. None of us was. We searched for them, but nothing. I would have never permitted them to go on their own," Renegade said in an obedient voice.

"Do you know where they ended up?"

"No, Teveras."

"At the Siobhans'— outclassed, outmatched. It seems you still have a lot to learn about Alias and his wife. Your men never stood a chance. And the sixth one, your stray. He fled after Alias and Doris answered. He's not missing. I took care of him myself." Renegade bit his lips and squinted his eyes, but Teveras continued. "You brought my name into your mouth with lies. You called me a trickster. Liar. You questioned my truth in front of others." His voice deepened, words dropping like stones. "You forget what walks with me, what listens when I speak? Do you hear me, you piece of shit?" The Petra darkened around them, its stone walls heavy with breathless anticipation. Renegade nervously nodded. Teveras stepped off the raised stone, his gaze cold. "The pit didn't call your name before because I held it back. But if you ever step out of line again . . . it will call you. And I won't be there to stop it."

Gesturing for Renegade and his followers to step to the side. He glanced at the others, "Where are the four Exuis?" He asked in an authoritative voice. The other Exuis began moving in unison while nodding.

Ohn shifted uneasily, exchanging a glance with Maera. "They never returned from their mission." A cold chill rippled through the room. The ancestors' whispers grew faint, as if the bloodline's link had been severed.

Teveras clenched his fists. "If they have fallen . . . this changes everything."

Maera's voice was chilling as she spoke. "We must prepare. They have made their move, and the old bloodlines across the waters have echoed this many times."

Teveras turned toward the darkness beyond the chamber's entrance, eyes raging. "Then let them come. We will be ready. Our bloodline is prepared." He then turned to Ohn, Maera, and the Exuis. "Alias and Doris Siobhan will be dealt with in time, and on our terms," he said. Then he faced Renegade. "But you will not go near them again. Touch the parents, and the pit will call your name, loudly this time." He paused. "The daughters, though . . . they remain fair game." The walls of The Petra pulse with ominous energy, swallowing their words.

38

Compartment 13

Fog rolled low across the tracks that morning, swallowing the sound of tires, footsteps, and the occasional honk from passing delivery vans and trucks. At the Aldan Station, the early trains had already come and gone, leaving behind the usual crowd of commuters headed to work and whatever else they had to do. The same could be said for towns and cities where the bloodlines of Lady's enemies lived. But what was coming would hit like a storm; Kramden wasn't the only place about to feel the shift.

Three nights later, far up the coast in Maine, the wind howled in the small town of Granmere as the Compartment 13 train slipped through unseen tracks. It was an old place, tucked between worn hills and rocky shores, forgotten by most, but not by Lady. And while Granmere braced unknowingly for what was coming, whispers were already stirring in Rivet's Hollow, New Jersey, where another bloodline had begun to feel the cold breath of something ancient.

Lady's enemies had planted roots here long ago, hiding their bloodlines among the working-class families that rose before dawn to man the canneries, tend the waters, and run the mills. They thought they'd been forgotten. They were wrong. But it wasn't long before the invitations began showing up in strange ways, scraps of weathered paper tucked in lunchboxes, odd symbols scratched into windshield frost, or the sudden chiming of clocks that hadn't worked in decades. Some dismissed it. Others felt something stir in their bones, a dread they couldn't name.

By morning, three families were gone, simply vanished. Their homes still stood, their doors unlocked, their breakfast plates still warm on the table. Neighbors said they saw them step out into the night . . . but no one saw them return. Granmere slept as Compartment 13 pulled into a station that hadn't existed since the 1800s. The platform rose from mist and ash, groaning as it recalled its old sins. The victims, descendants of the bloodlines that once hunted Lady's kind, woke in their homes to find black ash on their windowsills, the scent of rust in the air, and faint chanting beneath the floorboards. By dawn, their homes stood hollow. Chairs are overturned, and the food is still warm on the plates. But no bodies. Just claw marks in the wallpaper, mirrors cracked in spiderwebs, and scorched symbols etched into the ground where their shadows had been.

Those who saw the train, even for a second, never got the chance to speak of it. A fog unlike any natural thing chased them as they ran, thick as smoke, curling fast behind their heels, and then they were gone, taken alive by the train; their screams became one with the whistle that split the night.

Across the eastern states, Rivet's Hollow in New Jersey, the stone valleys of New Hampshire, Massachusetts, upstate New York, and as far south as Virginia, people began whispering of strange things. A train whistle where no tracks ran. Flickering lights at midnight. Entire families gone without a trace. But Lady left no mysteries behind, only messages. One home in Delaware burned in silence while a child's voice sang an old Siobhan lullaby through the smoke. Another in rural Pennsylvania had bloodlines pinned to the wall in ancient script, written in ash and bone.

In one small town near the Delaware border, a mother awoke to find her child standing motionless at the end of the hallway, eyes milky, whispering names no one had spoken in generations. When she reached for him, he collapsed, alive, but empty, as if something had passed through him and scraped his soul clean. Days later, an entire block in western Massachusetts lost power. Neighbors described hearing tracks grinding under their homes, followed by the echo of footsteps in their attics and the faint smell of burnt roses. No authorities came. No explanations were given. Only silence and ash.

Lady wasn't just cleansing bloodlines; she was making a path. A reckoning carved through generations, reclaiming what had been stolen. The train, once bound by time and myth, now moved on grief and justice. And as it howled into the night, those who had once hunted her kind, those who had buried, burned, and betrayed, were finally being summoned. Not for trial. But for sentence. The train didn't just kill, it marked them. And those who saw the signs knew: Compartment 13 was moving, and it wasn't finished.

After the onslaught, Lady stood beneath the Kramden sky, the stars hanging like quiet witnesses. She turned to the Sisters. "The East Coast holds many names. Many enemies. Granmere and the others are only the first. There will be more."

Eva nodded. "We'll keep moving. Until the bloodline is clean."

"Until the train is satisfied," Lady corrected her. "The train would find them all."

39

Ashes Between Bloodlines
Flashback, Kramden, Months Ago

Heavy rain was pouring across the crooked rooftop of the old slaughterhouse where Renegade had called the meeting. Inside, steam rose from the floor where water met blood. Sox stood with his arms crossed, a frustrated look on his face.

"You've changed, Ren," Sox said, looking him in the eyes. "You've gone too deep. There's no line anymore, just power."

Renegade didn't look up from the cracked table map. "This isn't about lines. It's about survival. Our bloodline. You either evolve, or you get buried with the others."

Sox stepped closer. "Then maybe I should've let them bury you back when the Barrs and the other families warned you about the old train yard."

That got his attention. Renegade's head snapped up, his eyes burning with anger. "Watch your mouth."

"No. You watch yours," Sox snapped. "You keep pretending we're still in control, but you're chasing ghosts and waking up worse. And you're gonna drag all of us down. Is this how we avenge our bloodline?"

Renegade didn't answer. Sox turned to the door, the rain cutting across his face as he looked back. "I'm done. You want to chase monsters? Fine. Maybe I shouldn't have returned."

"Now is not the time for this," Renegade replied, standing by the door.

Sox pulled the cloak's hood over his head. "I'm going back," he said. "I need more answers. Maybe someone there still remembers what we were before all this." Then he was gone.

The Old Country

The Old Country was stone and shadow, villages forgotten by time, thick forests whispering names that hadn't been spoken in centuries. Sox arrived in silence, this time a man burned by betrayal and haunted by purpose. It didn't take long to find them. Beneath a ruined monastery in a cliffside pass, the exiled bloodline stirred. They had been cast out long ago, their rites too cruel even for the old councils. But time had made them patient. Vengeful. Hungry. They greeted Sox like an echo, a man carrying the scent of lost power, a bridge between what was and what could be.

We sensed your presence when you arrived. You never came this way. Why now? What brings you here? a booming voice asked.

Shaking, Sox replied, "Answers. There are things I need to know."

Hmm. These grounds belong to the Wasiaks. Who gave you permission to disturb these grounds? several voices asked at once, cold and inhuman. *Was it the old gatekeepers?*

"It was," Sox replied, still shaking. "But I've come in the name of blood, our blood. In my travels, I learned I carry more of your bloodline than the Wicks."

An old woman stepped forward from the shadows, her eyes white with age, her voice dry like wind through dead leaves. *And what is it you want from us?*

Momentarily frightened by her looks, Sox mumbled, "I want Teveras and Abby to fall. I want to rip down what they've built with the same hands that helped raise it."

Hmm . . . Abby, she said, her voice filled with old disdain. *She and Teveras, their bloodlines crossed the great waters long ago, bringing ruin to our bloodline across the seas.* She turned slowly toward the others as their voices murmured as one, a low chorus of resentment and hunger. *And what will you offer us in return?*

Sox didn't hesitate. "The bloodlines. Their locations. Their weaknesses. I'll lead you to every last one. You'll get your vengeance; just leave enough for me to finish what they started." They smiled, not with joy, but with recognition. One of their own had returned.

Present, The Petra

Teveras had summoned Renegade and Sox to The Petra, the message delivered without explanation, only urgency. He stood in the center of the chamber, hands behind his back. Beside him, Ohn and Maera stood. Across from him stood Renegade and Sox.

"Step forward," Teveras said without turning. His voice echoed along the stone walls. They obeyed. Teveras faced Sox first. "Renegade told me you went to the Old Country. I'd like to hear from you. What was your reason for going?"

"To trace blood," Sox lied smoothly. "Old threads. I needed clarity . . . about my place in all this. There were pieces of my bloodline I didn't understand."

Teveras held his stare, "And did you find the 'Old threads' as you called it?"

Sox gave a respectful nod. "I did."

"But why was there doubt?"

"No, there wasn't any doubt. It was more curiosity."

Teveras studied him. "I see. So, you enjoyed your stay?"

"Yes, matter of fact, I did."

"Did you reach out to the ancient ones?"

"Yes. The old gatekeepers saw to it."

"So you must have learned a lot."

"Indeed."

There was a silence. Then: "Was there a fallout between the two of you?"

"Two of who?" Teveras glared at him. "No."

Renegade followed with a slight shrug. "Nothing like that. We've always understood each other."

Teveras turned to Renegade now. "Hmm. So, now that he's returned . . . does Sox take J.T.'s place?"

Renegade paused, then gave a slow answer. "J.T. has done a great job. Sox isn't replacing him. Sox knows what to do. He's here. He doesn't need a title to be with me. He's with me, and whatever we need, he'll handle it."

Something shifted in Teveras's expression. It was enough to suggest he was measuring every word. He stepped closer. "I expect nothing less," Teveras said, then turned his back to them. The chamber held its breath. And below the surface, something older was listening. "Because if either of you steps out of line . . . the pit won't spare you." Neither said a word.

40

The Visit

Sox had a lot on his mind as he contemplated his next move. He knew that he couldn't afford to make any mistakes as he walked the backyards of several houses. He had thought about driving, but for whatever reason, he felt this was the best option. The backyards and roads behind him were quiet. He moved with clear intent, just as he always had, but this time it wasn't Renegade or Teveras he sought. It was Alias and Doris. He was taking a chance. As he got closer, he wondered how they'd respond, would they welcome him, or strike out in rage? Maybe even tear into him. Either way, they'd feel the wrath of the Wasiak bloodline, he thought, just as a whisper began to stir.

As he approached, Alias was the first to sense something was off. He turned to Doris. She gave a slight nod; she felt it too. Without saying a word, they moved to the back door and stepped into the garden. There, beneath the withering branches of a hawthorn tree, stood Sox. Doris eyed him, brows raised, her fingers brushing the charm at her neck. Alias didn't move. He just watched and waited.

"I know we've had our differences, but I come in peace," Sox said. "I'm not here for Renegade, the Wicks, or the rest of my bloodline. I just need you to hear me out. Because what I'm about to tell you . . . you might think I've lost my mind."

"You speak the Erethal Tongue, the language of the High Spirits, the ancient ones of your bloodline who withdrew from the ruling body," Alias said, with raised eyebrows. "But I'll hear you out. Speak!"

"I was in the Old Country . . ."

"So, this is what this is about?" Doris said.

Sox stayed calm. "It's a different world now. I came back for the right reasons. Something's stirring in the Old Country, old enemies. Ones, neither you, Teveras, or Abby has named. They're watching. I figured it was best to come to you first."

"Us?" Alias said, glancing at Doris; her silence spoke volumes.

"Yes, the Old World sees us as newbies, babies, apprentices who have learned the ways of the older bloodlines. They're the ones we should be worried about. If I had gone to Renegade first, he would have laughed at me, but I knew you would hear me out."

"And what do you want from us?" Doris asked.

"Not a thing. Only that your daughters hear what I've seen. What I've learned. They need to be prepared."

Alias folded his arms. "Our daughters?"

"Yes, your immediate bloodline."

"You're not the same Sox we knew."

A sly smile was on his face. "None of us is. But you can trust me. I need to talk to them. Anne and Greta, too. Tell them I'll be at the old crossing in the barn near the eastern tree line where the old trees bend toward the river. If they're willing to listen, they'll find me there."

Alias exchanged a glance with Doris, reading the same suspicion in her eyes. "And why should we trust you?" he asked.

"As you said, 'I'm not the same Sox we knew.' You're right, you shouldn't trust me. But trust the blood. It has a way of calling us back, even when we don't want to answer."

For a moment, Alias's gaze was fixed on him. "We'll think on it," he said.

Sox gave a faint nod. "That's all I ask." He pulled his cloak hood over his head and was gone before either could speak again, leaving only a trace of cold air behind.

Later that night, when the sisters returned home, Alias and Doris told them about the conversation. The doubt was clear in their voices as to how they felt, but so was something else, a curiosity neither wanted to admit.

The next evening, the sisters, along with Greta and Anne, met him in the old barn near the eastern tree line. The women were wary, but curious. Sox stood at the center, his cloak hood drawn, as the wind whispered through the broken boards. "Strange, isn't it? I came in peace, just like I did with Alias and Doris," he said to Demetria, Eva, and Mattie. "Greta, Anne, you share the same bloodline. It's good to see you here."

"Alias and Doris told us what you shared. So, why meet up with us?" Greta asked, raising a brow.

"You're the younger generation. And if history's taught us anything, it's that every generation eventually dies out. But the earlier you start protecting yourselves, warding off those who want to wipe out your bloodline, the longer it survives," he said.

"We know that. But why should we listen to you, or even keep talking to you — an enemy of ours?" Demetria said, just before Greta spoke.

"I might be an enemy of yours, but as time passes, so does the bloodline's thinking. You've grown into your own," he said, his eyes glancing from one to the next. "But there are things that blood alone can't protect you from."

Eva stepped forward. "You're not just here to warn us."

Sox nodded slowly. "No. I'm here because of what's coming . . . And the writing is on the wall. It's beyond Abby. Beyond Teveras.

Beyond Alias and Doris, and all the other bloodlines. There are factions in the Old World who want balance, and they see too much power gathering here."

Mattie crossed her arms, a sarcastic look on her face. "And you're their messenger?"

"I'm a bridge," he said. "Trying to keep the war from getting worse."

Greta didn't blink. "Sounds less like peace and more like survival. Yours?"

Sox held her stare. "Maybe. But if I survive, so does part of you."

Greta watched him closely. Her eyes didn't trust him. "Or maybe you're trying to pick the winning side."

He didn't flinch. "I want peace. What the ancestors in the Old World want is obedience."

"And if they don't get it?" Anne asked.

"They will," Sox said calmly. "Because I promised it to them."

"You promised it to them? And how are you going to do so?" Demetria asked, biting into her lip.

"Just like I'm doing now, talking. Clearly, you've misread my intentions. As I said, it's about peace. I'll do the same with Teveras, and if I can, with Abby." He paused, his eyes on them. "Think about what I said. You'll know where to find me." Then, with a brief nod, he turned and left, his footsteps fading into the dark.

Eva turned to the others, an uneasy feeling in her chest. "Something's off."

"I felt it too," Mattie whispered. "Like he wasn't really looking at us. Like he was looking through us."

Demetria, with a sly smile, said, "We'll tell Lady tonight."

Far across the sea, in the catacombs of the exiled bloodline, chants echoed. Sox's name had already been spoken in smoke and carved into bone. And in Kramden, he stood on both sides of the fire, playing one against the other, at least for now.

41

Lines In The Blood

The fire crackled low in the small cast-iron stove inside Compartment 13. The steady rhythm of the train on the tracks pulsed beneath their feet as the Sisters stood before her. Whispers cried and shifted with each sway of the carriage, and the weight of what they were about to share.

"Sox visited our parents. Then came to us. He claims he came in peace," Demetria said. "He says the Wasiaks, and others, are stirring in the Old Country, ones we haven't named. He said neither you nor Teveras knows about them."

Lady sat back in her high-backed chair, pressing her fingertips together beneath her chin. She looked at the group of Sisters with a piercing gaze. "He said this to all of you?"

"Yes, including our parents," Mattie confirmed. "Even Greta and Anne. He says the war's changing."

Lady was quiet for a moment. Then she nodded. "I've heard the whispers, too. From the Sleepers in our bloodline."

"Sleepers?" Mattie asked, confused.

"Old spirits," Lady said with a smile. So did Elias, Bolshan, and Elowen. "Blood-bound to our line. Their voices don't come often, but when they do, I listen. And lately . . . they've spoken of movement. Of something shifting in the east." And as they listened, an eerie sound echoed through the compartment. Though they couldn't see the source, it came from the Veiled Twelve, a sound meant to remind them that the Twelve were of the Old Spirits.

Anne asked. "So, what do we do?"

Lady rose slowly. The polished floor of the railcar creaks beneath her boots. "We do what we've always done. Prepare. This will be a war to show you who still walks with us . . . and who's been watching long before Sox ever showed up. And if it comes to a fight to the death of our souls, then we take that fight back to the Old Country. If the Wasiaks and their allies want to test our bloodline? Let them try."

****

That same night, beneath a sliver of moonlight, Sox met with Renegade near the cliffs. Renegade paced slowly. "So . . . you met with Alias? With the sisters? Even Greta and Anne?"

"I did," Sox said. "And I told them what I needed to tell them."

"You're walking a thin line. They are our sworn enemies."

Sox shrugged. "I'm building a bridge. Trying to stop what's coming. Or at least steer it."

Renegade scowled. "You still working angles? Because if I find out you're playing both sides . . ."

Sox raised his hand. "You won't. I came back for the right reasons. I want peace, Renegade."

Renegade nodded slowly; something wasn't right, but he couldn't quite put his finger on it. The mistrust lingered, but for now, he said nothing more. Sox knew the silence was a gift, even if a fragile one.

****

Sox had watched Teveras and the followers of Dalo closely ever since he returned from the Old Country. Whatever hold Teveras had on Dalo and his followers, it ran deeper than loyalty. But Sox wasn't one to follow blindly. Not now. Under the cover of darkness, while the others slept or meditated, he made his move. He sent a message through one of the followers he trusted. It was meant to reach Dalo without alerting Teveras or any of the bloodline. If he could speak with Dalo alone, even for a moment, it might change everything.

Sox was aware of the vastness of The Petra and its sprawling underground chambers and echoing halls. But there was one area, walled off by stone and silence, where Dalo and his followers had been kept since their awakening. Few ventured there without permission. Even Teveras' own men treated it like sacred ground. Sox had studied the layout since his return, gathering information from his own bloodline without raising suspicion. There were back corridors, forgotten stairwells, and passageways that hadn't seen footsteps in decades. If he timed it right, he could reach Dalo's chamber without anyone knowing, but it was a huge risk. Reaching out to Dalo first made sense, and he agreed to meet.

Far from the cliffs and the watchful eyes of the bloodlines, Sox descended into the catacombs beneath The Petra. In the dancing candlelight of the crypt, Dalo appeared, cloaked in Shadows, eyes like cold embers burning beneath fleshless skin.

"Why do you wish to speak with me?" Dalo asked. "Where I once slept beside my followers, I now walk freely, as I did many nights ago. So, tell me, what does someone like you want from one who has slept restlessly, held and bound by curses?"

"You're exactly who I need to speak to. Teveras, Ohn, Maera, the Exuis, and others in our bloodline fail to see what's coming. And so does Abby, along with her followers, some of whom I can't even name . . ."

"And what is it that's coming? And why should our bloodline be spoken in the same breath as our enemies?" the Shadows around Dalo shrieked in a low voice.

"Old grudges are stirring up in the Old Country, and there are many bloodlines that are ready to war against their own blood. Some of them think I'm bound to their cause, but what I want is peace," Sox said. "But the Wasiaks threaten all of us, living or dead. They are the most powerful. We cannot afford old loyalties."

Dalo's ancient voice rasped like dry leaves. "Why should we follow you, mortal? What power holds sway over death itself?"

Sox met the gaze of Dalo and the Shadows. "Because I offer a future beyond this war, a way to survive what's coming."

A surge of energy hovered over them as the spirits exchanged silent counsel. Then, slowly, Dalo extended a black coin and placed it in Sox's hand. He clenched it tight.

"We will consider what you've said," Dalo said. "And if the time comes when we must walk in shadow and blood with you, then we will. But know this . . . if you lead us down a path unworthy of our dead, the ground will not only reject your bones, but it will also curse your name beyond the dust." Sox nodded as Dalo and the Shadows drifted backward and vanished into the dark.

<h1 style="text-align:center">42</h1>

Red Tape And Body Bags

The local Kramden train to Evansville and the nearby towns had fallen under intense scrutiny. Law enforcement could no longer ignore the complaints. Bits and pieces of human remains were being found along the tracks and inside abandoned cars where the trains passed. What drew their attention wasn't just the violence; it was how it was done. Demetria brought this to Lady's attention, knowing immediately it was the work of Elias, Bolshan, Elowen, and the Veiled Twelve.

Demetria stood at the edge of Lady's chambers. "They found pieces of bodies," she said. Lady didn't say much. Her silhouette sat still in the dim light, face half-veiled in the shadow. "They'll come looking," Demetria added. "They will check every house for information."

"You mean the police?"

"Yes."

"Don't you worry. Bolshan and the others leave messages, not evidence. They want them to see. They are drawing out something old that even the living will see or understand. This town will choke on its own doubt before it understands what it's facing. So, don't worry, our bloodline has nothing to worry about. As for Renegades, they are on their own."

Kramden was in a state of panic. People were dying on two fronts, on the train under Lady's grip, and in their homes, where Renegade and his followers moved from house to house, killing those not of their bloodline. The local police couldn't begin to grasp the supernatural angle, but when the bodies began piling up, they, too, had no choice but to respond. The first call came in just after dawn. A maintenance worker on the Kramden line spotted something strange lodged beneath one of the seats, which looked like a hand, and not a glove.

Sanders And Bundy

Detectives Vera Sanders and Jay Bundy were assigned to the case. Sanders didn't take kindly to the body parts turning up along the tracks. She'd barely slept since the string of murders began, bodies turning up in backyards, on front porches, even in church basements. By the time Sanders and Bundy boarded the train car, the air was stale and damp. Yellow tape already hung over the doors, and a few onlookers had gathered despite the hour.

"This is the one?" Sanders asked the cop stationed outside.

The officer nodded. "Car Seven. We've cleared the rest. It's . . . bad."

Inside, Sanders crouched by the seat. A hand, freshly severed, was wedged into the metal frame. Blood had soaked the cushions nearby. But that wasn't all.

"Jesus," Bundy muttered, staring at the back wall. There, smeared in something darker than blood, were symbols, jagged lines, curling slashes, an almost circular mark like a burned-in brand.

Sanders pulled out her phone and took a photo. "You ever seen anything like this?"

"Not in any textbook I've read," Bundy said. "Feels . . . wrong. What about the local sheriff and his officers? What've they done?"

Sanders replied, "There's been talk, supernatural stuff. Stories of demons and forces buried under the old Aldan Circle station. Some say a train shows up now and then to take revenge."

"A train? So we're investigating a train?" Bundy said with a bit of sarcasm. "Okay, let me stop. But revenge on who?" he asked.

"The living . . . and the souls that still haunt this place."

Bundy shook his head. "I'm guessing the train that is taking revenge is different from the local trains?"

"Yup, that's what it sounds like. And don't you notice that some of the townspeople seem to be living in a different time?"

"Yeah, I've noticed that. But as for the train and all the other shit, I don't buy any of it. Do you?"

"Let's just say I don't rule anything out. What I do know is this: the only ones I've seen with phones are local law enforcement. You ever seen that before?"

"No, yeah, that's strange. But nothing on the cameras?"

"Nothing!"

****

Meanwhile, in a neighborhood on Kramden's south edge, screams tore through the quiet morning. Renegade moved with his men like a storm. One by one, they breached the homes of outsiders, their enemies, people with no ties to the bloodline, but who they thought were giving information to their bloodlines. Renegade kicked open a door, his ethereal blade already dripping. A woman screamed. Her husband lunged with a knife of flame. Renegade cut him down without a word.

"Wrong blood," he muttered. Behind him, J.T. and Sox lit symbols on the living room wall with a bone-colored chalk. Flames sparked, then vanished. "We keep going," Renegade said. "We purge every crack in this place. Until it remembers," as they continued the onslaught.

****

Outside one of the homes, now swarming with deputies and CSU techs, Sanders stood just beyond the front walkway, arms folded, staring at the dried blood that streaked across the doorframe and spilled down the porch steps. The early evening light did nothing to soften the brutality of what had happened there. Emergency lights painted the town in red and blue, flickering across stunned faces and silent porches. There were whispers amongst some of the townspeople as they watched with wary eyes.

Deputies moved in and out of the modest one-story house. The air smelled of metal, sweat, and something faintly scorched. It was one of several houses that day. Bodies torn open. Their skins were peeled back in geometric patterns. Symbols carved into walls, simple at first glance, but too consistent to ignore. Sanders didn't need to ask how many died this time. She could tell by the look on the CSU tech's face as he backed out of the front door, pale and shaking, his gloved hands trembling as he clutched a plastic evidence bag.

Bundy caught the tech by the shoulder. "What'd you find?"

He didn't speak. He just held up the bag. Inside was a clock, antique, wooden, its hands frozen at 3:33. Blood crusted its edges. On the back, etched deep into the wood, was the same spiral mark they'd seen in the previous homes. The same one they'd seen carved into the steel paneling of the train.

Sanders had a grim look on her face. "Third one today, to be exact, same time."

Bundy's voice dropped. "This shit is coordinated. This shit is getting creepier and creepier."

Sanders looked toward the house again. The air around the doorway drifted, like heat waves off the pavement, though the evening had turned to night, and it was cool.

"No footprints are leading in or out. How do you rip a family apart and leave no trace?" Sanders said.

Bundy said nothing. The quiet was broken by a scream from down the street. They turned. A deputy sprinted toward them, wild-eyed, yelling, "He was just here, he was right behind me!"

"Who?" Sanders demanded to know.

"One of our officers," the deputy panted. "We were talking near the backyard; he went to check something out. I turned for one second, and he was gone. Just gone."

Sanders and Bundy exchanged a look. Sanders stared back at the house. "This isn't random. You're right, Bundy," she murmured. "It's targeted. Ritualistic. And it's spreading."

Bundy raised a hand to his mouth. "You thinking what I'm thinking?"

"The train," she said. "The symbols, jagged lines, curling slashes, and the circular burned-in marks." She shook her head slowly. "What if the train is the starting point? Like . . . cracked open."

Bundy looked at the vanishing deputy's flashlight, still lying in the grass, flashing. "Then we've got a problem we don't even have a name for."

Sanders stared out at the dark horizon. "If we don't stop it . . ."

Bundy finished it for her. " . . . the whole town's gonna burn."

"Let me know if you want to follow up with what happened to the officer," she said.

Just then, the deputy yelled in the direction of Sanders and Bundy. "Come, take a look. It wasn't there before, it just happened."

Sanders read the message scrawled in blood across the wall: *He recognized the signs. Even the hidden ones aren't safe. We remember every name, every branch, every betrayal. Blood answers blood.*

"What the fuck have we gotten ourselves into?" Sanders said, a stunned look on her face.

Bundy replied, "They got rid of him because he knew. Because his blood wasn't clean to them. You're right, Sanders, what the fuck have we gotten ourselves into?"

"Deputy, I need you to report what happened immediately," Sanders said to him.

43

The Thread Unravels

The detective stepped off the platform at Wilmer Station, the early morning filled with the wail of sirens. The crime scene had already been taped off, with uniformed officers holding back curious commuters. The train, Train 333 from Brookfield, sat still and quiet, as if it was stunned by what happened inside.

Meanwhile, Sanders and Bundy were on their way to the crime scene. Neither needed to say it aloud, but their expressions told the story. *It was likely the same brutal scene, the same haunting signs from the first train, and the houses.* They thought.

As they arrived at the scene, a female detective was already there, speaking to a local officer.

"Give me a quick brief," the detective said to the local officer.

"Six dead. All with similar wounds, clean slices to the neck, one had her arms broken postmortem. Their chests were split open, as though the killers had been digging for something inside. No signs of struggle from any of them. No weapon left behind."

"What do we have here?" Sanders asked, as she and Bundy exchanged worried looks.

Bundy whispered, "Looks like this nightmare isn't over."

"Any footage?" Sanders asked.

"We're reviewing," the female detective said. "The train's surveillance caught some glimpses, like someone-possible more than one, moving between cars, but it's distorted. The faces aren't visible. But passengers reported seeing an image of a tall woman in black. She acted like she fit right in."

"Witnesses?"

"Most of 'em are spooked. They said she looked like she didn't blink once. One woman said the killer sat beside her before vanishing, with a small group."

"Anything else?"

The detective didn't reply right away. She walked along the side of the train car, where the smell of blood remained.

Sanders and Bundy returned to the sheriff's office with more questions than answers. The ride back had been silent, both detectives stewing in thoughts they couldn't quite put into words. Sanders sat on the edge of her desk, flipping through her notes without really seeing them. Bundy stood by the window, staring out at the townspeople moving quietly through Main Street, faces tight, eyes darting, as if they knew something they wouldn't dare speak. What they'd seen over time, homes abandoned, trains full of lifeless passengers, no signs of panic or struggle, felt less like crime scenes and more like warnings.

Later That Day

Sanders and Bundy weren't looking for anyone that day, not anyone like her. The woman found them instead, stepping out from the shadowed doorway of a crumbling chapel just off the town square. Draped in layers of faded cloth and beads that clinked as she moved, her eyes held something ancient, like she'd lived through more than one lifetime of sorrow.

"You're digging in places best left buried," she told them, in a low voice, with squinting eyes.

"What was that?" Bundy asked, eyeing her with suspicion and curiosity.

"There are things here older than this town, things that wake when the wrong people go looking."

They exchanged a glance, Bundy half-smirking, but Sanders wanted to hear her. "What things?" she asked.

The woman's eyes darted between Sanders and Bundy, her fingers twitching at her sides like she was feeling something they couldn't see. "It moves through places where the ground was never blessed," she murmured. "Where bones were buried wrong."

Sanders tilted her head. "What moves through the ground, and which part of the ground is blessed, and which is not?"

The woman's expression changed. "You already feel it, don't you? Some places breathe easily. Others choke. The ground remembers what we bury, especially when it was never meant to be buried." She looked past Sanders, toward the distant tree line. "And what moves through it . . . that depends on what was invited in." She inched closer, her breath almost a whisper. "The town's been keeping its mouth shut for too long. Now the dead are speakin' for it." She stepped back into the doorway and whispered, "They always come in silence."

They never saw her again. Two days later, another deputy found her body just beyond the rusted gate of the Old Kramden Cemetery, laid out like someone had placed her there on purpose.

44

Lady's Night

Lady sat in her high-backed chair, her eyes closed, one hand resting on the armrest while the other traced slow, deliberate circles across the worn fabric, as if feeling something unseen through it. The steady roar of the train wheels filled the silence. The Sisters entered quietly.

"The job is done. We're ready to kill again," Demetria said.

Lady opened her eyes, black as night. "The spilling of blood will consume this dreaded place."

"We're ready," Mattie said.

"Our enemy's bloodline is ready," Anne added.

"Let them come," Lady said. "Fear is a blade we can wield. The train is more than metal and wheels; it carries our ancestors' wrath. Now . . . what about the one from the chapel?"

"The one that spoke to the officers, she's no longer amongst the living," Greta said.

"Good," Lady replied.

"Three officers on the outskirts of town disappeared. It wasn't our doing," Eva added.

"Hmm. Sounds like the work of either Teveras or Renegade," Lady said. "As the signs and blood messages grow, things will get darker. The townspeople are frightened, and the detectives are foolishly closing in on things they don't understand. But they'll learn soon enough."

Demetria stepped forward. "The detectives are asking questions no one should ask. The whispers say there's a cursed train, and that it takes lives."

A slow smile curled on Lady's lips. "Whispers are the oldest kind of mystics. They spread faster than fire. When those snooping detectives make their way to the Circle, it won't be forgetful. But in the meantime, I'll visit them. It's time; the bloodline must awaken fully. Fetch your parents. Greta, Anne, bring those bloodlines closest to us. We leave at dawn for The Hollow."

****

The wind had died down by the time Demetria, Eva, and Mattie got home. The porch light cast long shadows across the yard as they glanced frequently, checking out their surroundings. Demetria pushed open the screen door and stepped inside without a word, the others right behind her. Doris was up, standing in the kitchen, tying her robe at the waist. She turned at the sound of the door. "Something wrong?"

Eva spoke first. "Lady asked us to tell you something."

A curious look was on Doris's face. "What is it?"

Mattie stepped forward. "She wants you both at The Hollow. At first light."

"Is this about everything that's been going on?" Doris asked.

"Yes, Mother," Eva said softly.

Alias emerged from the hallway, rubbing sleep from his eyes, "Just us?"

"No, Father," Demetria said. "Anne and Greta are rounding up her family and others from our bloodline."

Doris walked over to the stove and turned it on. A flame flickered under the kettle. "Come sit down. You girls look tired. Have some tea."

"We can't stay," Eva said.

"She wants us to leave," Demetria added.

Doris paused, then turned toward the girls. "Tell Greta and Anne to stop by Hilda's. She'll need time to gather her things."

Mattie nodded. "And Naomi?"

"She, too," Doris said quietly. "If Lady asked for our blood, bring her."

Alias didn't waste time with questions. He went to the corner, pulled a canvas bag from the bottom of the old dresser, and began packing what he'd need. "First light," he repeated, as he walked to the door. "Be careful. There's movement everywhere now," he said.

Doris pulled each daughter into a brief embrace. Without saying a word, the girls slipped back into the dark. The porch light snapped off behind them. In the silence, the old house stirred to life.

****

Anne parked halfway down the gravel road and killed the lights. Greta jumped out before the engine finished ticking, scanning the woods like she expected something to move. Nothing but the sound of crickets and the rustle of trees overhead broke the silence.

"You sure this is the way to start?" Anne asked, shutting her door.

Greta didn't answer. She was already walking. Anne caught up to her as they stepped onto a side path that wound up behind a narrow two-room cabin. A dog barked once inside. Then the door cracked open.

Hilda stood in the shadows, glancing around. "Y'all come with news?"

Anne nodded. "Lady wants you at The Hollow. At dawn." Hilda didn't ask why. She stepped back to let them in. She reached for her boots and pulled the duffel bag from the nearby closet without saying a word.

"What about Naomi?" Hilda asked, lacing her boots. "Is she coming?"

"Yes, we're going to get her and the families off the old main road."

Greta looked to Anne. "We'll take the ridge road and hit Clay's place."

Anne nodded. "We'll get everybody and circle back before sunrise."

Turning to Hilda, Greta said, "We're parked halfway down the gravel road by the water. Meet us there."

Hilda got into her truck and sped off in one direction, Greta and Anne in another, splitting off beneath the trees. They reached Clay's trailer a little after two. Greta tapped on the window twice with her knuckles. A minute later, Clay opened the door in his undershirt and jeans, a pistol in one hand.

Anne raised a brow. "You always sleep with that thing?"

"Tonight, I do," he said, stepping aside. "Lady calls for me?"

"Yeah," Greta said. "We leave now."

"Give me a minute," Clay said, grabbing a few items. Greta and Anne climbed into his truck as he sped down the gravel road by the water, where Hilda was waiting. With Hilda and Clay following in their trucks, Anne smiled nervously, staring out the window.

"Doesn't this feel different?" Anne said.

"It is," Greta replied. "But I'm not worried."

"Let's get the families off the old main road," was Anne's response.

With several trucks in tow, they sped toward The Hollow. Dawn wasn't far off. By the time they reached the edge of The Hollow, the sky had started to lighten. One by one, the bloodline was gathering. Demetria, Eva, Mattie, and the others stood with Alias, watching the line of trucks roll in. Doris took a few steps forward, catching her breath as cousins and kin climbed down. No words. No questions. Just the sound of bags being dropped and boots crunching gravel. Whatever Lady was about to say, they'd come to hear it. And when dawn broke, none of them would see things the same.

45

The Hollow

Lady, cloaked in her midnight splendor, began to rise, her robe drifting like a dark mist beneath her. Her bare feet touched the ancient stone floor. She stood on the inner circle, a circle no other could enter. Around her, time held its breath. To her left, Elias stood still, one gloved hand resting on the black, polished rail that snaked through The Hollow's veins. His face bore the markings of the old trials, jagged and intentional.

To her right, Bolshan, half-burned but unbowed, leaned on his staff of twisted bone and ironwood. His eyes scanned nothing. He listened for Lady's voice.

Elowen held the lantern of cold fire behind them. Its flame, unnatural and pure, lit the chamber in pulses. It never sparkled. It lived.

The Veiled Twelve stood at the edges of the stone circle, their gauze veils unmoving, their silence not silence, but obedience. Beyond them, lining the chamber's edges, were the others. The aged followers. The last of the old believers. Men and women bent not by age, but by devotion. Those who had knelt when the first uprising fell. They had waited in The Hollow ever since.

Lady opened her eyes. "You feel it," she said. Her voice was calm, but it echoed across the stones like prophecy. "The veil is tearing." The lanterns pulsed once, blue, white, then back to blue. "The Old Country burns. The Wasiaks rise again, dragging what's left of their cursed bloodline behind them. I warned you this day would come." She stepped forward as Elias lowered his head.

"Both the Wasiaks and the Old Spirits seek to wipe out Teveras and our bloodline." A low murmur stirred among the gathered, but one glance from Lady calmed things. "Teveras and his kind are our sworn enemies, and it's strange that the Old Spirits and the Wasiaks would turn against him. It's possible that what he's become has frightened them because he's not a child anymore. He's a weapon. And his minions are no longer shadows hiding behind his back; they have names, faces, teeth. The Exuis, Ohn, Maera, and Dalo and his followers are loyal." There was a gasp at the mention of Dalo and his followers.

"Dalo?" Clay said aloud. "How is that possible? He was cursed to the pits of hell with his followers long ago. Who called him back?"

Bolshan answered in place of Lady. "The bloodline of Gerome Wicks, Renegade Jones." Several murmur rippled through the group.

Lady picked up where she left off. "I warned you this day would come," she said, her voice cutting through The Hollow. "They come for war."

A heavy silence followed Lady's warning. Then, from the edge of The Hollow's lower ridge, a voice cut through the gloom. "We're ready, Lady," Alias said. "And so is Doris."

"The souls of our bloodline are prepared," she replied with a reassuring smile, extending her hand toward Alias and Doris. Demetria, Eva, and Mattie watched, seeing their parents in a different light for the first time.

A gaunt woman stepped forward, her eyes blackened with ash, a harvest fang in her hand, her child clutching her tattered robes. "We've trained in the dark. Raised our young in the old rites. We'll bleed in your name." Others began to emerge, thin silhouettes with war markings scorched into their skin, some with hollowed-out eyes, some barely more than shadows themselves.

An elder man with rotted teeth rasped, "We were born in this pit. Molded by it. Our hate has aged well." Whispers turned to chants. The Hollow rumbled.

One of the Veiled Twelve stepped forward. Her voice rang out beneath the silk covering her face. "We are the last of The Hollow-born. Your word is ironclad, Lady. Speak it, and we'll burn their bloodlines from the Old Country to the new." Children stood behind her, their faces expressionless, holding blades of fire.

Elias, who had been making preparations, approached and spoke, his voice rolling like thunder. "The rails are ready. The blood path sealed. No one who dares descend shall return."

Bolshan raised his staff, and the sigil at its top flared red. "Their bones will rattle in the wind before they ever reach our gates."

Elowen stepped forward, her hands stained with ash and bone dust. She took a deep breath, then whispered an incantation that made the flames in the pit twist and darken. "Souls and bones never to return," she said coldly. "I've already carved their names into the stones of the forgotten."

Lady remained still, her presence towering. "Let them come," she said. "Let the Wasiaks and their ghost-fathers march. Let them summon their spirits, their beasts, their cursed ones." Her eyes glowed like coals beneath her veil. "They will find nothing but death waiting."

"But what about the detectives?" Demetria asked.

Lady smiled coldly. "Don't worry. I'll deal with them when the time is right. For now, stay sharp. Our time in The Hollow is just beginning.

46

Abandoned Train Station, Kramden

It was late, and the moonlight spilled over the cracked platform, casting long, skeletal shadows that stretched like reaching fingers. Sanders crouched near a rusted railcar, flashlight piercing the darkness. Bundy stood nearby, rubbing his chin, his breath visible in the cold night air. "These are the same carvings. What kind of place is this? Do you really think a train runs on these tracks?"

Sanders nodded slowly, her eyes scanning the empty tracks that vanished into the fog. "The witnesses say the train appears out of nowhere, a ghost on the rails. People disappearing, bodies turning up with symbols on them."

Bundy crouched, fingers tracing a jagged symbol etched deep into the debris. "Seems these things have been going on for years."

"As I said before, we're being pulled into something bigger than us." Suddenly, a movement caught Sanders' eye, a shadow slipping behind a row of freight cars. She tensed, raising her flashlight. "Did you see that?" Sanders asked, her hand close to her weapon.

Bundy shook his head. "No."

But something moved between the rusted-out boxcars, just past the old loading platform. Whatever it was, it didn't move like a stray cat.

Sanders stepped off the gravel, her boots grinding on the warped ties. "Over by that tank car. Thought I saw someone."

Bundy followed, drawing his weapon. "Could be some squatter."

"No," Sanders muttered, pulling out her flashlight and sweeping it across the rails. "Didn't move like one."

Behind them, a length of chain swayed gently from a crane hook, creaking in the windless air. Neither of them turned around right away.

Bundy brought the radio to his mouth. "Detective Bundy requesting backup . . ." static crackled instead. He lowered the radio. "Looks like we're on our own." The wind picked up, carrying a faint, guttural whisper that seemed to seep from the very earth beneath them.

Sanders swallowed hard, her gun drawn. "Whatever it is, it's angry." They exchanged a glance as an eerie train whistle pierced the silence, though the tracks were empty. She stared into the dark, a chill crawling up her spine. "Maybe we can get some answers now."

"Maybe, but whatever it is . . . it's coming for us next," Bundy said, his eyes sweeping the area.

She glanced at Bundy and yelled, "Let's get the fuck outta here."

Bundy didn't hesitate. "Right behind you." They broke into a run as the eerie whistle grew louder, then was shattered by a loud, piercing howl that echoed across the empty tracks.

Back at the sheriff's station, Sanders and Bundy sat across from each other, still catching their breath. The silence between them didn't last long as Bundy spoke. "What the hell was that?"

Sanders shook her head, "I don't know. But I'm not sure the sheriff or his deputies would believe us if we told them."

Bundy nodded slowly, rubbing his temples. "Maybe it's better if we keep this to ourselves . . . for now."

****

The truck rumbled forward as a sudden downpour of rain pounded the metal roof like relentless drums. Inside, there was an unspoken energy, grudges, and simmering rage. Renegade glanced at J.T., who had made his grievances clear.

J.T. broke the silence, "What of my family? The ones you let live? Why didn't you strike before they vanished?"

Renegade's glare hardened, his lips curled in disdain. "You were supposed to be the weapon, not the question."

Sox shifted, uncomfortable. "This isn't the time for doubt."

J.T.'s one eye half-closed. "They were mine to protect. And you threw them away. You didn't do shit."

Renegade pounded the steering wheel. "You failed." The truck jolted as it hit a pothole. In a reckless flash, Renegade lunged, one hand still on the wheel. The truck swerved.

J.T. shouted and reached for his dagger of fire, but Sox was faster; his hand locked around T.J.'s throat and started to squeeze. J.T.'s breathing became ragged. "You . . . don't understand . . . the blood . . ." he managed to say.

The truck came to a stop. Renegade stepped back, watching with heartless eyes as T.J.'s slumped body was shoved from the truck into the mud below. A tense silence filled the cabin.

Renegade turned and looked at Sox. "You went all the way?"

Sox met his stare. "You started it. I finished it."

Renegade gave a slight nod, then looked away as he drove off.

Unknown to him, a look of disdain was on Sox's face, followed by a sly smile. As the truck disappeared down the dark road, something unseen stirred, shadowy tendrils slithered from the mud, wrapping around T.J.'s broken form and dragging it silently into the thick, whispering brush.

As the two continued, a bit of guilt chipped in. "He was our blood. Maybe I let him down by not going after the Siobhans like I was supposed to. Even his cousins showed more grit than I did," Renegade said, a disgusted look on his face.

"You said he was a threat, and this war demands sacrifices, Renegade. What about Teveras? You said anyone acting without his approval would feel the wrath of the pit."

Renegade nodded. "You're right. The war and our bloodline are bigger than anything else."

"Good. When we get to The Petra, I'll tell Teveras about T.J.," Sox said.

Suddenly, a dark voice cut through the storm. *T.J. chose pride over order;* the whispers rumbled from nowhere and everywhere, heavy as the thunder that followed. *He broke the bond.*

Renegade froze, his knuckles tightening around the wheel. "You think they heard us . . . He must have spoken to the darkness. The ground took him."

Sox put a finger to his lips before glancing out the window, scanning the storm as if expecting the darkness to take form. "The whispers are never asleep. I don't hear them anymore. Do you?" he whispered. "I think you're right. They got him."

Renegade shook his head slowly. "Our anger almost cost us. We have to be careful."

"He knew what crossing Teveras meant. He wanted you to make a move before Teveras agreed," Sox muttered. "Orders matter; it's what our bloodline has always lived by."

47

Sheriff's Office Parking Lot
Evening

The sky was bruised purple and orange as the sun dipped behind the hills, casting an uneasy glow over the town. Two Tactical Assault Vehicles, dust-covered and battle-worn, idled side by side near the sheriff's office. Their engines hummed low, against the quiet hum of cicadas and distant dogs barking. Inside one truck, Sanders rubbed her tired eyes as she flipped through a worn file thick with photos and reports, bloodied bodies, strange carvings, and terrified witness statements. Beside her, Bundy sipped lukewarm coffee, his eyes glancing between the street and the shadows creeping from alleyways.

The town felt different. Something was in the air, and it wasn't love. Then, a soft, deliberate knocking at the passenger side window shattered the silence.

Sanders looked up. There she stood, impossible to ignore, Lady, appearing as Abby, standing there, waiting for the door to open. Bundy was transfixed, staring at her like he'd forgotten how to breathe. Sanders hesitated, then unlocked the door. Lady stepped forward.

"Detectives," she said, in a calm voice, "I've heard whispers. You're asking questions that stir things best left alone."

Bundy's hand drifted toward his holstered gun, his eyes on her. "Who are you?"

She smiled, a cold, knowing smile. "I wouldn't reach for that. And to answer your question, a friend, perhaps. Or a warning."

Bundy responded in a tense voice, "Are you threatening us? Ma'am, I'm going to need you to put your hands where I can see them."

Lady replied in her soft voice, "Would it matter if I were?"

Sanders stepped forward. "You want to be clearer before someone gets hurt? We might not be friends . . .," Sanders said, loosening her grip on her weapon and motioning for Bundy to do the same. "So, what's the warning?"

She looked Sanders in the eye. "The train is not what it seems. The blood running through this town . . . it has a memory. And the shadows are hungry."

Sanders swallowed, feeling the chill of those words sink deep into her bones.

Lady stepped back. She looked toward the darkened streets. "Be careful where you point your light. Darkness hides in many places, more than you'll ever know."

Without saying another word, she turned and walked slowly away, her silhouette melting into the gathering dusk.

Sanders grabbed the door handle. "Wait! There's something we need to ask . . ." But she couldn't get the words out.

The two hurried out of the truck, scanning the area. But she was gone. No footprints in the gravel. No sign she had ever been there. Only the fading echo of her words. Just then, the sheriff stepped out of his office. Sanders turned to him. "Did you see a woman walk by the trucks?" she asked, describing her.

"Plenty of strange things pass through here, but no woman by the trucks," the sheriff said.

They turned toward the town. Along the sidewalks, the townspeople had gathered in small clusters. Faces pale, eyes wide with an unspoken fear. Some glanced cautiously over their shoulders, others whispered urgently, as if haunted by something only half-seen. Sanders felt their eyes on her.

"Did . . . did you see that?" Bundy whispered.

"Yeah," Sanders replied, "Like they saw a ghost. Yet the sheriff said he didn't see anything." The wind shifted suddenly.

Bundy glanced back toward the trucks. "We're not just chasing a killer anymore. And these people know a lot more than we think."

Sanders nodded. "We've stepped into something much darker."

Bundy looked at her. "Let's not split up."

Sanders let out a dry laugh. "Wasn't planning on it."

As they turned back toward the Tactical Assault Vehicles, they knew they had to find out who the beautiful woman was. The wind whipped harder, and the townspeople's eyes seemed to follow their every step.

48

The Petra

The headlights barely pierced the dark as the truck sped down the muddy marsh road. Renegade's hands clenched the wheel, but he didn't speak. The terrain shifted subtly as they neared the boundary. The truck pulled to a stop, Sox stepped out first, his boots crunching the broken ground. "We're late," he muttered.

Renegade followed, wiping rain from his brow. "Then let's not waste time."

The entrance to The Petra opened, and a member of the Exuis greeted them. It didn't speak — only showed teeth without a face, then turned and drifted deeper inside. Renegade and Sox followed.

"I have never been inside this part of The Petra," Renegade said, as whispers bled like blood from the ancient, majestic walls.

"Me neither," Sox said as the pathway led downward, spiraling into the earth like a descent into damnation.

Finally, they reached the Sanctum of The Petra, where floating sparks that never burned out drifted through the air. In the center stood an altar that pulsed like a heart. Behind it was Teveras, surrounded by hundreds of demonic forces born of their own bloodlines that they never knew were theirs. They were flanked by Ohn, Maera, the Exuis, and Dalo and his followers.

Renegade and Sox exchanged a look of surprise. Teveras wasn't the child-like figure they remembered. He was taller now, imposing. Ohn, Maera, the Exuis, Dalo, and his followers had changed too, their forms darker, more twisted, no longer bound by human shapes. Teveras stood cloaked in layers of shadows and glinting armor etched in dark markings. His eyes were pits of molten dark, like looking into the moment before creation.

"Renegade. Sox," Teveras said in an angry voice. "You come bearing blood on your hands."

Renegade bowed his head. "T.J. questioned the path. He . . ."

"I know," Teveras said, stepping down from the altar. "I felt his soul being pulled from the world. I tasted it. That's why I reached out to you. But are you and Sox certain of the claims you've made?" He turned to Sox, "You acted without my command."

Renegade stepped in, his tone respectful. "He turned on us. On you. We couldn't take the risk. His ambition was revenge . . . alone, against the Siobhans, even knowing the threat we still face from the Old Country."

Sox added, his voice calm but calculating, "I'm yours to do with as you will. If I've offended the bloodline, then let my soul be cast into the pit."

Teveras studied him in silence. Then, slowly, he smiled. "Good." A pulse of heat rolled through the room as if Hell itself exhaled. "You've proven you're still loyal," Teveras said. "But know this, one more misstep, and I'll make your flesh sing with regret."

Sox didn't flinch. "Understood."

Teveras turned to the altar. "The bloodlines stir. The Old Country is awakening. The Wasiaks never sought revenge for those who killed Shadan. And Abby and her bloodline, we know where they stand. She will never fight alongside us nor with the Old Country. She has moved the pieces we thought were buried."

Sox's devious smile made its return as Teveras waved a hand. He didn't need to show them anything, but he did. A vision unfolded before them: Sanders and Bundy near the sheriff's office, inside one of the Tactical Assault Vehicles, talking to Lady, who appeared as Abby.

"So, she's revealed herself to them, but why? What are a couple of detectives supposed to do against Abby? Against us? They don't know the first thing about the occult, or the world our bloodline was born from," Renegade said.

Teveras's eyes twitched. "It's not what they know, it's what they might uncover. It's called knowledge, Renegade . . . and knowledge spreads like rot when left unchecked. She toys with them. Let her. But we'll meet her, and the Old Country, with fire."

Ohn added. "And this is something you two should know."

Renegade stepped forward. "What do you want us to do?"

"Gather our bloodline . . ."

A hesitant Renegade responded, "But . . . all of them?"

Teveras turned to Sox, "Every city, every state, wherever our bloodline lies, gather them. Have I made myself clear?"

"You have," Sox said.

"As for you, Renegade, prepare the gate," Teveras said, his eyes glowing. "The Hollow, and every place touched by the blood of the Siobhans, the Barrs, and the rest, they must bleed into each other. I want the veil torn open."

"And the detectives?" Sox asked.

Teveras sneered. "They walk too close to the truth. Kill them."

But something changed in Renegade's eye, doubt?

Teveras saw it. "Are you having doubts, Renegade?" he asked.

Renegade met his gaze. "No."

From the far end of the chamber, Maera, cloaked in a robe of ashes, approached. "Then prove it," she said. "Let's see how loyal your blood runs." Behind them, the altar began to beat louder, louder.

49

The Attempt

Sanders and Bundy were going over the information they had gathered from several of the townspeople they had to persuade. As they sat in one of the two Tactical Assault Vehicles, Bundy leaned forward, glancing over the train cam footage, "You feel that?" he muttered. Sanders didn't answer. She felt it too.

Renegade, Sox, and three others fanned out as they drew closer to the Tactical Assault Vehicle. One of the men pounded his fist against the side of the tactical vehicle. Another let out a bark that echoed through the alley, while the third shouted like a fight had broken out.

Inside, Bundy turned. "You hear that?"

"Yeah, sounds like a fight or something," Sanders said, already at the door.

They opened the door just enough to step out, then froze. Renegade and Sox were already there. "Back inside," Renegade growled, ramming a forearm into Sanders' chest.

Bundy reached for his sidearm, too slow. Sox had him covered.

"Easy," Sox warned. "Or I'll put one in your leg."

Though they carried their ancestral weapons, Renegade had insisted that Sox arm himself with a normal weapon.

"Who the hell are you?" Sanders snapped.

"Doesn't matter," Renegade said, kicking the door shut behind them. "You're not dying out here. Not yet."

Outside, the three men took their positions by the vehicle, facing outward, still as statues.

"Tell them to keep their eyes on the Sheriff's office," Renegade said. Sox cracked the door and told the men. Turning back to Sanders and Bundy, Renegade asked, "What did you find on the trains?"

Bundy held his hands slightly up, palms out. "Just bodies. Carved up like something outta a nightmare. Nothing human did that."

Renegade replied, "Things you don't understand? You think it's black magic, sorcery? What?"

"You fuckers are sick," Sanders said, pissed. "The whole fucking town is like this, huh?"

"You're in no position to disrespect our town and bloodline. You should have never come here."

"Wait a minute now," Bundy said. "If you do this, the arm of the law will kill everyone in this town."

Renegade and Sox burst out in laughter. Sox, a scowl on his face, asked, "And the woman?"

"What woman?" Sanders said.

"The beautiful one who visited."

Sanders shook her head. "She didn't come to us. She just . . . showed up. Asked a question, then vanished."

"What did she ask?" Renegade demanded.

"She wanted to know if the bodies were complete," Bundy said. "Didn't explain anything. We thought she was some kook."

Sox grinned. "That wasn't just some kook."

Sanders stared at the two. "Who the hell is she?" Neither Renegade nor Sox answered. They just exchanged a glance. Suddenly, a gust of wind hit the vehicle like a slap. Renegade froze as Sox handed him the weapon. Sox ran to the door, instinctively raising his ancestral weapon — a sword of fire. Sanders and Bundy were taken aback by the flaming sword.

Then came the screams, which were muffled. It was the scream from two of the men. The sound didn't last long.

The third man burst into the assault vehicle, face pale with terror, eyes wide and bloodshot. "She's here . . ." he stammered, but before he could finish, something yanked him back through the door with inhuman force. His boots scraped along the metal floor, then disappeared.

Silence followed for a second or two. Then a sickening, wet gurgle echoed outside, followed by a sharp crack, the unmistakable sound of a head being torn from a body. Then another. Then another. Bundy took a step back, almost losing his balance. Sanders gripped her holster but didn't draw. Renegade had her and Bundy in his line of fire.

Renegade's expression changed. He knew who and what it was. He looked at Sox. "Move." Sox didn't argue. The two backed toward the side hatch, the gun still on Sanders and Bundy. They vanished into the dark. Outside, three bodies lay twisted and headless in the dirt.

As Sanders inched closer, cautiously, she noticed a female figure in the distance, flanked by two taller silhouettes. They didn't move, just stood there, barely visible. Then they were gone.

Bundy whispered, "What the hell was that? I don't need this shit. They have to bring someone else in."

Sanders didn't answer. Her mouth was dry, her fingers still frozen over her sidearm. *Whatever it was, it saved them*, she thought.

"She took out her own kind," Bundy muttered, staring out the window. "But not us, why?"

Sanders nodded slowly, "I guess we'll never know, huh?"

"You think that was a warning? For them, or for us?"

Sanders looked at him. "Could've been both."

"She moved like she'd done it a hundred times. They knew each other."

"I need to talk to her, whoever or whatever she is," Sanders said.

"How is that even possible. Sanders, this is a devil-worshipping, evil town. I think we should stay out of this. Maybe, we should turn this investigation over to someone else."

"Bundy, no, please, stay on, and don't say anything to our superiors. I need you on this."

Bundy bit his lips, "Damn Sanders, okay, okay! Alright!" he gave her an assuring smile.

50

Failed

Renegade and Sox hurried their pace as they entered The Petra, where Teveras and the others waited. "Are they dead?" Teveras asked, not even turning to face them.

"No," Renegade said, out of breath. "Abby showed up."

Teveras slowly turned his head and stared at them. "Abby? She prevented you from killing two pesky detectives? She saved them . . . I see."

"And what of the others?" Ohn asked from where he sat.

"They're dead," Sox replied, without hesitation.

Teveras studied the two men, his jaw working, the muscle near his temple twitching. But instead of the tirade they expected, he gave a cold nod. "It's time," he said. "We must prepare for war." He stepped forward, his voice rising just enough. "Go. Gather our bloodlines. Alert the ones who can't make it here. Tonight, we wipe every last outsider off the map. Every bloodline in Kramden that's not ours gets slaughtered. House by house." There was no bluff in his tone. No theatrics. Just blood-soaked certainty.

Renegade and Sox exchanged a glance. They had failed to eliminate the detectives, and they expected Teveras to lash out, to make an example of them. But instead, he looked past it. That silence said more than words ever could.

****

Renegade and Sox didn't waste time. The moment Teveras gave his nod, they set out to gather the rest of their ancestors, silent souls who had waited too long to finish what had begun centuries ago. Dalo and his followers, eager to prove themselves, were allowed to accompany them.

Pulling Dalo to the side, Sox asked why he hadn't followed through on what they had discussed. "Now is not the time for this," Dalo said.

"So when?"

"I will let you know," Dalo replied, joining the others. Sox downplayed the brief conversation, convinced that Dalo would never take him up on the offer. Still, he wasn't worried about Dalo saying anything to Teveras.

Word traveled like the wind. Those who could feel the pull, who still believed in the old ways, began making their way to The Petra from far and near. Some had been waiting for the call all their lives. Others, alerted through whispers and dreams, would arrive later. But Renegade, Sox, Dalo, and the blood-hungry few who had nothing left to lose, they didn't wait. They moved under darkness, crossing into Kramden without a sound. The townspeople never saw it coming.

Flaming blades slid through throats in bedrooms. Axes of brimstone bashed skulls, littering the backyards of their enemies' homes. One man woke to see his wife gutted beside him, only to feel his own ribs crack under the swing of a rusted machete. Another tried to run barefoot through the woods, only to be dragged back, his screams muffled by a gloved hand and a blade sawing through his spine. They moved in the darkness. No one heard them enter. No one lived to tell how they left.

Meanwhile, Dalo and his followers formed a circle around the ancient graveyards surrounding Kramden and several nearby towns, their chants low and guttural. The ground pulsed beneath their feet as the rot from the ground ascended upward. Dalo's mouth opened wide as he summoned the souls and spirits of the bloodline.

One by one, they rose, moaning, whispering, clawing their way up through the cursed earth as the ground split open like an ancient wound. These were no ordinary phantoms. They were blood-sworn revenants, murderers, prophets, kings, and warlords, bound to Teveras' lineage by rites older than scripture, summoned by Dalo's hand. Smoke curled from their curved mouths. Eyes burned like dim coals in skulls worn thin by time. They had waited in silence beneath the soil, dreaming of vengeance, and now, awakened, they gathered to fulfill the ancient curse, to bring ruin to the Old Country and drown the Siobhans and Barrs in the blood of their ancestors.

By morning, the smell of rot hung in the air. Doors swung open on creaking hinges, revealing entire families butchered, blood soaked into walls and floorboards like paint. Even the animals in the barns were slaughtered. The killings were happening right under the noses of Sanders and Bundy, both still reeling from the recent events and facing pressure from the brass over the case's slow progress.

No one was spared, not even the sheriff who had gone to visit members of his family. This would come as a shock to Sanders and Bundy when told by one of his deputies.

Renegade, Sox, and the others wasted no time returning to The Petra, Dalo and his followers not far behind. The bloodlines gathered in force, thousands strong, answering the call. Teveras stood before them, welcoming their arrival like a general before a holy war. He told them what awaited. And they were ready.

As Teveras spoke, Renegade and Sox pulled Ohn aside.

"What is it?" Ohn asked in a low voice.

"It's the sheriff," Renegade said.

"What about him?"

"He's dead."

"Who gives a fuck, you?"

Before Renegade could answer, Sox cut in. "Law enforcement will get involved."

"Aren't they already?"

"This is different," Renegade replied.

"Different how? Wasn't an officer already killed? So why should we care about this sheriff? You undead are always full of riddles. Was he of our bloodline? Was he?"

"No . . . he wasn't," Renegade admitted.

"Then enough," Ohn snapped. "And if I were you two, I wouldn't breathe a word of this to Teveras."

He turned away, disappearing back into the throng. It was a sight, thousands of bloodlines invoking the darkest spirits, calling ancient evils from beyond. There was a stench in the air as they appeared, entering like a silent choir, no voices, only presence.

51

The Spirits Cross The Oceans

It had begun, across the ocean's blackened skin, they came, they moved beneath the waves like smoke in the water, formless, and cold as the depths they passed through. Other spirits boarded ships; their images seemed human but weren't. From the Old Country, across black seas they came. What once haunted the roots of bloodlines now traveled with intent, old whispers spoken in forgotten tongues pulled by unfinished oats, settled over the seas. And as they crossed, the winds quieted. Dogs howled at empty shores, and birds fell silent in the sky, as a deep, unnatural chill rocked the ships of those aboard. The tormented souls roared, their cries so fierce that even Teveras and his army of spirits felt it, and Lady and her bloodline did too.

Three vast groups of spirits tore across the night sky, splitting apart like a storm breaking over two fronts. One legion descended toward The Petra, heading for the bloodline of Teveras. The others veered toward the Hollow, pulled by the blood of Lady's line. Teveras and those in The Petra didn't flinch; they knew what stirred in the wind.

In The Hollow, the reaction was the same. Lady's blood stirred in the veins of her people. Children stopped crying. Elders stood tall.

Their eyes glowed faintly as the veil thinned. Demetria, Eva, Mattie, Greta, Anne, Alias, and Doris raised their heads to meet the storm.

A clash of spirits erupted just beyond the ancient stones of The Petra, as a division of Teveras's army, led by Ohn, draped in the shade of dark like smoke, warriors bound in chains of cursed fire and jagged death blades chanted their ancient hymns. They met the invading spirits from the Old Country. But the violence didn't stay outside for long. As the spirits broke through the first level, a fiery exchange of swords with fire tore into the approaching legions with a burst of fury. Maera and the Exuis led another division as their blades slashed through ethereal flesh, the soundless clashing of ancient steel ringing like thunder in the void. Wailing echoes spiraled through the dark as phantasmal forms tore at each other with relentless fury. Some erupted into bursts of black ash, only to reform with snarls of rage, their eyes glowing brighter with each rebirth.

Spectral chains lashed out like vipers, binding and crushing bones that existed only in spirit. Dark fire coiled and burst, lighting the battleground with hellish green flames that swallowed everything in their path. The ground of the first level itself seemed to tremble beneath the weight of centuries-old hatred.

At The Hollow, Lady's bloodline met the assault with equal ferocity in the surrounding woods before the spirits broke through, just as they had at The Petra. With the Artifact and the Stone exposed, their dark energy swelling, the Sisters claimed them. "They will listen. They will answer," Lady said.

Demetria's eyes blazed like coals as the chains of fire she called whipped through the air, lashing out and tearing apart the wailing spirits attacking her. As the fight raged on, Eva, Mattie, Greta, and Anne tore into the spirits, ripping out their souls. Black ichor spilled from them, hissing as it burned into the ground. Eva moved like a shadow possessed, her ghostly blades cutting through the fiends, leaving torn fragments of souls twisting in endless torment.

Mattie and Greta stood back-to-back, their hands glowing with deadly violet fire. With a fierce cry, they unleashed a barrage of ethereal flames, melting the ghostly attackers into pools of steaming ash. Anne's eyes were cold as she summoned sharp bone shards that cut through the enemies like guillotines, their ghostly screams ending as they were split in two.

Alias, Doris, Elias, Bolshan, Elowen, and the Veiled Twelve sat in a levitated circle, speaking in unknown tongues as flames and swirling fangs lashed out, snatching the souls and rising figures of those from the Old Country. The Veiled Twelve split off, racing toward a cluster of spirits who had just torn apart a group of children fighting for their lives. One by one, the children fell, limbs ripped away as their bodies melted into nothing. The Veiled Twelve's inhuman hands swept through the air, summoning walls of jagged, bleeding stone. The spirits lunged, only to slam into the barricades. Stones burst apart, shards slicing through the air like black rain, impaling and crushing them where they stood.

The battle was a grisly symphony of carnage. Spirits ripped apart by unseen hands screamed as their essence was devoured or torn limb from limb. Pools of black blood seeped into the ground, hissing with unnatural life . . ., while bursts of unholy fire ignited the battlefield in eerie green and violet flames. The Hollow itself pulsed with the rhythm of war, a living graveyard.

There was an eerie mist surrounding Lady; it curled and shimmered around her, forming a protective barrier that no spirit from the Old Country could penetrate. Frustrated, the dark wails grew louder as the malevolent presence of Wasiak and his wife materialized before her, shadowy-wreathed figures pulsing with furious energy. Their voices hissed through the heavy air, cutting sharp and cold.

"Abby," Wasiak snarled, "your bloodline has cursed us for centuries. You wear the name of your mother, but your blood betrayed us. Your ancestors forced us from our lands, condemned us to the shadows, forcing us into exile, as you flee from the reckoning we swore to unleash. Do you think we've forgotten the pain? The exile? The blood spilled in the Old Country because of your kind?"

His wife's voice, a venomous whisper, echoed in agreement, "You think your flight saved you? We are here to finish what was begun." But Lady stood unmoved, as she glanced at them behind the shimmering veil. "You escaped judgment once, but your time has come. You and your bloodline have haunted our nights for centuries. Now, we return."

Lady let out a cold laugh and lifted her chin. "You speak of blood and exile, yet it was your cruelty that forced us to flee. You twisted the old magics into dark sorcery, souls crushed, lands desecrated. If my bloodline is cursed, it is because we fought to survive your wrath. I will not cower before ghosts of your hatred."

Wasiak's eyes blazed. "Do you think a train can save you and your kind, or The Hollow? Defiance will be your undoing."

Lady smiled coldly, ignoring the warning. "When you speak of defiance, aren't you really talking about you and your kind?"

His wife floated, venom dripping from every word. "Your power means nothing when faced with the inevitability of our return."

The mists around Lady flared, humming with defiance. "Try, then. But I stand between you and this world. You will pass me only over . . ."

In a sudden flash of fire and shadow, Wasiak and his wife vanished, reappearing before Teveras in The Petra, where the spirits raged in brutal combat and were on every level. Wasiak's voice thundered inside the Petra. "Teveras! Your arrogance has blinded you. The blood that should serve is fractured and weak. We come not just for your enemies, but for you."

Teveras's dark eyes stared at him, his rage simmering under his breath. "Speak quickly. Why bring your venom here?"

Wasiak scowled, "You have fooled your bloodline with your childlike appearance for generations, and they have accepted it, but we from the Old Country, we know your true identity, and we'll never allow you to rule, never. We know your plan."

52

The Spirits Cross The Oceans 2

Teveras let out a chuckle, "You still haven't answered my question, why bring your venom here?"

"Because your bloodline harbors a traitor. It was he, Sox, who brought the Spectral Key. Yes, the very one. Stolen by the bloodline of Gerome Wicks, your bloodline, to this rotten place. Sox outsmarted Renegade Jones, found where the bloodline had hidden it, and delivered it to us. It unlocked the gates between here and the dark lands beyond."

"So, it was he who opened the gates for you. I suspected the serpent in my midst, but I never expected this . . . betrayal." Teveras's voice was a low growl. "Sox will pay. But know this, your invasion will not go unchallenged."

From where Teveras stood alongside several of the Exuis, Wasiak's wife stepped forward, her presence cold but not threatening. "Then prepare, Teveras. Because we have crossed the threshold. The Old Country returns, not as whispers in the dark, but as a storm to consume all."

Amid the chaos, Sox and a handful of followers he'd convinced moved unseen, guided by whispers from their protective spirits. They cut through the hills and valleys, delivering swift, brutal vengeance, slaughtering the undead without mercy.

Suddenly, without warning, a heavy stillness rippled across the battleground, and the fighting fell silent. Wasiak's voice, filled with revenge, echoed from where he and his wife stood, loud enough for Lady and Teveras to hear.

"I call you forth, Abby of The Hollow. Teveras, the shadow-cloaked king, come and face me, the true heir of the Old Country's wrath."

Wasiak and his wife, cloaked in remnants of war and ruin, shifted back and forth between their natural forms and their undead selves. Teveras met Wasiak's challenge without hesitation. Suddenly, Lady appeared ready to fight, her eyes locked on the trio. They recognized the ancient power before them, but both bloodlines had long resisted the wrath of the Old Country.

The four converged in the ethereal plane, where time warped and the air crackled with raw, untamed energy.

"Before I send you both and your bloodline to the darkest hells, this must be said. Old habits die hard, Lady, and the ancestors know that it was you and your followers who sent Shadan to the dark abysses. This is something that you cannot deny. And you, Teveras, we thought you would have dealt with her, but that wasn't the case," Wasiak snarled.

Teveras turned and looked in Lady's direction. "It was you all along. I should have known better," he muttered. "But today, I will take my revenge."

"You both speak boldly, as for you, Teveras, yes, it was I who struck down your mentor. I'll deal with you later. As for you, Wasiak, you're in a world where things and times have changed. You're in a world filled with lots of souls and bloodlines that couldn't care less about Shadan or you, and the ancestors that you brought with you, including that old bitch of a wife, Saline, you brought with you. Alias and Doris warned us about her long ago, and you, who was so busy, caught up in your evil, never knew about her and Shadan, the one you seek to take revenge for. Well, now you know," Lady said, roaring in laughter.

"Fuck you, Abby," Saline snapped. "What you've said about me isn't true at all. The rumors that you heard from Alias and Doris, who will not be spared, are exactly that, rumors. Your soul and theirs, and your bloodline, Elias, Elowen, Bolshan, Elowen, Anne, Greta, and the Veiled Twelve, and the one born under the crescent moon, along with her siblings, and what's left of your bloodline in the Old Country will not be spared," she said in an angry hate-filled voice, as Wasiak smiling and their armies of followers clamored around them waiting to attack.

"Enough of this nonsense," Teveras yelled.

Without warning, he unleashed gushes of infernal fire, twisting around him like a living armor. Seeing this, Lady summoned ghostly blades forged from The Hollow's deepest shadows. The Wasiak's icy flames clashed against Teveras's inferno, sending sparks that froze the air itself, as he launched devastating strikes, spectral chains whipping through the battlefield toward Lady's defenses.

Lady met the assault head-on, her blades slicing through chains with a hiss like a death knell, retaliating with blasts of cold flame that seared the ghostly forms of the Wasiaks. The clash rippled through the spirit realm, a violent dance of power and rage where neither side would yield. Seconds later, the creepy soul of an old, withered shadow sped towards Wasiak and whispered into his ear. Wasiak's wife looked puzzled, her eyes darting toward the sky as if expecting some unseen doom. Something was up, and they weren't about to question what it was, at least not now. It was at this moment that the fighting stopped.

Without a word or warning, Wasiak and his followers from the Old Country vanished into the shadows, leaving behind only silence and confusion. Lady and her bloodline, unsettled and unsure, retreated to the safety of The Hollow, their minds racing with questions they could not answer. Teveras and his forces, also baffled, pulled back to The Petra, uncertain why they had fled. Neither side understood the reason, only that the war was far from over.

****

The Hollow and The Petra lay eerily silent, the echoes of battle still trembling through the spirit realm. The Wasiaks and their followers had only just slipped back into the Old Country before the Spectral Key sealed the passage. That same key, which had carried them across oceans and ships, was bound to a cycle, open for only a time. Linger too long, and the way home closes, slowly but surely. Neither Sox nor Renegade had known this.

"How is this possible?" Wasiak thundered. "What did the bloodline of Gerome Wicks do to the Spectral Key when they stole it? It was never like this."

"What will we do now?" Saline asked. "Abby and Teveras's bloodlines must be destroyed."

"They must," the others murmured.

"They will," Wasiak growled. "But first, we burn the remaining Wicks family to the pits of hell." His voice broke into a roar. Several spirits loyal to the Wicks' bloodline tried to flee to warn them, but were quickly ripped apart, their cries devoured by the dark.

As planned, the Wasiaks set out for the old bloodline of Gerome Wicks. It was a spiritual fight as they clashed. Graves opened, the earth let loose the dead, and the night churned with groans. The Wasiaks struck with curses and chains of darkness, their forms swelling in the darkness. Wicks's bloodline rose in defense, but their souls were captured and bound in the chains. It was a fight that saw spirits fleeing but caught like flies in a flytrap as the cries rattled through the night.

In the end, the Wicks' bloodline was bound forever, trapped in the endless pits of darkness.

53

Payback

The betrayal stung deep as Teveras spoke to Ohn, Maera, and members of the Exuis. Teveras's eyes burned like fire. "He brought them here," Teveras muttered. "Sox . . . he outplayed us."

"It's time," Ohn said. The others agreed.

Two of Teveras's fiercest followers were summoned alongside Renegade. Their orders were simple: find Sox and kill him. They moved swiftly through the winding paths, hunting the traitor who had outwitted them. But the hunt did not go as planned. Sox was elusive, beyond even Renegade's expectations. They went to his home. The family said he hadn't shown up. Those were the last words they ever spoke before they were ripped apart. Furious that he had slipped through their hands, they strayed too close, too close to an area not too far from The Hollow.

Suddenly, the hunters became the hunted, as Demetria, Eva, and Mattie appeared. The two followers lashed out, firing chains of light and energy, while Renegade hung back. The sisters conjured balls of fire, hurling them at the two followers as the flames swallowed their twisted bodies. Their mouths were open, but nothing came out as the fire devoured their forms.

There was a scowl on the sister's faces as Renegade, now their prisoner, looked on with a dubious expression. "Your treachery ends here," Demetria whispered in a cold voice. "It's time you pay for your ancestor's treachery and the acts that you have committed."

Renegade spat and sneered. "Fuck you, all of you," he muttered, as they dragged him to The Hollow. His defiance stopped the moment the image of Lady appeared, flanked by the others. Hearing the roll call of names, he knew all too well, and the distant roar of the train, his knees weakened. *Is this the Aldan Circle?* he whispered to himself.

He was shoved to his knees before Lady, the circle of Sisters and the Veiled Twelve forming a silent tribunal around him. His eyes darted from one gaze to another, each burning with the memory of wrongs he could never repay.

"Renegade Jones," Lady's voice cut through The Hollow, "you carry the blood of those who spilled innocents' souls, who betrayed trust and trampled the sacred oaths of our realm. Today, you will answer for the sins of your ancestors, what they did to my family, and for your own treachery."

Renegade's lips twisted into a grin. "Do whatever you have to, I'm not afraid," he spat, though his voice trembled.

Alias stepped toward him. "You tormented my bloodline for years, especially my daughters. Now we're all here to witness your death, both in this world and in the otherworldly stages of the underworld."

Renegade eyes were on Lady as she levitated, "Abby, it wasn't me, it was all Teveras's idea," he pleaded.

"How quickly your position has changed?" she stared down on him, a disgusted look on her face. "You think this is about death?" she asked. "No, this is about reckoning. Your ancestors' debt is yours to pay." Renegade knew there would be no escape this time, only the trial, the verdict, and the price to be paid.

As the Veiled Twelve whispered in unison, chains of ethereal energy tightened around Renegade, lifting him from the ground as if the bloodline itself had risen to claim him. Faces glinted in the glow, shadows of Lady's kin stretching across generations, their grief and rage woven into the very strands that bound him. He thrashed, but the spirits were unyielding, pulling him toward a judgment no mortal hand could deliver. The weight of centuries bore down on him, and with a final shudder, his form was dragged into the unseen depths. His cries faded into silence, never to rise again.

Meanwhile, Sox, desperate and gasping, ran blindly. Seeking the distant docks where a ship might carry him from his nightmare, back to the Old Country, a smile appeared on his face as the moonlight glinted off the water, reflecting shadows of ships lined like predators waiting to strike. He sprinted toward the nearest vessel, his hope rising, but it was short-lived. From the darkness, Ohn appeared, his eyes blazed like fire, his intent was clear. Before Sox could react, he was seized and lifted from the dock. He struggled and cursed, but Ohn overpowered him. He was taken to The Petra where he collapsed to his knees, trembling as Teveras approached in his child-like form.

"Where is Renegade?" Teveras demanded.

"I . . . I don't know," Sox stammered, his sweat mingling with ash and blood.

"Did you kill him?"

"Why would I do that?"

"Because I told him to kill you."

Even facing certain death, Sox lied. "I never saw him."

"But you were heading for the docks. Where to, the Old Country?" Teveras's frown deepened as he circled Sox like a predator savoring the hunt. His voice softened, almost tender. "Do you understand what you've done? The Spectral Key. Your attempts at turning Dalo against me. You never thought he would bring it to my attention? You're nothing more than a hypocrite, a sham, a traitor."

Sox swallowed hard, a knot tightened in the pit of his stomach. Teveras raised his hand, his childlike face twisting and warping into a grotesque grin, teeth lengthening into jagged points. Sox's body seized as invisible hands clawed into him, bones snapping one by one beneath his skin. His scream was cut short when his chest caved inward, as if crushed by a force no one could see, leaving him crumpled and lifeless on the floor.

54

Lady's Plan

"The Petra stands," Elias hissed. "It's time we strike and bury Teveras and his bloodline forever."

Lady's eyes glowed faintly. "What do you think?" she asked the others. Bolshan, Elowen, Demetria, Eva, Mattie, Greta, Anne, and the Veiled Twelve agreed.

"Good. We won't storm the entrance. We'll need a diversion, and I think we have one."

"What is it?" Mattie asked.

"Wasiak and the followers from the Old Country. Teveras will be convinced it's them. We'll strike everywhere except the entrance. We'll make the ground tremble above them, then tear at the cracks until we break through. Once inside, we send everything, dead and undead, to their final resting place, forever chained. But I want Teveras and the leadership alive."

A figure rose in the circle, one of the old bloodline's torn souls. "What if the ground never cracks? The Petra has stood longer than memory."

Lady turned her head toward Bolshan. He answered in her place. "We know where his strength lies. He binds it in echoes, the bones of those he devoured, the shrieks he caged in his walls. Every Petra stone is swollen with his feeding. Break the stones, and the voices he hoards will turn against him."

The circle shifted uneasily. To shatter The Petra stones would not be a strike of brute force, but a ritual drenched in marrow-deep sacrifice. Blood would need to be given. The line would have to burn its own bones to summon that kind of power.

Lady stepped forward. "We draw him out with noise, with blood. We feed him a feast of the living, then poison it in his throat. He will be furious in his child shape or not, and when he does, The Petra will crack beneath him." They listened as she spoke. Then the whispers picked up again. Her voice grew. "Do you fear him? Good. Hold that fear; it keeps you awake. But remember this: Teveras may drink spirits, he may tear the flesh of men, but his arrogance blinds him. He believes no one dares to strike The Petra itself. But just as we were surprised by the Wasiaks, he will be surprised when we strike.

We gather what remains. Every fragment, every name forgotten, every soul too proud to kneel. We will walk into The Petra not as shadows scattered, but as one bloodline. And when we meet him, he will remember what true hunger looks like, and so will the Old Country."

A shiver passed through The Hollow; Lady, Elias, Bolshan, Elowen, and the Veiled Twelve extended their hands. Black smoke bled from their fingertips. "We are with you, Abby Barr. We were on the small ship when the journey began, and our bloodline from the Old Country will last in the pits, graves, and abyss of the underworld."

Lady turned to them and the others in The Hollow. "Prepare. The Petra will not fall in silence; it will scream."

Nights Later

Lady and her bloodline showed up at The Petra as planned. Chains of energy coiled around their wrists, sparks of cold fire dancing along their fingers. The Veiled Twelve swept their hands over the soil, summoning tremors that snaked through the ground. The earth cracked and shifted, and from these cracks, ghostly chains and spectral forms began to rise, and the haunting reflections of the bloodlines Teveras had consumed. Each stone in The Petra vibrated, resonating with the ancient voices trapped within. From above, Lady's presence spread like a pulse, confident that Teveras and his blood were unaware of what was taking place.

"We move together. Dead, undead, all that answers to our bloodlines," she whispered. The ground groaned in response to her command. Elias, Bolshan, and Elowen pushed forward, their forms blurring between solid and spectral. They struck first, splitting chains of shadow into the air, slicing at the wards that guarded The Petra's stones. Debris from The Petra trembled, dust and fragments swirling like a storm, revealing the cracks Lady had predicted.

Demetria, Eva, Mattie, Greta, and Anne circled The Petra except for the entrance, guiding the tremors with meticulous accuracy.

"The voices are ready," Bolshan said, his eyes scanning the fractures.

Elowen added, "Once we awaken them fully, they will turn on Teveras's walls, tearing from the inside." And just as she finished, the ground erupted. Cracks widened, releasing bursts of spectral energy that swirled in emerald and violet flames, devouring the barriers that had long kept The Petra sealed.

The Veiled Twelve moved like dark wind, appearing wherever a stone threatened to hold its place. They conjured walls of jagged, bleeding stones from the fissures, hurling them at the defenses that still held. When fragments struck them, they exploded in gurgling, black ichor that hissed and burned, forming puddles of shadow that writhed and attacked any spirit attempting to repair the damage. Each strike was exact and messy.

Lady's gaze turned to the skies above The Petra. "Now," she commanded, as Elias, Bolshan, and Elowen unleashed a chorus of ethereal fury. Chains of light and fire collided with the spectral defenses, each explosion shaking the stones further. Ghostly cries, some of anger and some of ancient terror, filled the foundations as it began to fracture. From the cracks, echoes of the bloodlines Teveras had consumed emerged, tormented spirits now allies of Lady. They surged upward, clawing at the walls, ripping through wards, and striking at the stones with ghostly apparatus forged from rage and sorrow. It was a symphony of destruction, a war beyond mortal comprehension. Every wall they tore, every stone they shattered, seemed to fuel Lady's power further.

Amid the chaos, Lady moved with predatory grace, her ethereal blades slicing through any spectral guardian Teveras had left to hold the walls. Yet she didn't lose sight of the fact that Teveras and his bloodline would hear the ominous signs and sounds and attack. "Keep pushing!" she shouted. "The Petra will fall from within. No stone shall remain!"

Demetria and her sisters pressed forward, along with Greta and Anne, forming a vanguard that battered the inner defenses. Every swing of their blades sent shockwaves through The Petra, causing pieces of stone and spectral energy to rain down like a blinding storm. Eva and Mattie ripped through the remaining undead forms that tried to defend Teveras's power, spilling black ichor that hissed into the cracks.

Elias, Bolshan, and Elowen channeled the soul of their bloodline, summoning torrents of energy into the cracks. From each crack, spectral chains shot outward, binding the stones themselves and amplifying the whispers of trapped souls. The Petra trembled violently. Lady's eyes glimmered with the thrill of the attack, her every movement orchestrating the devastation.

55

Lady's Plan 2

Suddenly, from the shadows of the crumbling ground, Teveras' fighters, led by the Exuis, Ohn, Maera, Dalo, and his followers, and their bloodline, attacked. Their forms changing between bone and smoke. Teveras stood heads and shoulders above them, levitating. He had once again changed his form. Black strands of energy snaked around him, binding him to the twisting fighters below. The two armies collided with a thunder that shook the unseen ground as their swords clashed against blades of shadows. Rituals, one after the other, fell the forms and spirits of both fighters. Both groups of fighters struck with shields of light, shattering ghastly figures that howled before collapsing into dust. Teveras's warriors swarmed like locusts, clawing and biting, dragging some of Lady's followers down into black pits that opened beneath their feet.

Lady and her blood did not retreat as Ohn hurled a wave of shadows, drowning The Petra in deeper darkness. Lady's hands rose, her fighters ignited a radiant but deadly light, as a searing pillar of flame tore through it, consuming Ohn's fighters in a single stroke. Dalo and his followers called upon the Embercleave, heavy axes of dark metal filled with flame. Using their tendril-like arms, they slaughtered a group of enemy followers. Maera darted forward, her form splitting into three, each slashing with hooked blades. But Elias met her charge, two falling beneath his blades before a spear of pure light pinned her to the ground, her scream rattling across the void. Still, Teveras pressed on. He descended lower, his hands spreading wide. With each movement, Lady's fighters were ripped from their positions, their essence unraveling into strands of smoke. Teveras' laughter was loud as a bell as it echoed throughout The Petra.

Lady's voice tore through the darkness. "You will not reign here," she thundered, her bloodline ripping into Dalo and his followers. With their tendrils turning to a smelly ash. Dalo began chanting, calling on his ancestors, but as he did so, a sword of ash and flame thrown by one of the Veiled Twelve pierced his body, leaving a pool of black ash.

Faced with a running battle, the Exuis sprang into action, their roars hacking through fighters like blades through flesh. Lady, seeing this, shimmered in her form, growing taller with treelike arms. She struck several of the Exuis with powerful blows, shattering them like glass.

As the battle reached its peak, Lady paused atop one of the broken stones. The Petra reeked of burned spirit and smothered flame. Around her, several fighters from both sides had been shredded into piles of squirming ashes, writhing and twitching as if refusing to accept death.

Lady and Teveras' eyes locked across the ruin, and in a flash, they lunged at each other, striking with a fury meant to end the other. The place shook with each blow as the two fought. Lady's figure stretched, changed, and snapped back again, part flesh, part shadow, part nightmare. Her talons raked the stone, shrieking like knives dragged over glass. Teveras stood his ground, his hands flaring with the same dark sigils that had given him dominion over men. He launched them at her, bolts of writhing power meant to tear her apart, but she tore through them, her body bending in grotesque, impossible ways. Her voice, a chorus of whispers and screams, filled the chamber: *You've fattened yourself on shadows not your own.*

Teveras roared, summoning every ounce of his will, forcing the shadows into a spear that hissed with venomous light. He drove it at her heart, but she caught it between her claws, smoke hissing from her grip as the weapon burned her flesh, and still, she held it. Her jaw unhinged, monstrous and wide, a cavern of teeth that were more bone than human. "Your rule ends in my jaws," she snarled, snapping the spear in two. The shadows recoiled from her as if recognizing their master, and Teveras, for the first time, stumbled back.

"It will be your rule that ends. I will take revenge for Shadan and my bloodline," Teveras roared, his eyes like pits of white fire. He began a slow walk towards her, raking the ground with a torrent of black fire that split the stone beneath Lady's feet. He lashed out with clawed hands, not just to wound but to tear her apart, each strike a reminder of who he was — the ancient spirit of the Old and New World, Teveras, the feared. A black surge erupted from his hand, slamming into her. Snarling, he twisted the darkness around him like a whip, striking her several times.

Lady, on her knees, fell back as Teveras lunged forward, levitating with unholy speed, his arms like twisted tree branches. In his grip, a flaming sword etched with ancient symbols spun in circles of malevolent power as he chanted aloud. The blade split into six, spiraling downward, each one aimed at the most vulnerable parts of her form. But Lady's eyes flared with raw, ancient power, just before they struck. She screamed a chant that shook The Petra, shattering stones and rattling every spirit it had ever held. Dead or undead, they fled in terror. The blades slammed into her momentarily, but the chants reversed their fury. With a violent snap, the swords were driven back into Teveras as he struggled, trying to get away.

He was pinned against the wall, trapped, where he hovered, as chains of fire sprang from the ground, wrapping around him. He thrashed, his form twisting into monstrous shapes, beast, child, man, phantom, but the chains held. His fighters rushed to free him, clawing at the bindings, only to be caught themselves. Ohn screamed as fire wrapped around his throat; Maera shrieked when her phantoms collapsed into one broken figure, shackled at Lady's feet. The Exuis, some wounded and others still fighting with desperate rage, screamed in horror as chains of fire lashed around them, yanking them to their knees and locking them in burning shackles. The last fighters of Teveras's Court cried out in anguish, charging to save their captured bloodline, only to be engulfed by pillars of flame that hurled them to the ground, where chains clamped them in place.

Teveras roared in defiance, yet even he couldn't break free as he glanced over his beloved Petra and what Lady had done. Lady smiled; it was eerie. The great Teveras and his chosen leaders lay bound before her, captured. Her followers gathered close, bloodied but victorious. The war was far from over, but tonight, Lady had claimed her enemy.

"Leave non-alive," Lady said, her command was a curse in itself. The Sisters and the others surged forward, bones snapped, spells were cast, and fire ripped through the undead and restless spirits.

56

The Fall

Lady hovered above The Petra, as Teveras looked on angrily. "It's time to witness the fall of The Petra," she said. With a single motion, she struck the tallest spire. The stone cracked, splitting with a thunderous roar that echoed through the spirit realm. Dust and shards exploded into the air, black ichor hissing as it met the ground. Chains of fire whipped through the remaining towers, toppling them in quick succession. Walls once thought eternal crumbled inward, their echoes screaming with the weight of centuries. The arches fractured, shards spiraling upward like blades before raining down in a storm of destruction. Lady's bloodline struck again, sending cracks snaking through the foundation, twisting The Petra's bones until the entire structure shuddered violently.

Even the floors and inner chambers buckled under the relentless force. Stone pillars bent and splintered, ceilings collapsed with deafening crashes, and the remnants of The Petra became a chaotic storm of rubble and dust. Smoke and debris coiled in the air, while the scent of scorched essence and shattered stone filled every corner.

Finally, with a last, echoing howl, the central tower shattered entirely, leaving The Petra a smoking ruin. Only blackened rubble, twisting smoke, and the eerie glow of residual energy marked the place where the fortress of Teveras had once loomed. Lady's eyes swept over the devastation. "It is done," she whispered. "Nothing of The Petra remains."

She turned and once again stared at the helpless Teveras and his bloodline. Their forms were still struggling as the chains of ethereal energy kept them bound. Around her, the Sisters and bloodline hovered like a storm of smoke and fire, ensuring no escape. Without a word, Lady lifted the captives, moving with terrifying grace over the smoldering ruins. The Hollow waited ahead. Each step, each shift of her form, and the others carried them further from the destruction.

Teveras's eyes blazed with fury and disbelief, but he was powerless, and the other leaders could only struggle, the chains cutting deep, sapping their essence with each movement. Lady's gaze never wavered; it was fixed ahead on The Hollow, where their trial awaited. As they neared The Hollow, Lady's form grew even more gigantic. The captives were brought down to hover above the ground. "This is where your judgment begins," Lady said, as they entered The Hollow. The bloodline formed a ring around them. "Your sins, your betrayals, your defiance, it all ends here. Teveras, you and your bloodline will answer for centuries of cruelty, for the torment you've unleashed, and for the blood spilled under your command."

Teveras sneered. "You bitch; didn't we have this conversation before? You speak as if you understand power. You know nothing of what it takes to survive the Old Country."

Alias stepped forward, "We understand enough to see your corruption. Every soul you've devoured, every spirit you've bound, we will see justice done."

Doris added. "You will pay for what you've done to our bloodline. Speak the truth now, or your lies will only make your end more certain."

The leaders of Teveras's Court murmured, trying to shift blame, but Lady's gaze locked on each of them. "It's time to pay the pied piper. Your time is over."

The Veiled Twelve turned up the palms of their hands as chains of fire and shadow coiled around Teveras, Ohn, Maera, the remaining Exuis, and the members of his Court. Their cries echoed through The Hollow. Lady's voice rang out, commanding the unseen powers of her bloodline: "To the great pits, all of you. Rot, decay, and vanish from this world and the next." The spirits were dragged screaming into the underworld, the air itself writhing with their agony. Below, the great pits gurgled, black ichor bubbling as their forms were swallowed, twisted, and bound in eternal torment. The Hollow fell silent, save for the distant hiss of fire and the faint, fading echoes of a once-mighty bloodline consigned forever to darkness.

Lady's eyes glowed with satisfaction, as did the others, as loud cheers echoed inside The Hollow. "Teveras was a formidable foe, and we took care of him. Now, it's time to send a clear message."

"What kind of message?" Elias asked.

"The Wasiaks brought this war to our doorstep. They will pay for what they unleashed. But we will not wait for them to strike again. "We will go to them. To the Old Country itself. And when we arrive, their names will be written in ash, their bloodlines broken, their spirits chained for all eternity. And we will do the same to whatever remains of Teveras's bloodline. Anything in Kramden that is not of our bloodline will be wiped out. Kramden is ours, our home!" A hush fell over The Hollow before a roar of approval erupted from her followers.

****

Meanwhile, Sanders and Bundy had asked for reinforcements, only to be told the department was stretched thin. The brass insisted the four men already with them were enough to put an end to the strange murders in Kramden. Sanders and Bundy knew otherwise. They were told that if things escalated, manpower would come, but both detectives knew by then it might be too late. They had come to realize that, as suspicious as the stories were, they would continue, no matter how wild they were. But what they were hearing now was different. No one said much, yet word of the spiritual clash between Lady and Teveras had spread, and it rattled the town.

"I'm guessing the woman they call Lady is the one who visited us," Sanders said.

"And Teveras?" Bundy asked.

"In their world, he must be someone of importance."

"You know, Sanders, I still can't believe these things exist, and somehow we're drawn into it. Not all of it, but enough."

Before Sanders could respond, an old man approached. "You two have been here long enough to see plenty, but take my advice, don't ask about the war you've heard of. And I know you have, because I've been keeping an eye on you. The few townsfolk who talk with you, I know what they've shared. What they fight for isn't yours. They fight in shadows, not daylight. Best you forget what you heard." But they couldn't forget.

Sanders eyed him closely. "If it isn't for us, then why are you warning us?"

Bundy added, "Yeah, it sounds like you know more than you're letting on, old man. Maybe you've fought in those shadows yourself."

"Maybe I do, and maybe I have. But the townspeople you see after dark are not who they seem. Take that as a warning." The old man smiled, turned, and walked away.

Sanders muttered to Bundy, keeping her eyes on the old man's back. "You catch that? He's saying the folks we see at night aren't really who they are. I don't like this one damn bit, Bundy."

Bundy let out a short laugh, though it didn't sound convincing. "Spirits, townsfolk, whatever the hell they are, it won't change what we came here to do. Just . . . keep an eye open."

What Sanders and Bundy didn't know was that the sound of the train they kept hearing was during the fight between Lady and Teveras. The sound of the train drove them to the Aldan Circle again. Sometimes it grew faint, like it was miles away, only to surge close again, as if it were grinding just around the corner. The strange part was that no train was ever seen.

Bundy slowed down and listened harder this time. "You ever notice," he muttered, "We only hear it when we are in the Assault Vehicles? Never on the way, never leaving, just here."

Sanders stopped, too, the thought digging into her. She glanced around the Circle. "Yeah . . . and it's always the same damn sound. Same brakes, same grinding. Like a fucking loop." Sanders and Bundy stood still, realizing neither of them had ever asked the obvious question. If there was no train, then what the hell were they hearing?

57

Teveras's Bloodline

The slaughter across the East Coast and the South had begun. Elias, Bolshan, Elowen, Demetria, and her sisters, Greta and Anne, and the Veiled Twelve led the charge, unleashing a terrifying warfare upon Teveras's bloodline. The East Coast was the first to feel it. The homes where Teveras' descendants believed they were safe erupted into screams as doors blew open without a touch. Families were pulled into the dark. Lady's army left no one untouched, names, faces, and children, all were stripped of the blood that tied them to Teveras. Incantations were spoken as graveyards stirred, and the evil spirits in high places were dragged down and cast into the pit of hell.

In the South, the plantations and estates where the bloodline had hidden for generations fared no better. Lady's followers moved through the fields like a tide of black fog, suffocating the night with their presence. Men who carried Teveras' name woke choking in their beds, dragged into darkness by unseen claws. Their cries carried out into the humid air, then faded, leaving only the creak of shutters and the rustle of trees.

Fires burned where families resisted, their homes collapsing into ash, their legacies carried away on the wind. In coastal cities, whispers spread of whole households vanishing overnight, their lineage erased as if it had never been. Teveras' name dissolved into nothing. His seed, his hope, his claim of immortality, all of it crushed. Lady whispered to the group upon their return to The Hollow. "The blood of Teveras is no more. The Americas are mine, and his line is buried."

Old Country Confrontation

The wheels were set in motion as the bloodline gathered. They moved on the currents of whispers that wrapped around them like a shroud. They did not walk, they did not breathe, they drifted, their presence dragging the air colder with each movement, drawn into her wake. "Soon, we will cross into the Old Country. The Wasiaks think the land protects them. They are wrong. Our bloodline has no borders."

The fog deepened around them, curling like smoke until the world behind vanished into gray. Then came the sound of the train catching the ears of Sanders and Bundy. They exchanged a glance, neither moving nor speaking of the Aldan Circle, though both were certain the eerie rumble marked another spiritual war taking place.

The earth cracked beneath the feet of Lady's bloodline to reveal another land, ancient and filled with history. Demetria froze, her breath coming in bursts. Eva's eyes widened, as if the sight itself threatened to swallow her. Mattie gripped Greta's arm, searching for something to hold onto in the unreality before them. Greta whispered a curse under her breath, unable to make sense of what she was seeing. Anne stood silent, her gaze darting over the strange horizon, struck by the sense that they had stepped into a place no living soul was meant to see. A place that had endured long before them and would endure long after.

The forests of Eastern Europe loomed around them, branches twisting like the fingers of the dead, the moon casting a pale light upon the ruined paths that led to the Wasiaks' ancestral home. Villages now broken to stone, fields strangled by weeds, and sacred grounds scarred with age all stretched before them. The living descendants still clung to these remnants, unaware that Lady's arrival meant their end. Lady's bloodline cut through the Wasiak descendants, then turned their wrath toward the other ancient bloodlines tied to Teveras and his kind. In the span of a few hours, blood that had endured for centuries was erased from the earth.

But death did not silence them. The ethereal bloodline of the Wasiaks and the other ancestral spirits tied to the land stirred at the slaughter. They drifted like wind toward the battlefield, their rage and grief binding them together. It was an awakening of the dead as the spirits gathered, coalescing around the towering form of Wasiak. His voice thundered across the battlefield, carried by the wails of the dead.

"How dare you set foot on sacred grounds, woman? To spill blood here, to desecrate what was bound by oath and bone, you think you can walk away from this unpunished?" Wasiak uttered.

"Spare me your outrage, Wasiak. Have you forgotten Kramden? It wasn't long ago that you and your wretched kin crossed the ocean and waged war against my bloodline and Teveras. You failed then, and you'll fail now. We have come to settle a score." A growl rippled through the spirits, but she pressed on. "Teveras no longer exists. His bloodline was erased in the Americas. I came here to finish what I started, to wipe yours from existence. And once that is done, the Spectral Key will leave with us."

Wasiak's face twisted into something between fury and amusement before he let out a booming laugh, the sound echoing like a dozen voices at once. "Erase mine? You think yourself capable of snuffing out the blood of Wasiak? You think because you toppled one bloodline, you can topple them all? Foolish Abby, the Wasiak blood is not so easily broken. Kill one, and a thousand more will rise. You've only awakened us, and now, you'll drown in what you've stirred. You will fall here, and your bloodline will be the one remembered only in whispers."

"Laugh all you want, but arrogance has never saved a bloodline. I am here to end yours." She lifted her hand and whispered words that hadn't been spoken for centuries as Elias, Bolshan, Elowen, and the Veiled Twelve joined in. They were summoning The Apo, a powerful spirit long feared even among the oldest bloodlines. A shadow darker than the night itself unfolded behind her, and the air trembled. Wasiak and Saline braced themselves, bristling at the daring of the call.

Suddenly, The Apo appeared like a living storm, black and writhing with a hunger older than the land itself. Wasiak and his bloodline and the others stood in shock, as trees groaned under its presence, their branches bending as though bowing to a king long dead. Elias, Elowen, Bolshan, and the Twelve Veiled stepped forward, their forms shimmering as one voice poured through them, merging with Lady's, creating a chorus of spectral authority that reverberated across the land.

Wasiak and Saline stared at The Apo, their spirits merged in anticipation of the attack. But they, too, spoke a name long whispered in fear and reverence. From the shadowed edges of the forest, a figure began to take form: a woman whose presence radiated both fury and command, bound eternally to the Wasiak bloodline. Her eyes glowed with fire as she stepped forward, and the air seemed to shiver at her arrival. The spirits and living warriors of the Wasiaks rallied around her, their allegiance uniting under the aura of her power. Her voice rose in a chant older than memory. Where Lady had summoned a force of pure terror, the woman's presence brought a powerful ancestral might, one that reminded everyone that the blood of the Wasiaks would not be so easily extinguished.

58

Teveras's Bloodline 2

The first scream ripped through the air as shadows surged from Lady's bloodline, spilling into the ranks of the Wasiaks like black fire. Steel met specter, but every blade that struck a shade passed through, only to find its wielder's arm frozen with an icy grip that ate away at flesh. The air filled with shouts, curses, and the guttural sounds of battle, but beneath it all was Lady's laughter, low, merciless. Several Wasiak fighters surged forward, striking the first group of Lady's fighters. Elias swung his darkened arms, slamming a spectral fist into the ground and sending roots snapping toward Wasiak's warriors. Elowen advanced, cutting through the front lines of spirits with deadly, slicing chants, while the Twelve Veiled moved as one, phasing in and out to slash at anyone in their path.

The powerful woman of the Wasiaks' bloodline stepped forward, meeting The Apo advance head-on. Energy flared from her hands as she sped some distance from the other with The Apo in tow. Sparks of spectral force exploded as the woman spun in the air, and a group of ethereal warriors attacked The Apo. Meanwhile, Wasiak and Saline moved through the fight, striking Lady's followers with deadly force, cutting shadows and flesh alike.

Demetria, Eva, Mattie, Greta, and Anne stayed close to Lady, their powers flaring in tandem as they pushed forward against the rallying spirits of the Wasiaks. Each swing, each incantation, met with equal force, the battlefield a blur of dark and light as both sides hammered into each other without pause.

The Apo raced toward the warriors the woman had sent, entering their forms. Smoke filled the air as cries of the dark rang out, their bodies torn apart from within. The Apo levitated, as did the woman, who spun once again, yelling incantations one after the other. Weapons from the spirit world were hurled at The Apo, but he dodged each strike and countered the incantations. The Apo raced towards the woman, forcing her to flee. Several fighters surged to her rescue, but they were hit with flashes of light and crumpled to the ground, their forms destroyed. Cornered, the woman spun one final time, summoning several child-like fighters who chanted in a child's tongue, hoping to distract The Apo. But The Apo saw through the illusion, firing daggers of fire into them until they vanished. Now, only the woman and The Apo remained, her eyes blazing with defiance.

It doesn't matter who wins here. We will meet again . . . somewhere in the depths of the Abyss.

I was called for a good cause, and I will see to it that those in the Abyss will imprison you for all eternity. With that, he struck. Blow after blow rained down upon her; each strike was fueled by fury and the power of his incantations. She stumbled, fell, tried to counter, but The Apo's assault was relentless. Finally, as she crumbled to the ground, defeated, he whispered one final incantation. A shadow spiraled around her, lifting her from the battlefield. In a burst of otherworldly light, she vanished into the Abyss, leaving only silence in her wake. The Apo sped back into the fray as spirits and scattered warriors fell before him. The screams of the fleeing echoed as they fled.

Meanwhile, Lady, Demetria, Eva, Mattie, Greta, Anne, Elias, Elowen, and the Veiled Twelve pressed toward the heart of the battle. Wasiak and Saline fought with everything left in them, rallying their bloodline, but the might of Lady's forces was unstoppable. Demetria struck first using the Stone, its power shattering the protective wards around Wasiak's core fighters. Greta and Anne moved like shadows, as the Artifact cut through defenders before they could react. Elowen's chants sliced through spirit and flesh alike, while the Veiled Twelve cornered them, leaving no room for retreat.

Wasiak roared angrily, in disbelief, seeing his bloodline fading in front of his eyes, but it was useless. Suddenly, Lady's booming voice cut through the chaos. "Your time is over. Our world will remember only the bloodline that stands today."

"This land will not remember you! My name will never die!"

"Your name dies here, Wasiak," she yelled.

With one final strike, Lady raised a blade of Shadowfire. Bolshan raised a symbolic staff, its symbols flaring bright as he whispered a binding chant that wrapped the spirits in chains of light. The Apo moved beside them, with twin hooks of flame and fire daggers. Together, they struck. Wasiak, Saline, and their closest warriors screamed as their bodies and spirits were torn, bound, and dragged into the void. They were erased in an instant, leaving nothing but ash.

Silence fell over the battlefield, broken only by the groans of the handful of minor spirits and scattered descendants who fled into the shadows, vanishing into the shadows of the forests and grounds. Lady's bloodline stood alone in the Old Country, victorious, but vigilant. As for those who escaped, they had no power to challenge her, but their existence was a reminder that even in victory, some blood of the past could linger.

Lady approached The Apo with reverence, and as he levitated toward her, she spoke in an ancient language. *You've done more than I could have asked. The Old Country stands because of you.*

I was called for a purpose. The rest was yours to see through.

Still . . . I owe you a debt, and not just for today. If ever the Abyss stirs against us, know that you have a bloodline willing to defend you.

Again, I was called for a good cause, and the cause was served. You and your bloodline now hold this world.

Then go. Return to the Abyss safely, Apo. The Old Country will remember your hand in its salvation.

Farewell, Abby. Keep watch. There are always shadows waiting, even here. With that, The Apo faded into the void, leaving only the faint ripple of his presence behind as Lady watched.

With the Old Country secured and the remaining bloodlines who had refused to join the Wasiaks warned to behave, Lady and her followers bid farewell to their bloodlines as they prepared to return to the Americas, with the Spectral Key as she promised. As they crossed the seas, Lady's gaze was on Demetria, Eva, Mattie, Greta, and Anne. None of the sisters had ever imagined their lives would lead them through the Old Country, carving out a destiny written in blood and spirit. Lady wondered if they saw it as a burden or the crown of their bloodline's triumph.

When the shores of the Americas came into view, a sense of homecoming and satisfaction of victory filled them. For now, the Americas were safe, and the balance of power had shifted. And with that, Lady turned away from the horizon, leading her bloodline forward, the legacy of her blood unbroken, unstoppable, and eternal. As they entered The Hollow, the living bloodlines and the forms of the spirits rejoiced in one voice. When the rejoicing faded, the living bloodlines slowly departed, stepping out of The Hollow and back into their villages, their farms, and their homes, ready to live again under the shadow of Lady's victory.

Meanwhile, Sanders and Bundy felt something like a natural mystic in the air as they sat in their Tactical Assault Vehicle. The other officers remained oblivious, unaware of the strange shift in their surroundings, while the townspeople of Kramden, some smiling, others wearing darker, unreadable expressions, went about their business as usual. The whistle of a train cut through the night, and a sudden breeze swept over Sanders and Bundy, carrying with it a presence that made the hair on their necks rise. They stepped out, glanced at one another, and silently shared the same thought: it was the woman who had visited them. And though they didn't know her true name, they both sensed that she had passed this way for reasons far beyond their understanding. And then, as quietly as she had come, the presence faded, leaving only the whisper of power that reminded Sanders and Bundy some things in the world were beyond understanding.